Splinters

Splinters

ERICA HELLER

CHAPMANS
1991

Chapmans Publishers Ltd
141–143 Drury Lane
London WC2B 5TB

Grateful acknowledgement is made for the following excerpts:

'Everything Happens To Me' – words by Tom Adair. Music by Matt Dennis. Copyright © 1940 (Renewed) by Music Sales Corporation. International Copyright Secured. All rights reserved.

The Golden Notebook by Doris Lessing, published by Michael Joseph Ltd, © 1962 by Doris Lessing.

'The Love Song of J. Alfred Prufrock' from *Collected Poems 1909–1962* by T. S. Eliot, published by Faber and Faber Ltd.

Men Who Can't Love by Steven Carter and Julia Sokol, © Steven Carter and Julia Sokol 1987, published by Bantam Books, a division of Transworld Publishers Ltd. All rights reserved.

'Moonlight Becomes You' (Burke/Van Heusen), © Famous Chappell. Reproduced by permission of Warner Chappell Music Ltd.

BRITISH LIBRARY CATALOGUING IN PUBLICATION DATA
Heller, Erica
Splinters.
I. Title
813.54 [F]
ISBN 1-85592-011-5

First published in Great Britain by Chapmans 1991

Copyright © 1990 by Erica Heller

Photoset by Rowland Phototypesetting Ltd
Bury St Edmunds, Suffolk
Printed in Great Britain by
Butler & Tanner Ltd, Frome and London

For My Grandfather,
Barney Held,
in Loving Memory,
and for My Grandmother,
Dorothy Held

With special thanks to J. Gregory Alderisio, Sara Giller, Anders Stephanson, Mike Chappell, Ellyn Peabody, Giona Maiarelli, Harriet Wasserman, my parents, family, and friends.

Part One

How fondly swindlers coddle their dupes!
—BALZAC

The damned rabbits had gotten into the petunias again. And scooping up the handfuls of pink and white confetti, I knew only too well that this did not bode well for me as an omen for summer. Every year, the rabbits served as my occasionally accurate barometer for what lay ahead. July after July, crouching down on dry elbows and fleshy knees, I persisted in playing this absurd little game with myself.

If I am anything at all, which I suppose I really must be, I am the type of woman who cannot stand suspense. And so, in some naïve way, I thought the ravaged petals could reveal to me each year what a gypsy reading grounds in a teacup, in a room swarming with flies, could not. I actually thought I could outwit my summer by anticipating it. Can you imagine an intelligent, forty-year-old woman with more than a tankful of savvy, with charge accounts at Zabar's and Rizzoli and an honors degree in English literature, seriously regarding a rabbit as the true purveyor of her destiny?

But so much for omens and gusts of flimsy hopefulness. Once I'd looked down and seen the colorful devastation, the elaborate feast that lay so brazenly at my feet, I more than got the message. And God help me, but I knew this summer was going to be an absolute killer.

So, this is what I happened to be thinking about early that morning in East Hampton while, as I gathered up the crippled petals, out of the corner of my eye I noticed a man jogging up my driveway. As soon as I realized it was my ex-husband, I knew my idiotic rabbit theory had been confirmed. In fact, I knew right

11

then that there was no more hope for me than there was for my petunias.

Unfortunately, there was no mistaking him. The hair was pure Marcello Mastroianni, wavy widow's peak and all. He moved with a grace that was all function. And although he did not look either thoughtful or complicated enough to have manufactured and supplied me with a virtually inexhaustible encyclopedia of lies, humiliations, and deceits that would paint *Gaslight*'s Charles Boyer green with envy, I assure you Boyer had nothing on my Charlie. Not when it came time to wriggling out of a drowsy marriage, he didn't. Boyer may have been the burglar who dreamed of vanishing with the family's heirloom silver, but Charlie had dreamed of the silver and the baby grand piano and had actually made off with both.

In deference to this wickedness, it had been quite a while since I had last set eyes on him; more than three years, in fact. We had been granted a divorce in a chilly, barely lit Manhattan courtroom that freaky day in March when it had rained, sleeted, thundered, snowed and hailed right outside the windows, making an elaborate light show out of the sticky coda of my ten-year marriage. That had been the day this nonchalant runner, who now approached me with the barest trace of a smile, had sat back, every inch the world-renowned playwright, and crushed me just like pepper in a mill. I can still remember his hands, crossed on the table between us. Long, slim, tapered fingers, they'd been born to play Bartók or Strauss on a Steinway, but had cleared a confident path to an IBM Selectric instead. Fingers still tanned from a much-publicized, pre-divorce romp in the waters of St Bart's, and looking very much like a neat row of polished knives. What a presentable picture he had made that day in court, in his crisp, expensive, pinstripe suit, his wild hair uncharacteristically tamed. I will never be able to forget the way he sat there, like a grape or pear in a bowl of fruit, posing for an oil study, so utterly detached and disembodied was he from what was taking place.

After the judge had concluded his business, I read somewhere, Charlie had gone to Chinatown with friends for something of a celebration. I, on the other hand, had run from the courthouse on

12

shaky legs, the hail slapping at my face. The way I figure it, just as Charlie was slicing his way into a whole, deep-fried flounder that had given up its life for his prandial pleasure, I was back at home, in our old Central Park West apartment, throwing up into a pair of Ralph Lauren pillows.

Sitting there in the dark, at the edge of our big clawfooted tub, I thought back over my muddled tapestry of a life, a bit frayed at the corners, and it made perfect sense to me that Charlie had so neatly become its cynosure.

After a quiet, unspectacular childhood, growing up on Riverside Drive as a quiet, unspectacular child, I had taken a good look around me and felt impossibly restless. My parents were Jewish liberals (so liberal, we had a Christmas tree every year). My father was in textiles, and my mother was into making sure he was a success at it. I had a saucy, eccentric younger sister who began smoking at ten and started a fire under our dining-room table.

I had one boyfriend in those days, in the sixth grade, a nasty semi-ruffian who once quite passionately threw me against a freshly painted fence in the schoolyard the day I wore my brand-new camel's-hair coat. From then on, this, to me, was love.

How I ever wound up on the Dean's List at NYU (where I changed my major as often as some people changed their socks), I will never know. I was so undriven I had zero mileage. But once I was in college, living in an apartment with two roommates, suddenly I was dating, and dating a lot. Oddly enough, no one person or face now stands out as particularly memorable. There were just a lot of unlaughing boys with beards, sandals, and rolled-up copies of *The New York Review of Books* in their pockets, quibbling in a coffee shop at 2.00 a.m. over dividing the tax exactly on two cups of coffee for much longer than it had taken to drink them. Whoever these people were, they were all the same. You went out with them. The second date, they analyzed the first date. The third date, they dissected the second, and it went on and on in this endless pattern until all you were left with was a pile of words and a nagging confusion.

13

Later on, one boyfriend, a dentist who played a sitar and had pleurisy, ran off to join some Buddhists upstate. Another, a wealthy, shallow Cape Cod loner-type, proposed marriage to me and then promptly vanished.

Sometimes I slammed their new coats against the freshly painted fence, and sometimes they slammed mine, but all the time I had been waiting, waiting as if in a dream, for that one great love to appear and jar me awake. That's why when Charlie came along I was so ripe for him, and why one evening when his powerful affection fell into my palm like a broken egg, my hand was open and waiting. And perhaps this explains why even now, so many years later, in spite of everything that had happened, he was still so sewn right into the invisible lining of my experience; why, unthinkingly, I carried him everywhere with me, like car keys, or a favorite folded handkerchief; and why I had sat there in the dark, clutching those pillows to me like life preservers. The fact is, I had never felt so affected by my husband as the night he was no longer my husband. And as for the tricks and plots he had connived, the twists and turns to his laundry list of public and private betrayals, I felt all the cumulative pain and despair from them sink to the bottom of myself, like waste in a fish tank.

We had started out together blinded with passion and promise, feeling insufferably invincible, to the point where our friends could not spend four minutes with us without requiring Dramamine in great quantities. Welded together as we were for days on end, month after month, in that first dazzling rush of hormonal imbalance and dizzying discoveries about each other, I remember the first time I felt Charlie's attention wander. We were bent over tuna-fish sandwiches and iced tea in an all-night coffee shop one evening, after suffering through some unredeemably esoteric foreign film, when I noticed that our waitress hadn't brought lemon for my tea. I made a half-joking observation, in this our third month together. 'Boy,' I teased, 'the thrill must be gone already, or at least going. Two months ago, if someone forgot to bring me a slice of lemon, you'd have been out on the street finding me a lemon tree,' at which his face darkened a bit, but he said nothing. The next day, when I arrived home from

14

work, my heart stopped, frozen, the instant I walked in the door. Everywhere I looked, under a telephone, peeking out of an open desk drawer, nestled behind a half-closed curtain, were bright splashes of yellow. Going through the apartment, I counted sixty-seven lemons (and I was always sure I'd missed a few). With that bold, dashing, tender, and impossibly romantic gesture, Charlie had more than made his point, and in the coming weeks, as I fed him the lemon breads I'd copiously baked, the lemon mousses I'd concocted, the lemon sherbets, lemon chicken, and lemon meringue pies, I managed to make my own point, one that took years for him to forget or take for granted. After the lemons, I looked at him with a deeper love, a more profound fascination and more intense appreciation than he could ever understand or I could fully articulate, even to myself.

I'm sure I know what you're thinking, but the truth is, Charlie's sexual infidelities had been the very least of it. Which is certainly not to say that Charlie wasn't an utter fool when it came to a pretty face. Or even part of one. A pair of gently haunting eyes, an impudently turned-up nose. A full overbite could instantly reduce him to a mass of quivering jelly. Poor guy. He didn't have a prayer. How many times I'd seen his head swivel a full 360 degrees whenever an enticing-looking woman was even in the same zip code. Feminine beauty was Charlie's kryptonite. It made him go all weak, feeble, and stupid.

Did I say he was a fool for beautiful women? Allow me to correct myself. There were also plenty that were not so beautiful who had halted the man quite dead in his tracks. Women whose faces could easily have stopped all the clocks of Switzerland.

Charlie couldn't see it though; he was too blinded by the bright glare of all things feminine. He couldn't make the distinction. This had always been, and I suspected would always remain, his Achilles heel, and unfortunately all I'd ever been able to do about it was kick it every once in a while and hope it really hurt.

But I am talking here about more than mere sexual indiscretions, about a coldly systematic breakdown of every last security I had. 'Pass the salt' said to me by him at the dinner table became

15

an indictment on forty-eight levels. I know I am equating his efficiency here with that of a psychiatric interrogator at a facility in Leningrad in 1962; I am aware of that. Indeed, as I crouched at the edge of my tub that evening in March, with my head bowed and my stomach unfit for life as we know it, I felt like the weary, misplaced traveler who has stretched and climbed the mighty Ural Mountains all on foot.

But I am getting away from myself. East Hampton had little to do with Leningrad even on a bad day. I was trying to nurture a cool and tranquil canvas of white violets, coreopsis, Scotch broom, Nepalese columbines, and heuchera. It was my summer vacation. I was just trying to clean up a beggar's crop of broken-backed petunias, and here was my ex-husband, startling my pulse by nearly stopping it, knocking the wind right out of me by loping toward me with the insouciance of a plumber strolling by an exploding sewer on his day off. Ah, if only my feelings had been as neatly pruned as, say, those Nepalese columbines. If only I myself had been. For three years I had worked hard, beating the feelings for Charlie out of myself the way a person might beat the dust out of a rug. Yet as we shall see, there is just no foolproof way to remove the last bit of microscopic dust from a rug.

However, if I have described for you something of a beast, it was only a man who stood before me then, his hands splayed on his hips and a bucketful of snazzy Hampton sweat soaking through his tattered navy-blue T-shirt. The shirt may have lost its shape, but I can tell you, I noticed right away that the man had not. Take a fifty-one-year-old world-famous playwright, spin him around the globe a few times on publicity tours, ply him with Parisian pastries, breads baked in the ovens of Tuscany, creamed herrings by the barrelful in chilly Scandinavia, doughy, meat-laden *pirogi* in Russia. Dip him head first into an endless sea of vintage wines, fizzy French champagnes, after-dinner brandies, and pour enough peppered vodka and *Kaffee mit Schlag* down his throat to drown a hundred sailors on a sunny day. Add all this together, plus the customary ravages of time and shifting flesh, and you'd expect this specimen to have lost his lean and hungry silhouette. But he had not. And neither had he lost his spectacular temerity.

'Can I get a cup of coffee?' was what he asked me between gasping jogger's breaths.

Can you blame me for laughing? I did laugh, I'm afraid, as soon as I'd found the courage to look up from my petunias and face him. The eyes, a harsh and bloodless green, like the jagged hunks of glass I imagine lying at the bottoms of oceans, passed over my astonished lips, then settled and locked into my own eyes.

'Coffee?' I asked incredulously, still laughing.

Had he lost his marbles?

'Well, yes, coffee. Evil men with sinister moustaches grow it in Medellín, high up in the mountains of Colombia, when they're not tending their drug crops,' he explained patiently. 'And then we drink it in cups. Sometimes to wake up. Other times to sober up. I'm here for the former,' he went on, 'so can I get some or not?'

'Oh, you can get some, all right. There's a Burger King north of the highway, up about a mile and a half. You know, hold the pickles, hold the lettuce.' I walked past him then, all atremble, up to the house. Luckily, it only required the strength of one unsteady arm to open the screen door to the kitchen.

'And maybe you could hold the sarcasm. I taught it to you and I'm much better at it than you are,' he called to me, a maestro admonishing his oboe section.

'Come on, can't a guy just get a simple cup of coffee? I don't even take milk anymore, or sugar. Be a sport,' he begged, squinting purposefully at the sun.

A sport? I'm not sure, but his voice may have even cracked at that point, like Oliver North or Alfalfa. Whatever, the whole picture absolutely horrified me.

I cannot tell you how I wanted him out of there and far, far away again, like a murderer whose very life is in peril if he does not quickly dispose of a stinking corpse. But where and how

17

could I bury Charlie? He stood there as sound as a parking meter, gazing silently past the sun to somewhere else, resolute. In the end, I just shook my head and went into the kitchen. Hearing the door slam behind me, I held my breath hoping it would not slam again, but of course it did.

'Half a bran muffin would be nice, too, if you happen to have one lying around,' he said as he sat down at my kitchen counter, beating his sneakered feet at his stool like a cranky toddler.

Holding my breath, I measured out the coffee with my back to him, seriously wondering what karmic debt I might be repaying. And then, as if this Kafkaesque tableau was not already quite enough, thank you very much, the man actually began to whistle.

'Moonlight becomes you, it goes with your hair' went the wobbly-clothespin treble. 'You certainly know the right things to wear . . .'

Well, if murder is against the law, thank God, questions are not, so I spoke up.

'I hate to seem ungrateful to my clientele, and I do *not* have any bran muffins lying around, but what on earth are you doing here?' My voice shook. 'What's the problem? Why can't you get coffee at home?' I asked him, seriously wondering. And right at that moment, it struck me like a bolt of bright lightning that I must look just awful standing there, sputtering and carrying on. In my shock at seeing Charlie again, I'd completely forgotten how I looked, which I judged to be a whole lot worse than the bedraggled Odysseus when he finally showed up after the wars.

Now, find me an ex-wife who tells you she doesn't give a hoot about how she looks when she bumps into her ex-husband again, even if she has made a sensational remarriage, and I'll show you either a woman with a head stuffed with straw or a magnificent liar. If I absolutely had to be held captive in my own kitchen with this surprise of a man who had gobbled up such a piggish slice of my past, couldn't I at least have had a little help from Yves Saint-Laurent? Couldn't my hair be swept up in some unthinkably hypnotic creation by the callused palms and fingers of Kenneth himself? Really, couldn't the shoes I'd casually kick off

18

be Maud Frizon or Bruno Magli? Was that asking too much? Why was I doomed to face my opponent in the arena again wearing faded, baggy jeans with soiled, frayed cuffs, and a bulky shirt that actually said FRED'S BOWLING LANES, with the name *Alvin* sewn in script over the left breast pocket, a gift from a friend at the office?

Moreover, not being one of the world's most accomplished sleepers, I had slept poorly the night before (I always do my first night away from the city), so my eyes were as puffy and ringed as a raccoon's. Oh thank you, I thought to myself, looking to the cryptic mysteries on high for answers that were not forthcoming and never would be. Thank you, God, I thought, standing there in my kitchen. It's not enough that you gave us the evils of something like the miniskirt and then had to bring it back again. You had to plunge the knife way in and twist it slowly . . . working it like the second hand of a watch. You had to let men age like elegant wines while we withered away like skinless grapes. You had to give our husbands lunch hours at their jobs, create things like *pied à terres*, male bonding, and hotels with hourly rates, so that they could have the kinds of satisfying lunches we could not pack for them in brown paper bags. And then, on top of it all, after these splendidly aged men had finally cast us aside, even then you could not guarantee us a reunion where we did not look like the Wicked Witch of the West.

So there I was, waiting for Lady Melitta to perform her task, as this heartbreaking revelation cracked over me like thunder, while Charlie just kept up his hopeless whistling. Of course he kept whistling. That was Charlie. See, even that early on I could tell the old boy still knew his stuff, knew his way around me all right. As the coffee filtered down, the thought percolated in my mind that across a stormy sea of three years, without a compass or a prayer, he could still reach my shores every time, the way Magellan finally reached the Moluccas and even got a strait named after him. To my knowledge, however, no one has as yet named a piece of geography for Charlie.

But meanwhile, stuck as I was in my own kitchen, with my captor and his impossible whistling, I remembered General

19

Dozier, who, I had read, was force-fed a continuous diet of loud, booming rock music when he was a guest of the Red Brigade. The blood probably ran like rivers down the sides of his face, but in the end they murdered him anyway. As I drew deep breaths and listened to Charlie and his serenade, my only fear was that I might not be as lucky. What I'm saying, I guess, is that I'd had enough.

'Excuse me,' I started, but he cut me off, suddenly abandoning his whistling in favor of singing. And as he sang, he looked me straight in the eyes. 'Moonlight becomes you, I'm thrilled at the sight . . .'

That's really what did it, the singing. He was a perfectly rotten singer. For the most part, he'd been a perfectly rotten husband, once we'd gotten our feet wet and were at last ready for a tryout in the deep end.

'Charlie,' I began in a low voice, my anger rising. 'What is all this really about? What are you doing here, of all places? This is not the Chinese laundry. This is not David's Cookies. We are not caught in some inexplicable time warp. You can't just stroll in and out of here and audition for the part of my new best friend,' I fumed. 'And anyway, why doesn't your wife know enough to give you coffee in the morning? Third wives are supposed to be great in the kitchen,' I finished, my face very close to his.

'Take it from me, third wives are great in any room,' he answered, but his cockeyed grin belied his words. 'Look, maybe for some strange reason, I woke up today feeling sentimental. And maybe I just didn't care any more about who you are or about what coming here means.' He looked at me then, and suddenly he was all business. 'Really, I just wanted some damned coffee.' Really. And I almost believed him, really, but then he resumed his impossible singing. 'And I could get so romantic tonight . . . so where is my coffee?' he also put to music, my crafty troubadour.

Where was it, indeed? Now, I must be open and frank with you and tell you that Russian roulette was not a particular passion of mine. I was not in the market that summer for intrigue, for bittersweet, or even semisweet, scandal, or, especially, for vague, wistful stirrings. The thing is, this man had stirred me so vigorously and frequently in the past, the mixture had nearly thinned itself out of existence.

The truth? I was a senior vice-president and associate creative director at LDR Advertising, a small but well-polished, respected, and successful agency, and I was feeling pretty good about myself. I had just stepped neatly out of the arena for some well-deserved time-out. True, not everything had gone absolutely perfectly, but enough had to justify my feelings. After I had worked on a long and concentrated new business pitch with my art director, Mara, LDR had indeed pulled in the $20-million account of Chin Airways, a posh new Chinese airline which more than a dozen agencies had hungrily vied for. Now, this had not been just a coup, but more like a coup and a half, and when the uppermost echelon of Chin Airways had invited a handful of agency people, myself among them, to their New York hotel suite for a lavish, elegantly catered celebration, Mara and I were only too happy to oblige. The evening went well, as we were the recipients of more than half a dozen toasts in two languages. The owner of our company beamed at us, and the owner of Chin heaped praise after praise on us, like rice at a wedding couple.

In the office the next day, the day I was to leave on my vacation, we were given an indecently extravagant bunch of flowers and a $10,000 bonus check each from upper management, which sent me off to face the steamy, crowded Long Island Expressway in a mood of delicious, hopeful, feverish abandon. If Chin was an omen, who knew, after this, what my vacation might hold in store for me? I only knew I was a partly reluctant advertising executive, a bit worn about the edges, with a special weakness for Ann Taylor, an occasional Sunday afternoon at the ballet, the inkish outpourings of Saul Bellow, a bit of charity work done during the winter months, the Jeu de Paume, before its contents were so coldly dismantled and moved, Adrienne Vittadini, the Triple Crown, Florence in May, with all the poppies blushing like pomegranates in the surrounding countryside, Bedlington terriers, *tiramisù*, Ray Charles, and the kind of

21

slow-moving, three-star foreign films that inevitably send you home to bed with a crashing, four-star headache.

At any rate, the very night before this peculiar reappearance of my ex-husband, I had packed up the car with battered paperbacks, casual clothes, and a rusty manual typewriter. You see, the plain truth is, and please don't wince, I wanted more than anything else to write the Great American Play and had nearly completed my attempt. Sure, I knew it would be American, but would it in fact be Great? That was anyone's guess and remained to be seen, just like the ending of my play. Although it had been laboriously plotted out in my mind, on paper I could see that it needed more than a bit of work.

Some women pine for Bulgari, for lavish Russian sables, for pristine castles nestled in redolent French valleys, for swarthy princes on milk-white steeds to spirit them away to the burning sands of the Sahara. I wanted only to write plays. Not just plays, but excellent, superior plays. I wanted to be the playwright's ex-wife, the playwright. And of course on my first opening night, I wanted to be draped in Bulgari and only the priciest Russian sables, and my date would naturally be a swarthy prince who would steal away with me to the Loire Valley but only after I'd gotten more kisses at Sardi's than the Pope's ring on a good day at St Peter's.

Now, having been married for all those years to Charlie Stamberg, world-renowned dramatist, was this wish to write plays a perverse one? Was I mad? Was Medea stable? All I can say is that I was a writer. I took pleasure in stringing words together on an empty page the way some people (certainly not myself) delighted in preparing piecrusts. Their fingers just sort of found their way. Without this undercurrent of innate crustmanship, recipes and instructions were useless. The English language was therefore my piecrust, although, believe me, many a half-baked shell had burned or crumbled apart right in my hands on its way into or out of the oven.

Still, the years with Charlie of out-of-town tryouts, rehearsals, writing and rewriting, the roar of the greasepaint, the glitter intermingling with the tension and the sweat of anxiety right up until that last final millisecond combined to make a shameless theater junkie out of me. So I kept inventing people and places and conflicts and pains and confusions and climaxes, in two or three acts. During the week, I wrote for a paycheck at the ad agency for a pack of dry-mouthed, ego-riddled semi-hysterics. But in the evenings and on weekends, when my time fell graciously back into my own lap and I could once again isolate and collect my thoughts, my heart always beat a little faster because I was working on a new play. And just at the point of Charlie's strange reappearance, it was coming along nicely, too. All during that year I'd kept at it, just peck, pecking away, inching along, charting and honing. I'd named it *Glad Tidings*, and punching away at it was what helped to keep me feeling glad. It was a closet in which I'd stored everything, and opening the door always reassured me of just how much there was inside. I suppose you could not have been married to such a man as Charlie Stamberg for ten minutes, let alone ten years, without inheriting his passion for bran muffins, electric toothbrushes, oral sex, and Balducci's unseeded rye, but mainly his unbridled thrill for the theater. In fact, life with Charlie had been so full of its own drama that most days I felt as if we needed an usher to hand out *Playbills* at breakfast.

So, I'd been bitten. Playwriting was coursing through my blood like rabies or malaria. Poised at my arthritic Olympia portable on my East Hampton kitchen table, as I sat facing the roses that inched and climbed up and around my garage, I'd hoped and planned to finish my play, spin out the last threads of my cocoon.

And so what if thus far, all of my painstakingly crafted cocoons over the years had come back to me with mostly polite little notes of rejection, except when one in a string of theater people actually took me out to lunch or dinner (before my divorce) in order to break my heart in person, as a professional courtesy to Charlie. The rejections had piled up over the years, and of course sometimes they really stung, depending on my connection to what I'd written, but sometimes not. Sometimes, I managed just to brush them off, like the dandruff on Charlie's tuxedoed shoulders in the years when we still stepped out together at night, like models in a Plaza Hotel ad, under a sky filled with bright, cold stars.

And so what if this man with the occasionally snowy shoulders had gone and won himself two Pulitzers, and four Tony Awards, as well as a host of other international accolades. All the more reason for me to try to plant my seeds in a similar garden. After all, when I'd met Charlie thirteen years before, I was just a copywriter taking an evening playwriting class of his at the New School.

Of course I was intimidated. Who wouldn't be? He had presence, he had character, he was the very essence of propriety, and he had depth. He had a voice that made Orson Welles sound like a braying ninny. He had a sexual voltage that could black out all of Manhattan on a steamy night. He had a classy, almost English reserve, but actually had matzoh-ball soup pulsing through his veins: a Jewish Lord Olivier, all decked out in his tweedy Meladandri, with just a whisper of a Bronx twang. And of course, he also had his first Pulitzer, which has seldom been known to hurt anyone's public relations.

Luckily for myself, as well as for most of the dazzled and dewy-eyed women in my class, he also had a wife stashed up in Westchester, whom he would refer to constantly in his lectures. Learning that she was Italian, I'd imagined nothing less than a contessa, a pearl of a woman, leaning upward and outward from a colossal oyster to the husband who cherished her for the prize she was. Imagine my horror and relief when she picked him up after class one wintry evening on their way to the theater, and I faced, instead of a pearl, a blackened rhinestone which had long ago lost its luster.

At a later date, I learned that Dolores had indeed come up the hard way, through the sewers of Red Hook, to be exact. She chattered ceaselessly that night at the New School when I first saw her, saying nothing. She was the sort of woman who often draped her mink coats on the floor, let them slip ever so nimbly

24

from her seat in restaurants, on planes, in theaters. She was said to be a consummate cook and, at the time I came to know Charlie, was in the dizzy process of redoing her oversized kitchen in only the milkiest, most translucent marble, shipped to her from the darkest reaches of Carrara, the floors in only the most beguiling tiles fetched from Spain.

Charlie had let it slip once that when they'd first met, she was nothing less than sensational – majestic, witty, and strikingly beautiful. She must have been, because he'd fallen for her like the ton of Carrara marble soon to line her kitchen. To hear him tell it (which, thank goodness, he had done only once), every man past puberty in the tristate area had pined for her homemade *brasciole*, her wild, scented, laughing kisses, and her passionate embrace. At this, I could only sniff somewhat haughtily and jealously and note how far the mighty had fallen. (As I recall, I had likened her appeal to dogs stopping at fire hydrants, and that had ended the discussion. Permanently.)

Rescued by Charlie, who plucked her from her humble beginnings as a handkerchief saleswoman at Lord & Taylor, she was now giddy with intoxication at being so securely tucked away in the leafiest corner of Katonah with her dogs, her pricey pots and pans, her minks, her Jaguar and her Mercedes, not to mention her pool man, her gardener, her plumber, and her tennis instructor, who could all be cheerfully coaxed inside for a beer, a chat, or an overexuberant romp between the strawberry-dotted Martex sheets. But to tell the truth, Charlie was no choirboy himself, so for a time their mutual, respectful coexisting duplicities balanced nicely with each other.

When Charlie met her at Lord & Taylor, in the heavy air of mingling perfumes battling for dominance, she told him that she was studying nights to become a graphic designer. Indeed, she'd had very graphic designs on Charlie about twelve seconds after she'd first spotted him. Right then and there, he took her out to lunch, even though it was only eleven-thirty, but first they stopped at her bank so she could deposit her paycheck. When she walked in, she was $127.56 overdrawn on her checking account. By the time they left, after chatting feverishly together on the bank line, she was worth a million at least. Talk about good investments.

But if the miracle of perfection could be found financially, it couldn't be found humanly, at least not within my own albeit narrow scope, which I must confess included neither Red Hook nor the certain saucy thrill of peddling monograms on the ground floor of a department store. I guess what I'm saying is that luckily for myself, as well as for the rest of the love-bitten female pups crowded into that overheated classroom at the New School, our celebrity of a professor, for all of his painstakingly crafted lectures on Chekhov or Ibsen, possessed one terrific imperfection, thank God: this man of impeccable grooming had nose hairs both long and strong enough to stir his soup.

It may have been thirteen years ago, but I can still remember the evening, quite early in the term, when he sat with me after class, going over a particularly insipid little playlet I'd concocted. If I was after his approval, I certainly didn't get it. Instead, I received a terse and fatigued speech on the perils of self-indulgence in writing, and the paramount importance of knowing how, why, and when to trim a scene. I was flustered, I remember, gazing into the dry glitter of those coldly disapproving, Pulitzer Prize-winning eyes, thinking of the great and cherished Contessa locked away in Katonahesque splendor, with her expertly handcrafted spaghetti carbonara probably clotting at that very moment right in the colander, all because my typewriter and I could not sufficiently suppress ourselves.

We were the last ones left in the classroom, and he seemed nervous, distracted. I had my coat on, and was eager to run the instant it was polite to. As he spoke, I could feel the sweat trickle in beads down my back. Taking his coat from a wall peg, he wrapped his cashmere scarf twice around his elegant neck, still speaking. But as he bent down to relace a shoe, I could, as always, see the tiny village of hairs in his nose sprouting every which way, pirating attention away from his otherwise perfect profile.

'Do you get what I'm saying, Stevie?' I can recall him asking, gesturing with his arms outstretched, getting into his coat. 'You've got to know when to cut. Be harsh with yourself, brutal.

26

Remember, you can always put things back, but start out lean. I know cutting hurts, but what isn't there can often be more important than what is. Trust me. Trimming is everything.'

By this time, his nose hairs were growing right before my very eyes, like Rapunzel's tresses dripping out the window. I couldn't take my eyes off them. Then, I'll never know what made me say it, but I asked, ever so softly, 'Like nose hairs?'

'Nose hairs?' he whispered.

I gathered up my books, looking away from him. 'Well, yes. If they're not trimmed properly, they can spoil an entire work of art, can't they?'

I wasn't being coy or argumentative. I was being thoughtless, stupid, but whenever I spoke to him, my head was filled with soda pop.

'But what has that got to do with anything? With play-writing?' he wanted to know. And he had a point there.

I scrambled then, forming words but not sentences.

'Are you making fun of me?' he asked shyly, his face beginning to break into something of a grin.

I stood to button my coat, drowning in sweat and fear. 'Not at all' was all I could manage, weakly.

'I think you are,' he said then, but it was as if he liked it. I could tell that he did. His hand brushed absentmindedly over his nose as we stood there, and then, for some strange reason, he reached over and took one of my hands in his and held it there. The awesome playwright was suddenly delighted with the tactless protégé, but she couldn't even begin to guess why.

'Your hand is like a block of ice,' he pronounced. All around us, the janitor was turning the lights out in the classrooms. In another moment, he let my hand fall to my side with a bit of a jerk. We walked together to the elevator then, and by the time we'd stepped inside, he'd reverted to his chilly professorial demeanor.

'You've got talent, you've got a good ear,' he said, more to his shoes than to me. 'You just have to know when to restrict yourself a little, pull in the reins. I'll be interested to see how your writing develops this semester. Don't forget about the trimming

27

now.' He leaned into my face as we reached the lobby. 'And neither will I,' he whispered.

We said good night and walked to the doors in opposite directions. You can imagine my surprise when, just before disappearing through the revolving door, he called after me.

'Hey, are you in love with anyone?'

'No,' I shrugged. Not unless you counted the sparkly-eyed, Pulitzer Prized, married man who lingered a moment to smile at my answer. A millisecond later when I had looked up, he was gone.

From that indelible moment on, we were locked in a dance that had taken years to wind down, if it ever really had at all. Love crashed in on me suddenly, exhilarating me at first, pinning me down in startled wonderment, and in the end it crushed me with a bitter disappointment that proved to be every bit as startling.

We began quietly, cautiously, with a good measure of shy and awkward reserve, with lunches I invited him over for at my apartment in the Village.

For weeks we didn't touch. Together, we'd sit and talk, listening to the strains of Schubert or Corelli, with me on the couch and him over in a corner, creaking away in my rocking chair (listening more, I thought, to the silences between notes than to the actual notes themselves). Occasionally, I would glance over at the table, still filled with our lunch paraphernalia, and I remember turning scarlet. (It always reminded me of an unmade bed with tangled sheets and pillows scattered everywhere.)

And then one afternoon, Charlie had suddenly had enough of these monastic meetings (which was not a moment too soon, since by then my own tongue was hanging so far out it could've mopped the sidewalk), and he came over to me, midway through our conversation, took a deep breath, and reached for me.

His first kiss was unexpected, not for what it was but rather for where it was, because Charlie kneeled down and, gripping me firmly, kissed me between my legs (and then proceeded to work his unearthly magic, with not a trace of his former shyness or reserve).

From there, things progressed quite normally and naturally. In the weeks to come, we were never out of each other's sight for very long. Hanging on each other's words, we could hardly believe our great fortune in finding ourselves together. In our minds, no one had ever before experienced the miracle of these feelings or ever would again. Sex was sublime, but all of our time spent together felt as if it had been ripened by some special sun.

Now, exactly why or how I fell for him so completely had caused me not a single second's confusion, but the enigma of why it was apparently reciprocated lost me many a night's sleep.

Of course, I was younger than Charlie, attractive, and I could be quite acid-tongued with him at times when he asked for it, rather than merely gushing and preening, but was all of that enough? Yes, he was in a loveless marriage, where he and Dolores each more or less lived as they pleased in their separate orbits, but did even this explain his apparent fascination with me?

There was, though, what he referred to as my 'gift', my writing talent, which he became quite obsessive about after a while. Convinced that I could do great work, sensational work, he kept pushing me to work harder, write better, breathing fire into the pages I wrote.

Well, perhaps that's it, I thought, way back when. Maybe it was the Pygmalion ingredient that had proved to be so compelling to his ego.

Whatever it was (as if anyone can ever understand these things), the day I finally knew for sure that I really had him was the day after we'd been up all night debating the merits of the first act of a play I'd been battling with. Charlie was more or less living with me in my apartment by then, and we'd rearranged some furniture so that we could work simultaneously, with him at a little living-room table, and me at my big mahogany desk in the bedroom.

Looking around me that morning, before I left for the office, I saw his clothes and things were everywhere. As I went about

29

straightening up, I realized I was furious at him for his overbearing manner in criticizing my work the night before. In a flash, without thinking really, I called my super and got him to switch the furniture so that when Charlie came back, he now had my desk and my play in his designated work space.

Well, that was the night I heard something fall, really fall, and I realized it was Charlie. Whereas his prior delight in me had merely been some delirious, hormonal, schoolboy's folly, this was the real thing.

That night, I knew he was mine.

He took one look around the apartment and his face began to color. His head was tilted. He noticed the desk. His eyes were dancing. You've made your point, they said. You are my creation, they also said, and, goddamnit, you're spectacular. I will never leave you, I also thought I heard them say.

And yet now, here we were, thirteen years later, and those eyes had lied to me.

Here I had had Charlie and lost him. He had first learned to trim his nose hairs, and later had neatly trimmed himself of me. But through it all, my sometimes nail-bitten fingers had never stopped itching to write plays, and I had kept at it relentlessly. Some would call this masochistic, I'm sure, but I would only ask them if van Gogh's wife (if only he'd had one, would she have saved him, or would he have done himself in even sooner?) would have dreamed of painting the side of a warehouse? I think not. I stalked the great American play the way a great blue heron stalks a tender frog for its midday meal: shoulders hunched down low, with mighty pale-gray wings outstretched. It kept my engine humming. After my divorce, as long as I was in my postlitigational shock, it did the trick. It kept me off the streets, or rather off the phone, bemoaning my fate to anyone and everyone who would listen.

One thing working at playwriting didn't do was supplement my alimony payments, which seemed to lose steam a bit earlier each month, now that I had divorced my husband and married my credit cards. I realized something had to be done when I began to notice the salespeople in Saks, Bendels, Bloomingdale's, Bergdorf Goodman, Lord & Taylor, B. Altman's, and Macy's – the real Seven Sisters – clearing a path for me and jockeying for position when I entered their departments.

At that time I was also logging a lot of time eating candy and junk food. How much time? Let's just say the shareholders at Hershey's were awfully happy that year. No pizza crust was too thick or lifeless for my palate. No fried chicken, purchased in waxy buckets in quantities sufficient to feed the entire island of, say, Staten, could ever bat at my locustlike appetite. Clearly, a problem was developing. I was almost ready then to return to advertising as a copywriter, the job I'd abandoned several years ago.

I had always been something of, well, I guess I might as well just say it, a looker. I stood about five feet nine on a day worth getting up for, and I had thick, straight, dark-brown hair that had often been compared to shiny chocolate sauce by more than one premarital blind date, as he made the messy slip from silly to sloshed, all under the beckoning moon. This cascading chocolate sauce fell in arched parentheses about my face, and was then cut at the jaw; very Cleopatra, but a hell of a lot sleeker than anything you might've found flipping through, say, the Egyptian Christmas issue of *Elle* in 29 BC. My eyes were blue and large, and had a habit of looking especially forlorn even when I wasn't, which wasn't terribly often in those days. My body was as neatly cut as the hair was; very hourglass indeed, with particular attention usually going to the hours of three and nine, if you know what I mean.

However, in those days, huddled deep, buried away in my bunkerlike cave of an apartment in the grim time after my enlightening brush with the judicial process, I was not a contender in any beauty contest. The skin was becoming sallow, and the hourglass was getting noticed more for the four and eight o'clock hours. I was spending too much time (which I did have), and money (which I didn't), roaming the shopping palaces and gabbing like a wild goose to all my new best friends, the saleswomen. A good example was the elderly, genteel Mrs Lutrell, in her eternal navy blazer in the skirt department at Saks.

31

'Well, I'm stymied, as usual,' I'd say to her, the store's first client on a Monday morning, exploding out of the starting gate as if shot out of a cannon, at precisely 10:01. Turning round and round in the circular mirrors like a spinning, wool-clad ballerina, I whined for her expert assistance.

'I'm torn between the blue, the brown, and the tan skirt, Mrs Lutrell. Please help me choose,' I'd say. At which point she'd pinch at one corner of her gondola-shaped, rhinestone-studded glasses, and say ever so softly, with the fragile diplomacy of a Henry Kissinger, 'Mrs Stamberg, this is extremely difficult for me. The blue picks up your eyes, which are exquisite. The coppery brown sets off your hair. Aah, if I only had hair that thick! Then, of course, there's the tan, which complements both. It's no wonder you're torn. King Solomon himself never had to make such a choice,' she finished, shaking her head and furrowing her floury-white brow. King Solomon? No empty vessel was our Mrs Lutrell. King Solomon had to choose, but she knew I didn't. She knew she had a live one, and that I'd end up with all three skirts, wrapped and bundled into a cab with me. And she was right.

Every sign pointed to the unavoidable truth that I was as unequipped for this new chapter in my life as the junior parachutist forced to make an emergency landing over the FDR Drive during rush hour. Mired in inertia and a gutless kind of misery, I needed a distraction gripping enough to wean me from myself for a time, a magnet the size of the Grand Canyon just to haul myself out of bed in the morning. But a job? Surely it would have been like teaching an aborigine to wear shoes. Still, I know that on one August day, I awoke with one temple beating like a wobbly metronome, in a lake of cold panic and perspiration, feeling nailed and bolted into a coffin while I was still breathing, and knew for certain that I had had enough. I knew it was time to try to get my old job back.

Believe me, given half a breath and an IQ out of the single digits, any woman will leap into a lifeboat when she is drowning, and the leaping doesn't mean she's any sort of a heroine or anything. It only means she prefers not to pass the whole of

32

eternity like a cask of sunken treasure, pressed to the bottom of the sea.

The thing is, I have never really had the stamina to flourish in the corporate world, with its ringing phones, machine-gun staccato of typewriters, its clash of mismatched egos and person-alities; the stale, endlessly recycled ideas had only helped to pile up my natural distrust and slimy creeping contempt over the years for an industry glued solidly together by Maalox, martinis, Valium, Librium, and Preparation H, like a heap of soiled clothes sitting in a laundry basket. I did not relish the thought of plunging myself once more into the executive shark pond, watching my limbs float out and away from me, stapled with the bloodied dental imprints of my colleagues and superiors. It was just the lesser of two particularly evil evils. It might've been different if one could actually get Frequent Flyer Bonus Miles for laps up and down the crowded aisles of the Food Emporium, and for those expensive hollow-feeling treks up and down the floors of the Seven Sisters. If so, I could've traveled free to the Big Dipper and back every day for a decade. But I not only needed pocket money. I not only needed a focus. I needed to stop calling my sister, who had her own problems, and my mother in Florida, who bemoaned endlessly the fact that she had not slipped a bagel knife neatly between Charlie's right and left ventricles when she still had the chance. I needed to stop watch-ing soap operas – and enjoying them – nagging my friends to have long and languorous lunches when they had jobs and lives to live. More than anything else though, I needed to stop mooning over my ex-husband, and replaying the final act so that it left him sitting across from me in the living room, drinking a dry martini, feet up on the glass coffee table, crossed at the ankles like a state trooper's, with eyes luminescent and so positively besotted with love for me that it embarrassed me and I could almost not look back. As you can see, I was in an appalling state.

If you find yourself wondering here about the children, there weren't any, and needless to say, it was the time in my life when I most regretted that particular lack of planning, courage, selflessness, and achievement on our part.

Actually, it was Charlie who had always put off the idea of having kids, much the way he considered having tandoori chicken for dinner. You know, 'We'll go, we'll have it, but some other time. Later, okay?' Sure, he liked Indian food. He liked kids. But always other people's kids. And so, somehow, we just never got around to having our own.

As it happened, I had occasionally considered the idea of trying to insist, of just putting my foot down about having children. The thing is, as Charlie became more famous, more celebrated, and caught up in the glamorous whirlwind of the demimonde, his plays became his children. He conceived and carried them, and sat up at night with them when they were ill. He rejoiced in their glowing report cards as they found their way to him from virtually all the patches on the globe. He went away to war with them and fought their every battle. Now this, you see, required all his strength and a colossal concentration, so it makes sense that he was a proud papa indeed when one of his plays took flight and actually set the world on its ear. Coming home at the end of a day of this sort of grand-scale nurturing, imagine the letdown he might've felt at having to cope with merely helping a little guy with a runny nose, unlaced sneakers, or, God forbid, things like ringworm and homework.

Was I bitter? Was I blue? Actually, at the time, I never allowed myself to reach the bottom of my feelings on this subject. If anything, my job in advertising was like a sponge into which I could absorb these feelings and blot them away every day. And that's why, a year after Charlie and I had fled the courthouse on that bleak and eerie day, with Nature crashing its approval or disapproval over our heads, I had once again found solace and stability in the predictable sameness, paycheck, and routines of the advertising industry.

But now, with the ghost of Charlie, past and present, intruding itself into my kitchen, the comfort of a job was truly the very last thing flashing through my panicked brain. I mean, there it was, the very first whole day of my well-deserved, self-imposed exile, and the tiny quiver in my entrails was already telling me that the greatest possible threat to this long-awaited slice of tranquil and precious time had already coiled itself around the legs of one of my kitchen stools, like a crafty asp inching along the muddy Ugandan banks of the Nile.

'Dolores is getting married again,' he announced to me, his sneakered feet still kicking away at the legs of the kitchen stool in an infuriating rhythm.

'So who is it this time?' I asked casually, pouring out his coffee. 'I know she loves a man in uniform. Is it the pool man? The man who comes to read the meter, or Roto-Rooter? Surely a woman with her refined sensibilities has standards that must be met.'

At that, he let out a jaunty yelp of a laugh.

'I can't believe how you still resent her. Even after all these years. And the funny thing is, there was never any reason to resent her in the first place. I mean really, if anything, she should resent you – which she doesn't. You're the one who broke up her marriage and rearranged her life.'

Clearly, we were off and running. I took a deep breath and hoped my adrenaline had gotten a good night's sleep, even if I hadn't. Did I mention to you that I wasn't up to this? That I just didn't have the juice? That I lacked the octane? Well, silly me. And silly you for believing me, for I could no more resist a challenge or a dare from Charlie than I could resist tapping my foot when in the presence of a marimba band. To fuel myself for the battle I was about to do, I poured myself a glass of seltzer, and sat down next to my opponent.

'I did not break up Dolores's marriage,' I began steadily, as he knew I would. 'If you remember, she was the one who called me when we first started seeing each other.'

'You must be kidding. You never told me that.'

'I've told you at least a dozen times, but your ego refuses to remember it.'

'Did she call to ask you to stay away from me? She was upset, I know, but God, I didn't know that she'd groveled like that.' He shook his head. Now it was my turn to laugh.

'Hardly. She called to ask me what was taking so long. She was hoping I'd be able to help her get out of her marriage because she'd had enough. I was her parachute.'

'Oh, come on. I can't believe you've never told me this,' he insisted. Can you believe how stubborn this man could be?

Still, I went blithely ahead.

'As I recall, her exact words were "For years I hoped he'd change. But a leopard doesn't change its stripes." Oh, she resented me, all right. But only because the ink on her divorce papers wasn't dry sooner.'

Was I dreaming, or was the master playwright actually at a loss for words? If so, it was only for a fleeting moment.

'What an amazing thing,' he said, shaking his head. 'I guess I did give her something of a hard time. Sometimes I forget *how* hard. It's just very tough living with a –, a –'

I knew this guy, and that's why I knew the word he wanted to say, desperately, was 'genius.'

'A celebrity,' he managed, weakly.

He was telling me. But this was a man who, with little or no provocation, would tell I. M. Pei how to construct a house out of Lego or Tinkertoy pieces, so nothing surprised me.

And the thing is, he was right, as I knew only too well. It is tough living with a genius. When I had lived with him, I had never thought that necessarily so, but I had read it so often about myself, in magazine articles, in earnest little pieces and in far-flung, always partly bogus biographies about my husband, the world-famous playwright, that toward the end I had finally swallowed it myself. When you are married to a man who reads his work out loud at the White House, who has won virtually every literary prize in existence, including a couple created just for him, with the particularly nagging (to him) exception of the Nobel (for which Charlie genuflected nightly, if only in his mind), a man whose face is impossible to escape on television (believe me, I've tried), who travels freely and luxuriously as the charmed guest of the governments of places like Sweden, Israel, Japan, Italy, and France as often and as effortlessly as you or I might step around the corner to the dry cleaner, when you've been tied up for more than a decade with a man whose work has inspired symposiums held in the courtyards of the Louvre, a ballet for the Bolshoi, and an entire meal named after one of his plays at the Russian Tea Room, whose plays represent, really, the backbone of top-flight American drama in our lifetime, a man for whom all the world is but a huge playpen, filled with temptations and distractions, well, it is hard not to be, shall we say, humbled and impressed.

'Actually, Dolores is marrying a minister,' Charlie told me. 'So maybe you're right about the uniform.'

Why wasn't I surprised? Who else would listen to her endless private litany of sins committed by and against her: of adultery, of greed, of viciousness and duplicity?

I would never forget the day soon after Charlie and I began together when Dolores, who must have been born with a stripe of evil perversity up and down her back like a skunk's, telephoned me to say if I wanted Charlie I was more than welcome to him. She was so accepting, she added with a hint of tinny munificence that she wanted to give me a gift via Charlie, to celebrate the fact that he and I had found each other.

'Oh, that's not necessary.' I squirmed in my seat. It was early on all right, but already I sensed she was not to be trusted.

'Oh, but it is . . .'

The gift, she claimed with a happy snort, was venereal warts and she hoped Charlie would pass them along to me as soon as possible, which, I'm sad to say, led to exactly what she'd wanted, namely a rash of nasty, tearful arguments, slammed doors and phones, bunches of flowers tossed down the incinerator, and many evenings lost in impassioned claims from Charlie about how he hadn't slept with Dolores in years. All of which added up to a hill of garbanzos until he finally dragged me into my doctor's office for a Pap smear, which tested negative. Oh, Dolores may have thrown away an old pair of unwanted slippers, but she really didn't want anyone else walking around wearing them.

And now Dolores, evil, contrary Dolores, was marrying a minister. Now this was a marriage with legs, I thought. It could go on and on into infinity, outlast us all. Perhaps her husband's confessional could fit right into the kitchen, provided not a single Spanish tile, whose value approached roughly the price of a one-way ticket to Barcelona, was scratched upon installation.

'Well, how very *Thorn Birds*. Where did they meet? Was she going for her confirmation?' I couldn't help asking.

'Actually, they met at AA. He runs the meetings at his church up in Bedford, and took a special interest in her. He's a recovered alcoholic.'

'Was she actually drinking too much, or did she go to the meetings to meet men and enhance her social life?' The image of Dolores lapping up the sauce Ray Milland style, with perhaps a broken blood vessel or two at the tip of her nose, tearing vulturously into Charlie's alimony payment every month with shaking hands and bleary vision, I confess, was not totally unpalatable to me. Don't get me wrong. I do not wish the broken, scarred life of drunkenness on anybody. But Dolores wasn't just anybody.

Ignoring my sarcasm, Charlie pushed on, full steam ahead. No quitter was this boy.

'From what I gather, she was drinking pretty heavily. She even started calling me late at night sometimes, and I really wasn't equipped, so I kept on pushing AA. It's hard when you're home all day with nothing to do.'

Now just what is it about certain women that makes men eternally prepared to make excuses for them? Dolores could butcher a family of twelve in their sleep with a straightedge razor and a smile on her lips, and I knew the man next to me would be the first one to arrive, unshaven and frantic, to post her bail money. 'It's hard when you're home all day with nothing to do,' he'd tell the phalanx of hungry reporters on the courthouse steps. Whereas I could step quite absentmindedly on the toes of some-one's grandmother in the produce aisle of D'Agostino's, and I know this same fellow would be petitioning the governor for the death penalty. What was it? If the Alps had unfrozen in a single second and had flushed into my little country kitchen at that very instant, there could not have been more water under the bridge.

And yet, even after all this time, Charlie's loyalty to Dolores still bothered me, just as it had when we were married, even though, as he had never been tired of telling me, he had left her for me.

The real question was, had she ever really left him? How well I remember those late night calls from her, before she ever needed the excuse of alcohol, in the days after Charlie had moved in with me. She'd misplaced her accountant's phone number, or it was his mother's birthday the next day and she wanted to make sure he didn't forget, or what was the name of that movie she liked so much, you know, the one in black-and-white by De Sica, about the boy and the father and the bicycle? It was on the tip of her tongue. And the thing was, he'd always answer her patiently, tirelessly, even if only three minutes before he'd been gushing forth with an endless vitriolic tirade on her various failings as a wife. The time quickly came when we imposed a ban on talking about her, but I knew she was still in Charlie's thoughts, probably more often than not. And it was from that long-ago, pent-up reserve of angry frustration that I could call upon my Dolores demons, even to this day, and have them speak for me. And look at how well they rose to the occasion. Just give me a few regurgitated petunias, startle me with a dazzling ex-husband on a quest for caffeine, and put a lifeless glass of seltzer in my hand. I'd regress thirteen years.

'Well, Dolores always did need a father figure. And just think, she can even call him that and no one will bat an eye.'

I met his eyes then, which were looking at me somewhat sadly.

'But I'm not planning to be thinking about it,' he said, barely above a whisper. 'At the moment, I'm thinking of other things,' he said quietly, setting off the worry alarms in every chamber of my heart, sending all my survival instincts scrambling for cover.

'I just don't know why you ever divorced her if you're still so concerned about her.' I spoke to the chipped nail I was picking on my left hand.

'Maybe I don't know why I ever married her, but divorced you.'

'Well, being married to her must've been –'

39

'Being married to her was just too much goddamned trouble, just the way talking about her is, Stevie.'

'But –' I sputtered.

He threw up his hands then, and spoke to my kitchen ceiling, watery blotches, cracks, and all.

'A mandarin fell in love with a courtesan. "I shall be yours," she told him, "when you have spent a hundred nights waiting for me, sitting on a stool, in my garden, beneath my window." But on the ninety-ninth night the mandarin stood up, put his stool under his arm, and went away.' He paused. 'Roland Barthes wrote that.'

Well, of course I was moved. But not too far. The man was a walking library, a mobile companion to the *Oxford English Dictionary*, and had memorized every piece of drama, poetry, and fiction ever written, that's all. If he ever tired of his current preoccupation with the theater, he could always make the rounds of quiz shows. Stump Stamberg? I was convinced it couldn't be done. I could name any subject, from dung beetles to oysters, and it'd take this man only about four seconds, on a slow day, to sift about and summon from his microfilmed memory bank not just an interesting but also a perfectly correct, identified, appropriate quote.

'A lover's a liar,' he'd begin, perhaps. 'To himself he lies. The truthful are loveless, like oysters their eyes!' Then would follow the full, preordained pause, necessary for his audience to feel the full force of awe, jealousy, and esteem. 'Kurt Vonnegut said that,' he'd finish, not without a trace of self-satisfaction.

In the beginning, when you are in the first mindless, weight-less throes of reckless abandonment and discovery about one another, when the revelation that someone uses unwaxed dental floss seems a crucial enough part of his puzzle to keep you awake nights, when he tells you things like your hair smells of apricots, or whispers to your neck that you look absolutely adorable eating popcorn in a movie, even though you know you look like a rodent chowing down in a reform school – during that blissful, feverish moment in time, burned into the hide of your memory until long after you'd like it to be, it is not hard to find yourself disgracefully impressed with a man whose storehouse of a brain seems to you to be something of a national treasure. Later, though, when the smoke clears and you see it's all been done with mirrors, the magnificence of such a memory seems only tedious and a bit ludicrous, yet another reason why you feel the man should be boiled in oil. So, if you're bowled over here with this business of Charlie quoting Barthes's mandarin, of course I don't blame you. (I wonder if even Barthes could have quoted Barthes that casually.) It's just that by now I expected it from him. Charlie, even when he was at his very worst still effortlessly gave forth the blinding incandescence of ten thousand candles glowing right out of the face of the sun, like some colossal birthday cake. But more and more over the years, I'd come to regard his incessant quotes as the Charlie McCarthy to his Edgar Bergen, a way of saying things to me without being ultimately responsible for their content or import. That's why when 'Proust said that . . .' or Dante or St Augustine 'said that,' I gradually came to resent it, to regard it as an unwillingness to talk to me himself.

'If you'd like more coffee, now is the time to ask for it.' I said that, going over to the Melitta on the other side of the kitchen. 'The kitchen is closing.'

'Yes, please. Your coffee is still the best,' he said quietly, as I refilled his mug.

'You know, I jog farther and farther every day,' Charlie said then, very softly. 'Soon I'll be in Toledo,' he smiled. In spite of myself, I looked into his face then, and suddenly felt the full force of a violent electrical storm. In fact, at that very second, I felt my whole kitchen crackling with such stupendous voltage, I knew the entire South Fork must be frying. Certainly Craig Claiborne himself would caution me against ever trying to make mayonnaise in that kitchen again.

'Well, you always were a little compulsive about staying in shape. It was just never quite as fashionable before,' I responded coolly, thinking back to all the years of his predawn runs, long before it was considered *de rigueur*. In those days, it was just de ridiculous.

'Look at me,' he said, gesturing at his sweaty T-shirt and slimy

41

sneakers with the proud, detached confidence of only the very beautiful or the very ugly. 'Do I look fashionable?' Outside, the whiney bobwhites called to us in their monotonous, rhetorical lament. 'Watch . . . out,' the clipped, endless trill seemed to say to me. Charlie's question, too, required no answer, or else he would never have asked it.

'I'm not jogging because it's fashionable. Actually, I'm having . . . a bit of a problem working at home lately. I seem to end up doing most of my thinking away from the house, when I'm running. My family only gets to see me between acts,' he said, a little grimly.

Did Pandora hesitate before she opened the box? We'll never know, but Lord knows I didn't. Instead, I flung myself at the open door of catastrophe, shoving both feet through it at once.

'What . . . sort of a problem?' I managed to get out, ever so casually, with soggy visions of my sanity, my stability, my summer vacation, my future passing tragically before my eyes, like the entire villages that float away in floods on the eleven o'clock news.

'The baby . . . screams a lot. And my wife . . . Patsy . . . talks a lot. More than a lot, actually. It's becoming insufferable. I had no idea, really, of what I was getting myself into.'

At that, I had to laugh. 'Charlie, babies scream. Wives talk. It says so in the catalog, so you knew what you were getting when you ordered them.' I guess that got him, because all of a sudden he began to squirm, and the regal brow began to furrow. Well, so much for child brides. So much for babies having babies, I thought.

'Well, I'm afraid the whole damned package may just not be for me,' he tossed off, as if he were refusing a cheese sandwich in an Automat. 'Look, does this house have a living room? I keep waiting for a waitress to bring us a check.'

'It has a living room,' I answered. How I had always loved dancing with my husband.

'Did I buy it for you?'

'The living room or the house?' I wanted to know, my hackles up once again, as ready for warfare as the National Guard.

42

He shrugged. 'Either.'

'No.'

'In that case, I'd love to see it,' he laughed.

'The living room, or the house?'

'Both.' He tilted his head a little then, for added sincerity. 'Come on, Stevie, let's try to have a nice conversation,' he said softly, following me out of the kitchen.

With his back to me, he began to inspect the contents of my living-room bookcases, emitting an occasional groan or sigh.

'So that's what happened to my *Treasury of Russian Literature*,' he said, taking down a weighty, dusty volume that had long ago lost most of its pages.

'As I recall, we bought the book together.'

'Well, then maybe I could sue you for shared custody. How's my story about the guy who keeps getting more and more land, gets too greedy, loses everything, and dies because of it?' he wanted to know, turning to it. 'Here it is. "How Much Land Does a Man Need?" I was always extremely proud of this one.'

'I didn't realize you wrote it. I thought it was Tolstoi.'

'I mean proud of Leo,' he paused, thumbing through the book. 'I'm definitely taking this one home.'

Over my dead body, I thought. I knew this guy. I knew I could give him an inch, and he'd take Czechoslovakia, give him a book, and he'd leave with the dining-room table in his back pocket. I went over and took the book away from him very gently. 'And then you can write a story called "How Many Books Does a Man Need?" The book stays here, buckeroo,' I announced, sitting down on a couch.

'Well, can I at least come over once in a while and visit it?' he wanted to know, settling down on an opposite couch, his muddy sneakers missing my cherished chintz by about an eyebrow.

'No, but you can photocopy the whole book if you want to.'

'It's over a thousand pages.'

I couldn't resist, so sue me. 'I know, but just think of how much of your baby's screaming and your wife's talking you'll miss.'

He shook his head. 'I want you to know this is killing me. How does it feel to look at a dead man?'

We stared silently at each other across a glass-topped coffee table coated with a sugary film of dust.

'What,' I took a long breath, 'is it that's killing you? The coffee . . . or the company?'

'Neither. Knowing that all my best Billie Holiday tapes are probably here, right under this roof' – his eyes narrowed – 'and not only will I never get them back from you, you probably won't even let me hear them.'

Before I could even tell him what I thought, which was, that's right, buster, the phone began to ring. It rang and rang, and in my underwater, disconnected state, it took quite a while for me to understand that in order for it to stop ringing, it was necessary for me to answer it, which I finally did. On the seventh ring, I picked the phone up in the kitchen and heard my mother's voice.

'How are you, Mom?'

A low moan followed. 'I don't even want to tell you the color of what I was coughing up this morning.'

Even though she was calling from Florida, thanks to the eerily flawless connections of AT&T, the nearness of her voice always startled me, kept me teetering on the itchy rim of paranoia. She always sounded no more than a short cab ride away, and whenever I hung up after speaking to her, I half expected the doorbell to ring ten minutes later.

'Who's there?' I'd ask, with false surprise, my blood turning to ice, knowing full well who stood waiting to shock me on the other side of the closed door.

'Surprise!' she'd scream as I opened the door, eyeing the twelve pieces of luggage my elevator man was already lining up like bowling pins in my foyer. 'And you thought I was calling from Florida,' she'd say, pressing herself to me. 'Now, let's sit down and figure out how to pull your life together,' my mother would say, steering me with an iron grasp into my living room. At this point, if I was lucky, my fantasy of horror usually broke off and deposited me, most thankfully, back at the door of reality.

44

'You sound as if you're right around the corner,' I told her then, trying to outwit her, just in case she really had just stepped off a plane at Kennedy, or really was, God help me, calling from a phone booth in East Hampton.

'I'm surprised you can even hear me at all. I have a terrible sinus infection. I can't tell you what I feel like . . .'

'Well, don't feel obligated.'

'I just wanted to make sure you got out there all right,' she stated, a trifle defensively.

'The trip out was just fine,' I said, breathing a little easier now, for we had safely passed the three-minute point and no coins had dropped. She was not calling from a pay phone. She was calling from Florida. Just then, a loud boom of unexpected music burst forth from the living room.

'I make a date for golf, and you can bet your life it rains. I try to throw a party, and the guy upstairs complains,' a beaten, miserable Billie Holiday sang, louder than she was ever meant to. Louder than anyone was ever meant to. 'I guess I'll go through life just catching colds and missing trains. Everything happens to me.'

'Who's there singing?' my mother asked. I could barely hear her, the music was so loud.

'Billie Holiday. It's an old tape.'

'I'm calling long distance, and you're blasting tapes in my ears?'

'Can you turn it down?' I yelled in to Charlie. Apparently, he could not.

'How's the garden?' asked Mom.

'Eve Arden? How should I know?'

'No, the garden. The *garden*.' She raised her voice. 'I'm making a toll call, and you're forcing me to compete with a dead, Negro dope addict,' she wailed.

'Hold on a minute, Mom.' The music had gotten even louder. 'Can you do that?' I screamed.

'Of course I'll hold on, but first let me apply for a bank loan to pay for this phone call,' she yelled back.

I went into the living room and found my ex-husband sitting

45

cross-legged on the floor, surrounded by a sea of records, tapes, and books, every bit at home as a two-year-old in a playpen. His eyes were closed as he mumbled along with the music, which I turned down, much to his displeasure.

'If you don't mind, my mother's on the phone.'

'Tell her I can't talk right now. This is absolutely my favorite song. Remember it?'

'You're incorrigible' was all I could manage, and got back on the phone.

'Who's there with you?' my mother asked.

'No one.'

She paused. 'Is no one about six feet one, with brown hair, good posture, an eating disorder, and about ten million dollars in the bank?' she wanted to know, referring to a man I'd made the mistake of letting her know I went out with once in a while.

'No. Listen, let me get off the phone. I have a million things to do, Mom.'

'I thought the point of this vacation, Miss Solitary, Miss I Want to Be Alone, is to do nothing but work on your play.'

'It is. But there are a lot of things I have to do before I can do nothing.'

She stood, I could tell, right at the precipice of sulking. It could still go either way.

'All right. Will you call me soon?' she relented.

'Tomorrow.' The music was blasting again.

'Early tomorrow or late tomorrow?' Seventy-five years old, and she could still leave me in the dust every time.

'Tomorrow tomorrow.'

Billie was by now launching into an especially compelling rendition of 'I Must Have That Man,' which had abruptly brought my mind back to the thought that *I* must have that man . . . out of my house.

'Bye, Mom. Talk to you tomorrow.'

I hung up. There was little else to do. There was just no way I could swallow Charlie and my mother all in a single gulp.

Even during the best of times, which in retrospect had seemed to last only about as long as it took to reheat a Weight Watcher's pizza in a microwave, my mother was no great fan of his. Even with those Tonys and Pulitzers paving the way for familial benevolence, she could never quite see what all the fuss was about where he was concerned. And then, when it was finally all over, her main preoccupation regarding him was all the different ways she could've done away with him when there had still been time.

'I could've smashed him over the head with an omelet pan,' she'd announce sweetly to the air, usually midway through a conversation that had nothing to do with Charlie. Or else, 'I could've just shot him and said it was in self-defense,' she'd say, perhaps while mashing the tuna or egg salad she perpetually served for lunch.

'Jews don't shoot each other. They're not shooters, Esta,' my father, still alive then and a most patient man, would pronounce to the sky.

'No. Jews aren't drunks. But they're shooters when it suits them.'

'You think Charlie Stamberg is worth spending the rest of your life in prison for?' he'd ask her.

How her silence would resound its positive reply, like a mighty wall of trumpets, blaring her convictions, which rang out yes, yes, a thousand times yes.

As far back as I can remember, which is entirely too far to suit me most of the time, my mother has always had her own highly perverse version of reality, her own method for twisting and shaping the truth like some cockeyed sculptress, for meting out justice or salty malevolence as thoughtlessly, as mechanically as she deals out the hands in a card game when planted beside the pool in Florida with her bejeweled cronies. I think the story that says the most about her is the one my sister, Leslie, and I still shake our heads in amazement at – and even a little fear, even after all these years. The one our mother told us that shows, more than anything else, what a shrewd cookie she is, and reminds us of how unlikely it is that she'll ever turn stale in the cookie jar.

A long time ago, you see, before open marriages, prenuptial

contracts, and divorce lawyers, there were only things like lust and love, romance and jealousy. The things you could really sink your teeth into. What the human heart and the human mind fashioned and surrendered themselves to, the miracles and the madness, all started out from – and led back to – these, like the roads that must all lead to Rome. (Unless one is on the Long Island Expressway between June and September. That must lead one to insanity.) In any event, back in those days, we're talking late 1940s here, my father was an elegant and strikingly hand-some devil, as well as something of a crackerjack businessman in his field, which was ladies' sportswear. He owned a showroom on Seventh Avenue, replete with a never-ending chorus line of models to cavort and parade around in his tasteful, pricey merchandise. Since he was also cursed with a fool's generosity, my mother was forever sending her friends and their friends over to his showroom for entire complimentary wardrobes. Oblivious for the most part to beautiful women, as only an equally magnificent-looking man could be, he generally failed to take much notice of his models, or so he claimed, including the lovely, curvaceous and freshly employed Hannah Moscowitz, until my mother's friend Selma brought her to both my parents' attention when she came to our house one night for dinner.

'You should see this Hannah,' Selma began in hushed tones, daintily wiping away the last crumb of chewy, buttery, home-made rugelach from her cherubic chin. 'Such a face, such a figure, like a dream. I tell you, she took my breath away, Esta, and I'm only a woman. Ask Jack,' she prodded, gesturing to my father, who just shrugged with disinterest in the subject matter. But like a dog with a bone, this Selma was only just getting started.

'Go ahead. Ask Jack if she hasn't got the most irresistible shape he's ever seen. Intoxicating, even,' she pushed, the viperess.

The way my mother tells it, it was then that she first started listening; it was then that she raised a carefully pruned eyebrow and got every last one of her neuroses to stand at attention.

She looked over at my father, but he said nothing, answered

48

nothing. In moments of great crisis, he could always be counted on to impersonate a tree.

'Well, I'm listening, but I'm not hearing anything.'

At last my father relented, shrugged a shoulder and said, 'What's it to me? A pretty girl is a pretty girl. But she's really not worth making a fuss over.' Which got him off the hot seat only for as long as it took my mother to go waltzing down to his showroom the following afternoon (his traditional afternoon at the racetrack), in order to scrutinize the potential competition. My point here is that no grass, not a single lowly blade, ever grew under this one's feet. She took one dreaded look at the hapless Hannah prancing daintily about in the very plainest of white ducks and a sunny striped-cotton shirt, big sellers that year for my father, asked her to turn around for her, like a cake that rotates itself into oblivion in a glass case at a diner, caught her breath, mopped a bit of perspiration from her upper lip, spun right around and set out for home, like a bale of hay afire in a burning silo.

I'll give her this though. At least she waited to pounce until late that night, until they were lying in bed and it was almost time to go to sleep. Then, as my father read over his customary slew of inventory reports, with an intensity Boris Becker and Ivan Lendl only dream of, she casually mentioned that she'd stopped in at the showroom while running some errands downtown, and had seen the new model, Henny.

'Hannah,' he spoke to the pages, penciling some numbers in the margins.

'A pretty girl . . . but ooh, that problem of hers,' my mother left off cryptically. The way she tells it, and trust me, she tells it well, she had to say that about sixty-five more times before he finally heard her and asked her what the hell she was talking about. You could, you see, lead my father to water, but if you seriously expected him to drink, you had to come prepared to sit down and wait awhile, like possibly until Colonel Qaddafi demanded and got a bar mitzvah. (Not for nothing was he nicknamed 'Push' Seligman at Princeton.)

'All right, already. So what kind of a problem?' he finally asked his wife, sneakily stealing his eyes away from his reports, turning with love to this woman, both the vessel and the betrayer of his trust.

'Oh, Jack, don't tell me you haven't noticed. Poor girl. I could smell it out in the street. You'd better be careful that it doesn't spoil any of your merchandise.' She closed her eyes and pinched her nose clothespin style then, just in case the full import of her nasty words had somehow whizzed past him like an errant bullet. She was taking no chances, but she hadn't a thing to worry about. You see, she had spoken the magic word. The truth is, World War III could've exploded all around my father and he would probably have just gone blithely about his business as if it were a day like any other. But just mention her merchandise, and he'd spring into action like a rabid cheetah before you could say the words Chapter 11.

'She *smells*, Jack,' my mother whispered to him then, and his horror filled him like a heart attack. He removed his glasses and rubbed his eyes. He focused his shock on my mother, staring at her with eyes that were almost misty with an uncanny, invincible love, fairly brimming with his inexorable trust.

'I never . . . noticed, Esta. Are you sure? A beautiful, hard-working, intelligent girl like that smells? How could she? It's impossible.'

My father had been the kind of man who always tried to make sense of everything, to pigeonhole what he could and scale down what failed to fit neatly into his compartmentalized consciousness – or, if possible, to make excuses for it. A rich man would not steal money . . . A happy man would not weep . . . A weak man would not fall apart. He slept better at night believing the best of people. The world was a sweeter, tidier place. How unlike my mother he was, who barely slept at all, and always with one eye open, warding off the catastrophic possibilities of her nemesis, the unexpected. In this way, my father put himself into an early grave, taking with him his extravagantly kind beliefs in people, while my mother still continues to fiercely patrol the borders of the unknown, which may say a great deal about a great deal, but I am straying from my point.

50

'Nothing's impossible,' my mother answered my father's incredulousness about Hannah. 'Who's to say Betsy Ross didn't work up a good sweat and also smell like day-old herring after a big workout with her needle and thread. I wasn't there, Jack, were you?' It was in this way, building layer upon layer, that my mother continued to mold and shape and manipulate my father into the man she wanted to have married. And it worked. This sculptress of Riverside Drive could've successfully unveiled and exhibited her work at any gallery or museum and received a standing ovation. (Isn't it strange? In truth, my father was the more intelligent of the two, and yet a marriage such as this made them both feel happy, complete, kept them giggling and thrilled with each other, with the whimsical combination of themselves together right up until the day he collapsed and died at the racetrack, in the sweltering heat of July, while placing a two-dollar bet on a horse named Final Curtain.)

'I just never noticed it,' my poor father kept muttering, as my steely-nerved mother kept swatting away at her invisible demons.

I can picture my father at this point quite easily, confused and ashamed, pausing in the anteroom of true vexation. 'What will I do with her?' he asked my mother then, who was already smothering a secret smile, for she had won and she knew it. That night, she put all of her toy soldiers away in a box and went to sleep without a care in the world.

The next night, both of my father's feet were barely in the door before he announced to my mother, who was no doubt bending over a meat loaf made with too much ketchup, or a chicken roasted with more savagery than was appropriate to the occasion, 'You know, Esta, you were right about Hannah. I couldn't even breathe when I walked into the showroom today. I can't believe I never noticed it before. It's overpowering. Thank you so much for bringing it to my attention.'

Knowing my mother, she probably went over to him, patted his elegant hand, smiled shyly up at him with her inestimable love, and told him to get ready for dinner. And as he did, he

51

called out to her in the kitchen, 'She took it pretty badly, I'm afraid, poor kid. She cried when I fired her.'

'What reason did you give her?'

'I thought the best thing I could do would be to just tell her the truth.'

'She'll thank you one day, Jack. You did her a big favor and you're a good man. Now sit down. Dinner is getting cold,' proclaimed the cheerful cook, by now almost believing the lie about Hannah herself. No guilt for her at banishing the lovely, sweet-natured, hardworking, and, I might add, sweet-smelling Hannah to the unquestionable grimness of the unemployment line at a time when jobs were as scarce as the flavor in a poorly prepared chicken.

Unfortunately, many years later, when it came time for me to jump ship, and by this I refer glibly to the SS *Charlie Stamberg*, as it pitched and careened in deeply troubled, bimbo-infested waters, suddenly this genius at marital witchery claimed to be all out of tricks and embalming techniques. Which was deeply regrettable, given that Charlie had never quite cut the mustard where she was concerned. He could pile up those vaunted prizes as easily as jelly beans (and maybe even one day reel in the prize he was convinced came showered with the blessings and honeyed kisses of the gods, the mighty Nobel), but he could never quite win over his vituperative mother-in-law. I would never forget her unbridled glee when my divorce became final. I thought she'd break a bottle of Korbel right over my head, so eager was she to launch me on the open sea that led me away from Charlie. Is it any wonder then that I had bitten my tongue and chosen not to tell her that the specter of her darkest nightmare had popped over for coffee and a 'nice conversation'? Hardly. Just look at the sad, ineluctable fate of the divinely voluptuous Hannah Moscowitz, wherever she may be. No one could glory so much in the thorns of a rose, while neglecting totally its lush and eloquent beauty as my mother could, and just now I knew that I could not

52

afford her own special brand of brutal, jaundiced, botanical observations.

Charlie, you see, was not only in my blood and in my past, he was still sitting in my living room, and looking now as frustratingly comfortable and at home as a Japanese beetle brunching away on the leaves of one of my rambler roses.

'Mmm . . . Good couch for me,' he muttered approvingly, pushing down on it with both hands, testing its hardness.

'I know you've got a bad back, but the couch really wasn't chosen with you in mind.'

'Maybe not, but it's nice the way things sometimes work out, isn't it?' he beamed at me.

At the mention of Charlie's fickle vertebrae, I could not help but think back to the time he'd ruptured a disc, the third year we were married, and had had to have surgery.

It had been four weeks before Christmas and Lenox Hill Hospital was hardly the place people went in search of holiday cheer. Nevertheless, there we were, with Charlie in utter, unrelenting agony, overmedicated on painkillers, anti-inflammatories, and muscle relaxants. But not too oblivious, he claimed to be more terrified than he'd ever been in his life.

Charlie's supercilious surgeon bowed and scraped, practically davened before the famous playwright, but despite his panting efforts to get Charlie a private room, he couldn't quite pull it off.

My husband's roommate was a tough, wisecracking teenager from the Bronx (who was admitted for what he described as 'domino pain'). The afternoon Charlie went in, his roommate's girl friend was visiting. Twinkie wrappers littered the floor and the television was blasting, but not quite loud enough to drown out their moans and giggles as they wriggled around together in his sickbed.

'Must I endure this?' Charlie asked his nurse repeatedly.

That evening, I settled Charlie back against his pillows, fed him dinner from a good local deli, and hooked him into his Walkman with some favorite Mozart. The nurse finally brought him a sleeping pill and he dozed off holding my hand.

I spent the night curled up in the chair next to his bed. When Dr

53

Important and his lackeys showed up early the next morning to connect his IV and take him down to surgery, I can still picture Charlie's face and his last-ditch effort at a stay of execution.

'Doctor, you must tell me,' Charlie whispered urgently, with grim desperation. 'Isn't there *any* alternative to this? If this were your wife, would you insist on surgery?' Well, at this the doctor could only laugh broadly, shaking his great stomach like a tambourine.

'Most doctors hate their wives. Ask us about what we'd advise for our sisters' was his answer, as they led Charlie away to his operation.

Left alone in his room, the floor nearly ankle-deep with food wrappers and with flowers and fruit sent to him from every country I could think of, I felt my heart turn over for my big and strong husband, reduced now by fear and pain to a pale, weak, powerless six-year-old. And I thought, with a shock that seemed profound, of just how much he meant to me, of how much we loved each other.

But all of that seemed very long ago and far away now, and here we were, not in a hospital room but instead, inexplicably, in my East Hampton living room. And here he was, all nestled into my couch like a deer tick in a blade of tall grass. And, I suspected, just as treacherous. But what could I do to thwart the possible advance of Charlie? And more to the point, what did I want to do? Already, my mind was scurrying, looking for an escape hatch and coming up empty. What, precisely, were my options? To crush him quickly beneath my heel, like one of those glinty-eyed beetles, or to pull him to me with the dry, cold force of some supersonic mistral; press him to me with a powerful, persuasive energy that eradicates all sensibility, all faint echoes of a past together, all hungry whispers of a present or a future together, and just entomb him somehow, in the transparent confines of a chilly, Lucite block. Which would it be? One foot stepped forward while the other held back. Inside, my left auricle sparred with my right ventricle, leaving my heart in a state of bewildered confusion. I realized that a lightness in the head had stolen over me like some airless, tightly wrapped cap of Nantucket fog. As it closed in around my neck and forehead, I knew it was prepared to choke the life out of me as I returned to the room where my quilt of self-preservation was threatening to come apart at any moment.

There, the prospective unraveler spoke to me. He asked, 'So, what exactly are you doing out here, you're on your summer vacation or something?' I nodded dully.

'For how long?'

I shrugged. 'Two weeks, give or take a little.'

He laughed. 'Well, since you mention it, I might like to take a lot.' Again that smile that could melt the marble-hard ice palaces of Switzerland in a single tremulous shimmer.

'You're impossible,' I said, under my breath.

Oddly enough that seemed to shock him.

'Impossible? That happens to be the last thing I am, Stevie. I'm extremely possible. Hey, for all we know, I may even be probable.'

Right there, I decided it was time to disperse all of these noxious fantasy fumes and try to take command. An angry expression and my hands on my hips seemed an enterprising way to begin.

'The only thing that's probable is that I've got a lot to take care of today, gardening and shopping, and it looks as if you're determined to let me get to neither.' Did smoke shoot out of my smokestack? I doubt it, but at least I'd said it, said something. Spoken up. Made a gallant, if anemic, attempt to beat back the enemy.

'I'm sorry,' he began, and I actually believe he was. 'Of course you've got things to do, but don't worry about it.'

'Worry? You're telling me not to worry? There are petunias out there with legs longer than Anjelica Huston's. And my coreopsis needs to be deadheaded. Even as we speak, my own private nation of Japanese beetles is deciding to give me the Nobel Prize for curing world hunger.'

His long, tanned hand flew right up to his heart, like a fearless bird.

'Now you've got me.' Aah. If I had wanted to drive a red-hot stake through the most private cabin of his heart and burn it right to the ground, I could not have poised my arrow more artfully. I had spoken the word, you see. The word that had spun out like a spider's web over many thousands of hours of marital conversation: conversations in our bedroom as the sun came up, in our bathroom as the same sun sank into the horizon, conversations over the rattle of cutlery in our dining room, or in our big, old rustic barn of a kitchen, in taxis, on speedboats and ocean liners, on planes, on telephones when Charlie was somewhere around the corner or on the other side of the world. The Nobel was nothing less than a religion to this man. He talked to it, prayed to it. If sheer wishing could make someone a winner, I had no doubt that one day the man who stood before me would be summoned to Sweden. I knew, as I had always known, that even those sawdusty old Swedish highbrows with the juiceless emotional lives of scrod could not remain immune indefinitely to the bright twinkle of Charlie's star, to that great tornado of suction that was his talent, his contribution to our dramatic history.

At any rate, here I had thoughtlessly stepped on the land mine of Charlie's ego by daring to make that little crack about the Nobel. And I tell you, I knew enough, even in the time that had passed in the wake of our untidy divorce, to know that making this sort of remark represented a body blow. It wasn't suitable, any more than it would've been suitable to put a family of Jews at Hitler's dinner table and expect him to stand and toast them. With Charlie, you could joke about cancer, about the IRS, or the time his spanking-new silver Porsche with the quadraphonic Blaupunkt was stolen as he emptied his beer-filled bladder into a potato field in Bridgehampton; this, he could joke about. The Nobel, however, was quite another matter.

'Oh, God, sorry about that.' I winced.

'What do you mean? I'm not *that* sensitive about it. I mean, it's just a goddamned prize like any other. I've won enough stupid prizes, after all.'

Sure it was. And the Rolls-Royce Silver Shadow was just a

jalopy. Still, his casualness, real or intentional, surprised me. But when he shifted quickly to another topic of conversation, I knew that I had indeed done some damage.

'So what did you say, you've got to work in the garden, go shopping?'

'That's what I said.'

'All right, so let's do it.'

'I hadn't exactly planned on making this a group activity,' I offered gently.

'I'll just watch. I won't disturb you or anything. I always wanted to see how to deadbeat a coreopsis.'

'Deadhead.'

'Don't call me names, Stevie. It's so undignified.'

What can I say? I felt a huge surge of fatigue overtake me at that moment. My bones felt as if they were suddenly pinned down by the Holland Tunnel. I went with him outside, and showed him how to pinch back my snapdragons.

'Seems unnecessary to me,' he balked, this instant genius in the garden, whose only previous contact with greenery had been whenever he counted his cash.

I squinted up at him, right into the sun. 'Do not . . . question me in this area. Either slave or go home. And by the way, either option is fine with me.' With that, I set about cutting all the faded and fading petals of my cosmos.

'I can't imagine why you're cutting off flowers that are still blooming. It's just mean of you,' he hissed over at me, on his knees, squeezing away at my delicate snaps with all the delicacy of Mike Tyson in gloves.

The sun was beating down like bongos by now, and I was truly in no mood for any more of his nonsense. I kept quiet. But once hunched over my flowers, he was back on his favorite topic again. Lord, where was his new wife to listen to this broken, old record? It was old and broken when he used to play it for me, and that was many, many snapdragons ago.

'Christ, those squarehead Swedes even gave the Nobel to Eugene O' – as in oh-how-*boring* – Neill. The man drove two sons to kill themselves.'

'They don't give out awards based on how good a parent someone is.'

'Well then, what about Sinclair Lewis and Pearl Buck? Their work was absolutely awful, unreadable,' he barked, beheading my delicately nurtured flowers with such violence, I was sure I heard them shrieking.

'Easy with the flowers. They're not the Nobel Committee,' I couldn't resist saying.

His voice climbed an octave at least.

'Too bad they're not.'

'I thought you didn't care anymore if you ever won it.'

He looked me full in the face and threw down his little handful of savagely severed buds.

'I don't. It's just that T. S. Eliot won, Stevie. The whole world knows the guy had bad breath.'

I laughed. 'Obviously his personal hygiene wasn't relevant.'

'Goddamned herring lappers,' I heard him mutter. 'Ice monkeys.'

'They give good massages and make good meatballs,' I offered.

'Fucking fish-brains. They all look and think alike.'

'But what if they all thought to give you the Nobel?'

He paused for about as much time as it used to take Ronald Reagan to fall asleep during something important.

'Well, then I'd think they were a bunch of goddamned brilliant fish-brains . . . herring lappers . . . squarehead Swedes.' He grinned, a grin that made my toes curl and my palms itch. Suddenly my throat felt pinched, my eyes were watering like sprinklers. What was I doing? Why was he here?

I took off my gardening gloves and stood up, ever so full of good intentions. My brief but perilous flight of fancy into the Theater of the Ridiculous was evaporating like a damp mist right before my eyes. The path I was to travel laid itself down before me stone by stone, step by step. It was time to act like a grown-up.

I groped in the darkness and found a beam of light.

'Just out of curiosity, doesn't your wife get . . . nervous or anything when you're out this long running?'

'Nervous as in jealous . . . suspicious?' Hmm, that was precisely what I meant.

'Well, I know I would.' I thought about it. 'In fact, I know I did.'

He looked so sheepish then, I could've cut a winter coat out of him.

'Maybe we should go shopping,' he posited, like a babysitter casting about for activities on a rainy day.

'Maybe I should go shopping and you should go home.'

'Patsy knows I'm not cheating on her,' he offered, a trifle smugly. This man had been out of my life for what seemed like ages, but he could still make me feel as small as a worm and as luckless as a Brooklyn baker who wins the lottery after working his fingers to the bone twelve hours a day for fifty years, and then is run over by a meat truck on the way home from picking up his check. Welcome back, Charlie. It feels so good to have you around.

I glared at him through hot little jet flares of jealousy.

'How does she know you're not?' I asked, really wanting to know.

'What difference does it make? I just know it never enters her mind, that's all.'

Well, of course I was crazy to pursue this, but I knew I wouldn't have a second of peace until he answered me, even if it wasn't the sort of answer I was hoping for.

'Are you . . . both so much in love?' I asked with astonishment. I couldn't imagine him so entrenched in the cozy quicksand of devotion, and if the truth be known, it was for me, at that moment, a horrifying thought. If he hadn't been faithful to me, how could he be faithful to anyone?

'Oh, Stevie, love's got nothing to do with it,' he said with a shrug.

Now, this intrigued me, and suddenly I realized I was hanging on his every word. God, he was charming. Lethal, but charming.

'Well, what is it? Did you see *Fatal Attraction* or something?' He was walking toward the driveway, and damnit, I was following him.

'Come on, let's go shopping. I guess I'm not much of a gardener,' he said.

He stood at my car, the red Honda with more dents in it than Jake LaMotta. 'What do you need?'

Oh, boy. I only wished I knew.

He asked me two more times, and I finally answered him, tonelessly and methodically. I needed milk. More coffee. Peaches. Toilet paper. Yogurt. Light bulbs. Raisin Bran. Typing paper. Windex. Lettuce. And now that I thought about it, plenty of Extra-Strength Tylenol. If the telegram my head was sending my stomach was even the slightest bit correct, I'd be slugging down those white pellets of mercy by the barrelful during the next two weeks, like fistfuls of M&Ms. And it wouldn't be because of the anguish over writing the last act of my play.

Oh, how well I knew this man. It had been some time, but not long enough for me to forget that while most of us whiled away our lives, caught up in feeble little plots and the complacency of daydreams, this man never so much as left his bed in the morning without brewing up some grand scheme. This was someone literally incapable of wasting time, who never 'wandered' any-where, or 'drifted into or out of' a relationship. It was unthink-able, unheard of. Without a doubt, he'd already set some machine in motion which had begun cranking its way toward some inevitable conclusion. I couldn't escape or deny this, and neither could my trembling hands or now aching head. Here I'd opened the door barely an inch, and he'd gotten a bulldozer through it.

No wonder I was so leery. And no wonder I just felt, goddamn everything: the rabbits who gobbled up my petunias and pansies; the Japanese beetles who left behind their jagged little holes, like so many kisses planted on the bellies of my roses. And goddamn ex-husbands, who reappear with all the welcomeness of cholera, and somehow worm their way into your kitchen, your garden. The next thing you know, you're turning the key to your car's ignition, and heading out for the store, sailing down the Montauk Highway on a dangerously pretty day in July. The strawberries are ripe and blooming, the air is swollen with their perfume. The corn and the grain are swaying by the side of the road in the breeze and the potatoes are burrowing underground, awaiting their purposefulness. And you just glide along in the merry old carnival of life until your car stops moving, until you stop moving it, in the big, crowded parking lot of the East Hampton A&P.

'Damn. I left my shopping list at home,' I remembered.

'Just like old times,' he dared to mutter, as he opened the door to the A&P and we stepped inside.

Well, not quite. In the old days, it would've taken a ten-ton crane to get him into a grocery store with me. And now that he was here, although God knows why he was, it just felt creepy, slimy, and peculiarly illicit. Good Lord, it was broad daylight and there I was meandering down the overpriced aisles of the A&P with someone else's husband. So what if I had held his head for him one night years ago, over a porcelain chamber pot as he vomited again and again his reactions to a bunch of bad reviews. Sentiment had nothing to do with it. The issue of postmarital propriety seemed not to disturb him or even to skip across the untrimmed lawn of his complicated consciousness, but as we stopped to inspect a table of cheeses it paralyzed me with anxiety and embarrassment.

What if someone saw us? What would I tell them? What would I tell myself? When I was married to Charlie, did he disappear from the house at random to escort the sweet-faced, thighless damsels of the South Fork between the Morbier and the Saga? I could barely remember, but I do know that back in those days, he was more concerned with what was going on between the sheets, and I'm not talking about phyllo or the breathless, papery-thin *mille feuilles* of a napoleon. I looked at him, and he seemed a little bored, like a child who has perhaps gone too long without a nap, and I decided I could not go another step without speaking. So right there, right in front of the cheeses, looking around and behind me with the hawkishly guilty glare of an unpracticed

61

shoplifter, I put before him yet another one of the burning questions of the day.

'What if someone saw us?'

He blinked. 'What if who saw us?'

'Anyone, Charlie. What would they think?'

'They'd probably think it was sweet,' he smiled. 'I do.'

'Sweet? Who would think it was sweet?' I whispered, with the rasp of an electric razor.

'I don't know who, because you won't tell me who "who" is,' he laughed. 'Peter Jennings? The little hairy guy who rolls my tennis court?'

Suddenly, my shopping cart was moving again, flying, breaking all decent speed limits, as it shot away from him. Jackie Joyner-Kersee, of course, caught up with no difficulty whatsoever.

'Anyone, everyone,' I muttered, throwing up my hands, which were full of overripe peaches. 'I'd just like to know what you'd say.'

He hooked a hand around my cart then, and put a sneaker in front of a wheel to prevent future takeoffs. After stopping to think for a moment, he answered me.

'Well, I guess I'd say what I'm about to tell you, Stevie.' He paused. 'That the Spanish olives here are the best in the world, and they happen to be on sale today, so if I were they, whoever "they" happen to be, I'd buy enough to fill my pool with them. Unless it's the guy who rolls my tennis court. He can afford better. I ought to know.'

You can see what I was up against.

'Why,' I put to him as we sallied together past the frozen foods, 'have you still always got such a neat little non-answer for everything, even after all this time?'

'What do you want me to say? Maybe the questions aren't tough enough, Slim.' Ouch. Now he was skating on very thin ice indeed, and without skates. With the invocation of a private nickname from our prior life together, he had crossed the frontier from merely low to verminesque.

'I'll wait for you in the parking lot,' he said, and promptly slunk past the hungry gaze of several women shoppers and checkout girls. Oh, you can damned well have him, I thought, and then realized, for all I knew they already had.

The thing about East Hampton (and East Hampton parking lots) in July is that they're crawling with people you know and who know you, and with people you don't want to see who don't want to be seen. Regardless of who you are or where you've been, even if you spend the day crouching under some dank rock with a flashlight, reading *The Magic Mountain*, there's a 99 percent possibility that either the guy with bad skin you dumped in high school, or your sister's best friend who's on the committee of some charity she'd like you to get involved with, or the man who uses the same dry cleaner in the city as you do will poke you somewhere between your shoulder blades, and start up some flimsy excuse for a conversation. I suppose some might see it as a plus that you couldn't even get into the shower out there without expecting to see a face from *60 Minutes*: some boozy, overrated novelist who boasted of supping with Irwin Shaw and James Jones during their halycon days in Paris, a controversial sportscaster with more vowels in his name than the menu at Sabatini's in Florence, or some ex-Hollywood starlet, a little bit past her prime, and now looking for somebody's husband to flirt with. I was just never much of a stargazer, I guess. But then, that's the Hamptons. And never mind what anyone tells you about windmills, about unspoiled beaches and soil rich enough for the Sultan of Brunei. The real scenery in East Hampton walks, it talks, it looks around to check that it's being noticed, adored, envied. Just step inside the Candy Kitchen in Bridgehampton on a Sunday morning. You can cast a major film, start a television network or a publishing house, all from the potluck sitting inside, slumped over their newspapers, their coffee and excellent scrambled eggs.

And sure enough, as I stepped into the parking lot of the A&P on that particular day, I spotted the familiar face of a man I worked with in the city, an advertising creative director who

63

happened to be an old friend of Charlie's. Indeed, I held my breath when I emerged with my groceries and found the two of them clapping each other on the back and laughing uproariously. When we were married, Charlie used to call Spike Church his evil twin, the embodiment of all his wicked, outrageous thoughts and behavior.

If you were throwing a party and you weren't sure whether any of the guests would have a single piddling thing to say to each other, the first name on your guest list might well be Spike's: *bête noire extraordinaire*, three times divorced, and quintessential conversation piece. He was truly the very wildest of wild cards; you were never sure what Spike would do or say next. Would he entice the shy, giggly, Irish serving girl into the Jacuzzi he'd filled with Cutty Sark? As big and burly as the state of Montana, he liked to joke that he and the Leaning Tower of Pisa had three things in common. They were both round and off center, and there were days when he felt that his plumbing, too, had been built by Bonanno Pisano in 1350.

His imp's face can most respectfully be described as perpetually florid, and I could never pass by Spike's office and spot him hunched over his computer without thinking of a great, Asiatic sloth bear, tinkling away at a toy piano. Now, I am tempted here to call Spike a 'man's man,' but that would truly do no justice to the exceptional crop of women he skewered like shish kebab, unless, of course (and believe me I can't stand the thought of this), that helped to make him even more of one. These were women who, more often than not, cooked him their most impressive dinners, cleaned their apartments, shaved their legs, did their hair, and spent hours selecting just the right flowers, the right music, the perfect wine for him. In great battalions, they deveined shrimp for him, braised endives, wept with the cruelty inflicted by the juices of the pitiless onion, regardless of menstrual cramps, broken air conditioning, or a bad day at the office. Everything had to set the proper mood, no matter what. The thing with Spike, though, was that there was no such thing as a proper mood. He struck where and when he struck, like lightning, without rhyme or reason. And as we know, since lightning almost never strikes twice in the same place, that left most of these beleaguered women badly disappointed. Spike was the kind of man women didn't tell their therapists about.

Spike loved women in his own way (and never for very long), but loved his lovely house in Sagaponack even more, and so every year since I could remember, he had thrown open the doors on July 14, just as the doors of the Bastille had opened wide in 1789, for a party that was as eagerly awaited all year as an IRS refund. Since my divorce, forever the diplomat, Spike still invited me, but every year I declined. It was Charlie's night to howl, you see, and we never, absolutely never, let our signals cross or overlap socially. Hosts knew better than to even attempt this impossibly intriguing social gaffe. Hosts except for Spike, that is.

As I approached them in the parking lot, I knew they were talking about the much-anticipated party, and I watched with great trepidation as Spike's eyes opened as wide as garage doors at the sight of me. 'Well, holy shit. Will you look at this,' he said, shaking his big, sunburned mop of a head. 'Tell me I'm dreaming, in a time warp. Tell me I fell asleep. It's 1980 and Bonzo is president.'

I walked directly over to the car and put my groceries inside. 'I had nothing to do with this, so don't get excited.'

Charlie threw his head back and laughed. I mean, the man was a playwright. His play *Now, What?* had just won two Tony Awards. Again this year, like every year, as predictably as Succoth or Ash Wednesday, his Nobel nomination had materialized. Such a man, such a theatrical craftsman, certainly knew when a scene was being played well. He also knew the intent of the scene and where it was to lead. Unfortunately, that made only one of us.

'I *am* excited. I'm extremely excited,' Spike said then, slapping Charlie's back a few more times for emphasis. 'This looks . . . very good, very domestic. Very déjà vu. The thought of you two together again . . . aah! I can die a happy man,' he pronounced, a bit too magnanimously for my own tastes.

'Hopefully, within the next four minutes,' I told him, amused

65

at his amusement. I looked up at the big, open sky which was positively cloudless, yet full of mystery and surprise, and wondered if this day would never end – if my vacation would never begin.

'Does this mean I'll see you both on Bastille Day?' asked Spike, so full of hope he could've taken off at that very moment in a balloon right across that cloudless sky, and fueled himself all the way to Pukapuka. I hated to haul him in for an emergency landing, but I had no choice. I bit my tongue and swallowed all the things I could've said. The truth was, his silly little party was one of the few that I was bothered about staying home from. Every July 14, I made other plans to distract myself, but regardless of where I was, it found me and hammered away like a neglected toothache.

'You most certainly will not,' I answered, a trifle haughtily, I hoped.

Now that, of course, did not sit quite right with Charlie. Clearly, he was in the process of designing some sort of mosaic, whose each and every tiny shape had been cut and planned for a very specific place, and here I was, muddling the plan.

'Leave it to me. I'll see what I can do to get her there,' Charlie assured his old friend.

With that, Spike executed a low and dainty bow, and told Charlie he had the utmost confidence in his powers of persuasion. That worried me, because despite the gravity of my stoniest willfulness, I knew somewhere deep in myself Spike's confidence was not entirely ill placed. I got into the car and turned the key in the ignition. Charlie quickly got in with me, and we said good-bye to Spike, who came around to my side and stuck his head in, a bird's breath away from my face.

'Seven o'clock on Bastille Day, and don't be late. *Vive la réconciliation!*' he sang, waving to us as we sped away.

The minute we were moving, Charlie reached into my groceries and started eating up my grapes.

'Where would you like to be dropped?'

He just blinked and kept on blinking.

'Dropped has such a cold, painful connotation,' he mumbled, with a mouthful of grapes.

'How about dumped, then? Where would you like to be dumped?' My mood was far from improving.

'But I have to pick up my Walkman from your house. I left it on the kitchen table.'

'You're slipping, old boy. You're letting the seams show. You didn't have a Walkman and you know it.'

'I always run with my Walkman,' he insisted.

'Maybe always, but not today. I'm dropping you a block from your house. And your wife. And your baby,' I couldn't resist tacking on.

I knew where his house was because I had been the one who originally found it, renovated, and decorated it. I had even managed to live in it for about seven seconds, or to be more precise, for about a summer and a half, before the Changing of the Guard.

'You can drop me near my house now, but that'll only mean that I'll have to come over and get the Walkman tomorrow.'

I sighed with exasperation.

'Are you absolutely sure it's on my kitchen table?' By now, my memory was so foggy, I could barely remember my own name.

'As sure as I am about anything,' he nodded. 'As sure as I am that you and I would have a terrific time together at Spike's party. Or that I just might win the Nobel this year, once and for all.'

'You can't possibly know anything about that yet. No one does. Not even the Swedes.'

'I've heard rumors. I was nominated –'

'You're always nominated.'

'Well, for once, they may actually have their heads screwed on straight, because I've been led to believe that my nomination this year is being considered more seriously than in past years. Who knows? Maybe I'll actually get it. They may drink too much and kill themselves more than anyone else, but I'll give the Swedes the benefit of the doubt. Sooner or later, they've got to make the right choice and pick me. Even you know that.'

He wasn't wrong. But was he right?

'Aah, we'll see. Anyway, about Bastille Day . . .' he started.

Who invented the Walkman? I have no idea, but whoever it was, I cursed him silently and colorfully as we breezed along the Montauk Highway. How could he do this to me?

'Look,' I kicked in, 'I am not French. I never could stand Edith Piaf or Maurice Chevalier. The mere thought of "The Marseillaise" makes my hair stand on end. I don't feel any more compelled to celebrate French holidays than I do to dress like a leprechaun on St Patrick's Day.'

'Oh, come on. You'd have a good time,' he said then.

'Every year you and your wife go, and every year that's perfectly fine with me, so why should we change things?'

He shrugged. 'I'd just like to see you there, that's all.' But I knew better. With Charlie, it was never 'all'. With Freud, a cigar may indeed, upon occasion, have been just a cigar, but I doubted that, too.

'And what about Patsy? Would she like to see me there? Oh, I forgot. She doesn't get jealous or suspicious. She knows you'd never look at another woman.' I couldn't help but laugh, as we pulled back into my driveway. 'You know, Charlie, airtight love is a wondrous thing in this day and age. But the day you're totally faithful to anyone is the day I'll mow my lawn with my front teeth.'

We got out of the car and he followed behind me up to the house.

'I didn't say anything about love or being faithful. I just said I don't screw around anymore. If you don't believe me, there's nothing I can do.'

'How could I, though? Remember me? We put in a little time together once upon a time, sailor. I know you.' I went on into the kitchen, slamming the screen door with a force I was certain would bring the house crashing down around our heads, continuing on with my shrewish peroration as if I'd rehearsed it for years, which perhaps I had. 'I know you, and I know the mere thought of a single wasted opportunity would keep you up for a month burning with indigestion, and you love your beauty sleep.'

68

'I'm going to tell you something, Stevie, although God knows I certainly don't have to. I don't fool around anymore, because –'

A light flashed suddenly in my head.

'Is it because of AIDS? The thought of mingling those Pulitzer Prize-winning body fluids just anywhere *is* pretty risky isn't it?'

He stayed cool. He could walk right into a burning building and out again, I had no doubt, and look as if he'd just stepped around the corner for the newspaper or a pack of Camels. The man was unflappable.

'The truth is,' he smiled, 'I got tired of bragging and lying all the time. And of holding my stomach in, in women's bedrooms. When I was single, after you –'

'For all of twelve minutes,' I added.

'Oh, it was longer than that. I didn't meet Patsy until two months after.'

I shook my head. 'Gee, two whole months. That's a long weekend.'

'Anyway, it just all got to be too much effort, you know. And then I met her and –'

'I know. I read all about it in *People*. You went to get contact lenses, right? And she was the doctor's assistant who helped to show you how to wear them, taught you the in and out process, so to speak.'

'That's right,' he said softly.

'And aren't you living happily ever after?' I held my breath.

He paused. 'Let's just say I'm thinking of going back to wearing my glasses.'

That was when he finally looked over at my kitchen table, but I was way ahead of him.

'No Walkman,' I gloated.

'No kidding,' he threw in, gushing with a surprise every bit as tinny as a diamond ring buried in a box of Cracker Jack. 'Are you really going to make me go home now?'

'Perhaps you should,' I offered quietly.

'Well, perhaps I shouldn't.'

I threw up my arms, marbleized from my morning's gardening with veiny, blue streaks of Miracle Gro, making them look like Gorgonzola.

'You know the thing Picasso said about his ex-wives? The thing about burning them?'

'No, but I'm sure it was extremely feministic.'

By now, he'd taken my groceries out of their bags, and was moving through my peaches like a machete through a field of brush.

Holding out a peach pit, and biting into a plum, he said, 'What do you do with the pits? Throw them out, or do you have a compost pile?'

'My compost pile is standing right in front of me.'

'Picasso said, "Every time I change wives I should burn the last one. That way, I'd be rid of them."'

'Well, isn't that lovely . . .'

'"They wouldn't be around now to complicate my existence,"' he went on. '"Maybe that would bring back my youth, too,"' he finished. 'Just be glad I happen not to agree with him. Be glad I have such a high regard for my ex-wives, Stevie. Play your cards right and I'll even take you to Sweden with me for the Nobel ceremony.'

'Look, my card-playing days are over. And what about your current wife? Why wouldn't you take her?' I began circling him like a vulture. 'What's going on with you, anyway?' He just stood there silently.

When he spoke next, it was in a small boy's frail and faraway voice. 'Sometimes, I still think of *you* as my wife. My real wife.'

'That's just ridiculous.' My voice cracked. 'You know how ridiculous that is. And I don't even believe it.'

He smiled serenely. 'You know, O'Neill inscribed the Nobel Prize edition of his plays to Carlotta, "the Noblest Prize of all!" I might write that to you if I win, Stevie. In fact, while I'm on the subject, it really might be a neat trick to win you back, the two Tonys *and* the Nobel, all in the same year.'

'Get it through your head, Charlie' – I laughed, I couldn't help it – 'I'm not your wife, and there's no way I'm going to Sweden with you. I wouldn't even go to see *My Life as a Dog* with you at this point if you asked me.'

'*Is a Dog*,' he mumbled, going to work on a velvety nectarine. 'It's *My Life Is a Dog*.'

'*As*,' I insisted.

'*Is . . . Is a Dog*. I'm sure of it,' he pushed relentlessly.

I put my face very near to his.

'I don't care what it's called,' I said slowly. 'It's a Swedish film, and I wouldn't go to it with you.'

'Who's asking you to?' he barked.

'You're insidious,' I bristled.

'You're magnificent.'

At just that moment, the heady smell of privet, like sweet sour milk, rose up and came through my windows, catching me off guard, and I had to steady myself. Sirens, car alarms were going off somewhere in my head.

'I want you to leave this house, Charlie, and I don't want you to ever come back,' I whispered, putting it to him simply, while holding on to my kitchen counter to help regain my sea legs.

He seemed surprised, which surprised me, and he handed me his plum pit, and started for the door. When he got there, he said to me, 'Do you know why water swirls counterclockwise above the equator, but clockwise below? Do you know why water doesn't swirl at all right at the equator?'

Well, he certainly had me there. I shook my head.

'Neither do I. I haven't the slightest idea.' He took another step toward the door, then walked back over to me and put both hands on my shoulders. Aah, I thought, those hands again. Those same hands that had taken me through thirteen-plus years, ingenious little devils, instruments of passion, of affection, of scorn and rejection. I could never forget their wily, smooth, persuasive powers. They could reverse, I had no doubt, the swirl of water draining both north and south of the equator, but with luck, they couldn't reverse me. I shook his hands off the shirt that said FRED'S BOWLING LANES and stepped neatly away from the man who carried them around with him.

'I'd really like it if you'd go now. This was a . . .'

'No it wasn't,' he finished for me.

'It was.'

'It wasn't,' he persisted.

'It wasn't what? What? How do you know what I was going to say?'

'A mistake, right? You were going to say that this was a big mistake, right? That seeing each other again was a terrible idea.' The curl of his mouth began to creep into the seeds of a smile. Right again, buddy.

I walked over to the door and opened it.

'Good-bye, you,' I said to him then, staring at my feet.

Seth Thomas, the clockmaster himself, was never such a genius at timing. Poised right there in my doorway, between in or out, come or go, he grabbed my face in his hands with something resembling the ferocity of his old, early days, kissed my mouth quickly, sturdily but softly, as if with the wings of butterflies, and whispered to me, '*Vi ses i morrou*, Stevie,' and walked through the door and outside.

'What does that mean?' I asked in a voice so shaky it needed crutches.

'It's Swedish. It means . . . have a good vacation.' He smiled his most winning smile then, and jogged right back out my driveway, my nightmare in reverse. The phone was ringing, and I let it ring. My heart was racing, and I let it race, for what was my option?

I left the food out on the counter, right there in the midday sun. I couldn't be bothered with it. Let the milk turn to cheese, let the bread turn to penicillin. It made no difference to me at that point, as I climbed the stairs to my bedroom and fell into my bed with a shiver of exhaustion and release. The house was baking, as still as a needle in a tapestry, as I fell into a sweaty sleep and out of it again, over and over until darkness began to fall. And as it did, in one shattering moment of clarity, it suddenly came to me. A thought so horrific, I could only grasp it in fractions, in stages. *Vi ses i morrou*, oh, *vi ses i morrou*, indeed. In my heart of hearts, in my skin of skins, I suddenly knew how false Charlie's translation had rung, and I could still hear it as it clanged again and again, as I pictured the smile of an eel that played about the corners of his mouth as he had whispered it. I did not know what the Swedish words actually meant, but I knew enough to know it barely mattered. The sense of peril I felt had sunk so deep down into my bones that I did not need words to claim it.

When I closed my eyes and drifted toward sleep again, I dreamed I was walking across a mountain that was salted with wet sugar, crunching down with every step as if on a carpet of dead beetles.

My room was pitch black when I awoke, and my limbs were still pinned down as if with lead. The whole South Fork could have gone up in flames, and I would not have budged toward safety, even a single lonely millimeter.

There was no doubt about what the immediate future held for me. The dank and dirty summer heat would no doubt suffocate the trees and all the crops, would hurt people, hurt me, damage natural systems, choke the very life out of us all until even a bottle of wine could not breathe.

The radioactive and chemical contamination levels would shoot up dramatically in our drinking water, until we were not drinking water, but strontium 90, which would seep into all of our bone marrow and shrivel it to nothingness.

My mind swam with these thoughts, these dangers. With the thought of the ticks of every prancing deer in civilization alighting on my property, and crippling us all with ten thousand consecutive cases of Lyme disease.

It filled with thoughts of the raw sewage and hospital debris that was surely washing up on the shores of the beaches surrounding me, even as I slept and half slept, of the soggy condoms, the filthy syringes, and the fishy-smelling test tubes filled with tainted blood that would wash up across the pale bleached sand.

The roots of my mightiest weeping willow tree, I had no doubt, would grow and creep and climb, like great outstretched claws, weaving their tangled way to my house and pool pipes.

73

The rabbits would be out after my pansies and petunias. Foxes would be prowling for chickens. Owls would be hunting rats and mice. Raccoons would stalk turtle eggs and lily bulbs. Deer would munch away at grass, twigs, at juicy roses and tender young azalea buds.

In the darkness, I knew that whole acres of wild buttercups, of chickory, of portulacas and morning glories would just clam up, slam shut like prison doors.

I felt dazed, dizzy from the thought of all this activity, this evil and sadness in the darkness, which I could not keep out of myself. And still, I could not move. The truth was, none of it frightened me nearly as much as that little smattering of Swedish spoken through that half smile of an oily eel. *Vi ses i morrou* took me through the night and on into the next morning without a single breath of peace. I can remember all too clearly the me I was that night, and looking back helps me to see how silly we are. And how little we know.

Here I felt it was surely the end for me, and it was only the beginning.

Part Two

Do what we can, summer will have its flies.
If we walk in the woods, we must feed mosquitos.
— RALPH WALDO EMERSON

W as it a bear? Was it a moose? Was it a 747 jumbo jet, straying from its charted appointment with a Queens runway, in for a crash landing in my pool? For the life of me, I couldn't even begin to imagine what it was that slapped me out of sleep the following morning as the sun climbed into the sky to hover over yet another day laced with curious, nasty, ironic dilemmas. I only know that when I heard that slam, that certain crash outside of something splashing about in my pool, I looked over at my digital clock, saw it was only 6.54, and held my heart with absolute terror. What could it be? kept running through my mind like a broken recording, as I tugged on a robe, c. 1958, and stumbled half blindly down the stairs. And then halfway down, it hit me, like a ton of bricks. Fearing the worst, I found it, towel-drying itself off, and wearing what appeared to be nothing more than a little sliver of a triangle, bright yellow with thick black stripes. I'd say it looked something like a bumblebee, but it was too small to even cover one. The image of Charlie, as he stood there oblivious to my presence and every inch the lord of the manor, filled me with rage and then with a weary feeling of impotence that made me feel as if every bone in my body had been twisted and broken. It was too early for all this, I thought, rubbing the near-sleep from my disbelieving eyes. And even more important, it was too late for this. Far, far too late.

'How dare you,' I started, finding my voice, as he spun around to face me, not without a hint of surprise pasted across his fine face, this nefarious, scantily clad, evilest of bumbling bumblebees.

My finger pointed directly up his right nostil. 'You have no business being here.'

He put his towel around his shoulders, then grinned sheepishly. 'Well, yes, but I just thought . . .'

Bumblebee diaper notwithstanding, I took off then, shouting and threatening, speaking in a harsh whisper meant to inspire fear and shame, which did little, however, to raise the specter of either, I'm afraid.

'Get off my property,' I finished mightily, drawing up my shoulders. I wasn't quite Gary Cooper in *High Noon*, but I was doing my best. 'Go back to your wife, go back to your house, go back to Jasper.'

'Jeremy,' he offered lamely.

'I'm surprised you even know his name, you're around him so rarely.'

'I can't help that,' he yelled, and then finished quietly, 'The whole scene at my house drives me crazy. That whimpering, flat-chested *au pair*; stepping on toys in the middle of the night; Patsy's hysterics every time Jeremy's bowel movements aren't the right color.'

'Well, guess what? That isn't my problem. Go home and be miserable; God knows you've probably already driven them all to the brink of despair. You're even better at that than writing plays.'

He just stood there, his hands pressed like handles into his tanned little dancing teacher's hips.

'You should be ashamed of yourself,' I tossed in, 'as if you could ever live that long.'

'Oh, come on, Stevie. I just came over for a swim, I didn't pillage and plunder. I didn't rape the dog.'

'Like I said, you should . . .'

'"I should have been a pair of ragged claws, Scuttling across the floors of silent seas."'

I raked a wobbling hand through my hair and implored him please, please, not to start throwing T. S. Eliot at me at this ungodly hour, at any hour, but please not at this one, before I had even tasted my forty-ninth cup of the morning's coffee, before the *New York Times* had even been thrown at my door, with a force and a thud I always likened to a pot of geraniums being thrown at an errant husband.

'Instead, I was a lovelorn ex-husband, scuttling across the floor of your pool, you doll, you,' he smiled.

'Don't start. Don't you dare start,' I warned him then.

'So I guess you figured it out, huh? I mean the Swedish?'

Again, that eel's snippet of a smile.

'You know what it meant, right? It meant "See you to-morrow."'

I just stared at him.

'So I've gathered.' The words were barely out of my mouth when I heard my phone ringing. Who on earth could be calling?

'Go home, little boy,' I sneered at him, with more than a bit of the eel snaking its way through my own words. Then I turned my back to him, raced up to the house, and got the phone.

'I'm sorry to bother you, but is Charlie there?' a tiny, cheer-leader's voice wanted to know. Only one message unit had been shared between us and I already knew this was a woman who had cried her eyes out at *The Sound of Music*.

I stood there for a second or two, actually speechless. Since when did the current wives of ex-husbands call ex-wives in search of, groping pitiably about for current husbands? And even more to the point, when did my house become the house of Hades? It was all just too much for me, too modern, too surreal. Woody Allen might make a film that had characters like us, floating into and out of each other's feelings and miseries as effortlessly, as inconsequentially as clouds, but deep down, we all really know that life isn't a bit like that. Still, there I was, forced to play a part I hadn't even auditioned for. The little voice spoke again, called me back to the present as I watched one of the wings of one of the Goddesses of Vengeance disappear behind my dishwasher.

'Is he there?' the breathless baby's voice asked again.

'Let me see if he's still here,' I answered finally, putting the phone down. And, of course, he was, pulling on a T-shirt, and lacing up his sneakers.

'Hey, Buster Crabbe. There's a call for you,' I called to him. He walked slowly up to the house and, picking up the phone, covered it just long enough to say to me in a low, low voice, '"I grow old . . . I grow old . . . I shall wear the bottoms of my trousers rolled."'

'This has gone far enough,' I spat at him, not without a little urgency.

'Hi, honey,' he said, pouring on gallons of runny sunshine. He talked to her then, briefly; he nodded and said yes a lot. Lord knows what she said, why she had called. Was the baby sick? Was the house, the house I originally chose, burning to the ground, collapsing in on itself like a house of cards? I couldn't possibly care at that moment. Or even the next, when he hung up.

'How did she know you were here?'

'I don't know. I may have mentioned that I might be stopping by.'

'In English or in Swedish?'

'Oh, come on, Ace. It was no big deal.' He held his palms out to me, those smooth, feathery palms that looked so innocent yet held so much promise for wickedness.

'Again, I am asking you to leave. And to not come back. Not "morrou," or the day after "morrou," do you understand?'

'Aah, Stevie,' he sighed. '"I have heard the mermaids singing, each to each."'

Hah! For once I was too quick for him, even at that hour of the day, even with my brain all in a tizzy and my thoughts coming out in slow motion, underwater.

'You do not think they will sing to you? Well, this one won't. And don't come back. Not for coffee, not for talking. And not for my peaches.' I laughed. 'I've already seen how you "dare to eat a peach," old man,' I finished, just as he was going back out through the screen door. 'Really, Charlie, now this has got to stop. Seriously, I mean it,' I added. It had to.

With all the blitheness of a newborn babe, he reached out then and tugged on a handful of my hair. 'I think you've got it all

wrong.' He grinned a little. 'I think now this has all got to start.'
And with that, he pranced across my back lawn, stepping down
on all the flowers I had nurtured so tenderly, just as they were
getting ready to stand up, and open for a day of business. He
even narrowly missed a baby rabbit's tail. Charlie was quick,
masterfully quick, but even he was no match for a rabbit.

A bit later that morning, I invited my friend Mara (who was out
visiting friends for the weekend) over for lunch. When she said
yes, I set about looking at myself, at my dusty, disheveled house,
and at my kitchen, which was by now once again utterly
peachless, plumless, and, in fact, as fruitless as I was by now
beginning to suspect any effort to relax on my vacation would
prove to be. And, of course, knowing Mara, this simply would
not do. Mara with the swan's neck and the tanned and graceful
dancer's legs craved fruit salad at lunchtime the way a lizard on a
rock craves sunlight.

It was for this reason that, after dressing quickly and a fast
mental realignment of priorities as I shaved my legs, I found my
way to the Farmer's Market in Amagansett. I guess I have been
known, upon occasion, to let friends down in life; good Lord,
haven't we all, but it has never been known to come down to a
couple of plums or a mouthful of watermelon.

Now this being a weekend, a Saturday morning in July, I knew
it would be as possible to get quickly in and out of the Farmer's
Market as it would be to, say, get a reservation for Santa's knee
on Christmas Eve. As I parked and made my way through the
tented hood of gold and white stripes, I overheard a woman,
with spindly nails that looked as if they'd been dipped in sheep's
blood, exclaim to her companion, a shorter, more pallid version
of herself, weighted down with every item in the Louis Vuitton
catalog, 'I'm telling you, Cherry, I should have let him beat the
hell out of me. I would've gotten rid of him long ago.' As I passed
her, I looked unavoidably into her face for a second, expecting it
to be scarlet with something like shame, but it was not. She piled
a few ears of corn into her basket with a jangle of thick, steely arm

bracelets that seemed to me to belong on the ankles of a chain gang and went stolidly about her business with Cherry. Using my elbows to part the sea of voracious shoppers around me, I made my way across the imitation brick floor to the back of the market, for the wooden shelves crammed with oils and delicacies, jammed with jams imprisoned in their jars. There was no air to breathe. I jockeyed for a sliver of space within arm's reach of the mustards, but abandoned the idea as a face that passed me caught my attention, held my breath for me, and would not let it out again.

There stood the new Mrs Stamberg, her mouth parted wide enough to let in a dozen fluttering moths. She knew who I was and I knew who she was, and suddenly Mara's big lazy bowl of lushly colored fruits – the sugar, the water, the vitamins and the seeds and pits – all went right out of my head as I watched this woman actually come toward me. All I could really think of as she took her first awkward, tentative, galumphing steps was that this was the sort of woman who licked her fingers before turning the pages of a book, who considered making a Betty Crocker cake baking from scratch.

'I know who you are' were her first words, delivered shyly, with her head on a tilt, almost coyly, without the merest trace of venom or reproach.

'Well, yes. I guess you would,' I muttered to the fake bricks of worn linoleum beneath my feet, waiting for the words that would be spoken between us.

'It's kind of funny, isn't it, I mean, don't you think? I mean, not funny like laughing or anything, if you get my meaning. Just funny in the way that things are funny.' She shifted her weight from one faded espadrilled foot to another. 'I mean, us both being here like this. But not like a joke.' All right, I was thinking already, relent. But she was not about to. 'I mean, like as a coincidence, more like, if you get my meaning,' she groped about, more just trailing off than finishing her thought. If you get my meaning.

She went on speaking, defining and redefining herself to me, apologizing for the early morning phone call, seemingly oblivious to the stupendous inappropriateness of her response, and it was while she was in the midst of this great mass of twisted, recycled words that revolved and repeated that I got my first real chance to look at her. Of course, I had seen her blond Kansas farm girl's face staring out at me beside Charlie's from more pages than I could remember in all the toniest magazines, little 'People in the News' bites that described how an optometrist's assistant from Poyntz Avenue in Manhattan, Kansas, had followed her own road right into wedded bliss with a national literary treasure from Manhattan, New York. And now here she was, standing in front of a table overflowing with ripe, yellow peppers from Holland, close enough for me to pinch her.

For nearly three years I had restlessly dreamed of this meeting, and had determined just what my attitude would be. I had honestly meant to buy a one-way ticket to the icy tundras of indifference, carrying with me a pronounced air of having someplace far better to be, honestly I did. According to my plan, I would direct my frosty-as-marble eyeballs to a specific point on her clothing and just stare at it, insolently, unwaveringly, as if there might well be a spot or two of ketchup that had spilled. (How could that possibly fail to wither her on the vine?) In fact, I had imagined this moment more times than was actually dignified to recall, and yet how many ex-wives, finding themselves in less than advantageous circumstances, are not occasionally lulled to sleep at night by the sweet solace of this most fangless of fantasies?

There in the market that morning, however, all prior strategies of anything resembling imperiousness left my mind. Impressions at that moment meant less to me than, say, the price of those fiery yellow peppers, which cost an arm and a leg, with quite possibly the cost of one year's tuition at Exeter thrown in. What I'm saying is that I simply didn't care about all that, although I knew I might later on.

Instead, for the moment, which felt indecently long, I just stood there under her great torrent of words with what I'm sure must have been a dopey half grin painted across my face. We were soon interrupted by a short, youngish woman chewing bubble gum, and my fascination skyrocketed with the baby she carried, a drooling, yelping bundle of wetness which was, I knew instantly, none other than her son, Charlie's son, Jeremy. Even though I sensed it was the right moment to part company and proceed with my original quest for fruit, I just stood there, gazing with great curiosity into the baby's wrinkled face, so contorted with tears. Right then, I felt Patsy lay a clammy little hand on my shoulder, and heard her whisper that she wanted to ask me something very important, and really, I just couldn't resist.

Important, *very* important. What on earth could it possibly be, I thought, racking my brains. Did she want my family's special pot roast recipe? (Fat chance she'd ever get it.) Did she want to know why Charlie always shuddered when you traced the bottom of his left ear lobe with your tongue, but not his right one? Did she want my advice on just how to keep her trophy of a husband on the mantelpiece? I doubted it, since she was living proof that I had failed at it so abysmally myself. (For a brief moment, I actually felt for her. Was she up to the task? Was anyone?)

In the meantime, as I waited for her words, I managed the obligatory 'Well, this must be Jeremy' in a voice I could only pray sounded natural, unpanicked, positively unstricken. My motor raced even more wildly as I stared into the baby's face, which was such a stark replication of his father's that I had to suppress a manic shriek of a laugh. And then, as I watched Patsy take him from her little gum-chewing employee and try, unsuccessfully, to quiet him, I turned my incredulous stare to Patsy, aware but unconcerned that anyone, that she, might notice and object to my excessive curiosity.

Her small, round, chinless face, so arrogantly without even a trace of makeup, was the color of milky oatmeal, but she had a pair of watery blue eyes that swam right out of that pasty face and managed to stand their ground. The little teeth were passively aligned, making no statement of their own. She was, as I'd read countless times, a tall, willowy string bean of a girl, but seemed to me to be utterly without texture, contour, or dimension. She looked, more than anything else, all liquid and unfocused. Dull and a little slow. So watery, in fact, that I wondered how, when Charlie swam into bed with her at night, they didn't both just float out to sea in opposite directions. (Or did they?) I can't exactly say she was pretty or attractive, but I don't exactly have to because everyone else was forever saying it. She was all of twenty-six years old, and I had crow's feet that were older, so I would not necessarily trust my own opinions on this particular topic, but this is what I saw. The other thing I saw was a pair of simply terrific knees beneath her creaseless khaki shorts, and they turned out to be what got to me, affected me in a way I could not quite fathom. Got to me, indeed. They made me want to cry. They were those scissor-hard, sharp-edged kind of knees, the kind that could neatly pare cheese, or sand the deck of a Fire Island house. I didn't have them. No matter what I tried to do, I never could. They were the knees that every tall, blond and bony, watery-eyed, non-Jewish girl had and they just broke my heart. You couldn't have them just for being a decent person, for being truthful on your tax returns, reading to the blind one night a week, or walking your elderly neighbor's dog on a rainy day. They just weren't in the stars, or the catalog. Better luck next time.

So this is what I was thinking about when she finally turned back to me, about knees and about good fortune, as Patsy handed the baby back to the whining au pair and, taking my arm, led me a few steps away from the crowd.

She leaned down a bit into my face as her own seemed to darken for a moment.

'The thing is this,' she started, with some difficulty. I waited and waited while she cast about for the proper words, starting and stammering so that I began to worry that she'd never spit it out, that my friends and I would spend the rest of our living days guessing at what Patsy Stamberg might have asked me that day in the Farmer's Market.

Whatever color had been in her bloodless face washed right out of it then, and she whispered to me, in the direst, darkest possible way, 'Did he use to scream in his sleep?'

85

'Did he what?' I whispered back, the hope in my heart afraid to take flight in case I had heard wrong. But I hadn't.

'Did Charlie use to scream in his sleep at night when he was married to you? I've wanted to ask you that for so long,' she muttered miserably, a few drops of humid perspiration beginning to bead her oatmealy upper lip.

Well, I was positively speechless, floored, blown away.

For a second I nearly giggled, so light-headed did I suddenly feel, as if the air at the market was suffused with champagne or with helium. Aah, but what would my answer be, I wondered to myself, tugging myself reluctantly back to earth and reality. What could it be?

I looked up into that trusting face, the blue eyes searching my own for an answer that could relieve her despair, just as Jeremy began wailing. 'Well, no,' I started. 'I can't say he ever did,' I told that pale but somber face, although, of course, he did. He did more than he didn't. And I don't mean he talked in his sleep. I don't mean he giggled or made little gurgly sounds in his sleep. The man screamed at the top of his lungs. God only knows what used to provoke those gut-wrenching, bloodcurdling shrieks. Charlie always said he didn't know, that he couldn't remember. At any rate, if he did, he wasn't telling. Of course, my attitude about these nocturnal arias varied with the subtle shadings of my feelings for him. If I happened to know, for instance, that Charlie was in the midst of one of his spicy little peccadilloes, I would sit up, turn on the light, and watch him almost without emotion, coolly, even hoping that his midnight agony was as unbearable as my midday agony was. But if he was behaving himself, having a dry spell between adventures or a temporary crisis of conscience, I would wake him gently and murmur a few genuine, comforting words. Needless to say, this did not make for a particularly relaxing or restful sleeping pattern for myself, never knowing if or when I might be awakened by the cries of a thousand bloodthirsty banshees, but I did the best I could.

Did he scream? Oh boy, yes, he screamed, but I was not about to tell her that. That could be my little secret, and she could take home her own conclusions regarding it, along with her gum-

86

cracking nurse, her wet, cranky baby, and her basket of corn and ripe avocados.

'Are you absolutely sure? I mean, this is something I need to know.' She bit one corner of her mouth petulantly, which annoyed me a little. I didn't at all appreciate being asked this question by her, let alone being pressured.

I looked into that watery depthless face with those pristine eyes of blue swimming around in it and said with what I hoped was at least a trace of sincerity, 'Look, good luck with your problem,' and stepped, finally, past her and out of the store, aware that what I was bringing home to my lunch guest was far more delectable than any fruit I could possibly find. Indeed, I knew that she and I would chew this over for many days and nights to come, would pick it apart and put it back together again in every possible sort of permutation and probability, would just drain, sap, and deplete it until there wasn't a drop of juice left to it. And I couldn't wait.

When I arrived home, however, and went into the kitchen, I did not find Mara (it was still early), but instead a brand-new IBM Selectric II typewriter sitting on my kitchen table, all alone, apparently with nothing to explain its sudden appearance. I circled it suspiciously, understanding full well how it had gotten there, but not knowing why. It was then I spotted the tiny typed note snuggled beneath the paper bail.

'Your old one will simply not do,' it began. 'Great plays must be written on great typewriters, or at least passable ones. Give yourself a break, and *me* a call when you get home, and tell me how grateful you are.' It was signed 'Your Ex,' and the PS read, 'Loved the robe this morning. Did I give it to you?' I sat down at the table and crumpled the note in my fist.

Well, this was a fine situation, I thought ruefully to myself, thinking in the bleak and immediate instant that from now on, I'd have to lock the door when I left my house. So much for the pleasures of the country.

I took a closer look at the typewriter, which sat detachedly on

87

the table looking like a smug and angry enemy about to come in for the kill. Could it see the fear in my eyes? My hand that trembled just a bit? Could it smell my wavering temptation to just give in and embrace the enemy rather than retreat? I hope not. Machiavelli wrote, as Charlie had so often reminded me, 'If you can't kill your enemy, embrace him', but somehow I don't think this was what Machiavelli was talking about.

Lady Mendl wrote, however, in quite another context, that when entertaining friends, one should 'Never build a meal on a lake,' referring to meals that commenced with soup, either hot or cold, and this seemed a bit more pertinent to my day's activities. I lifted the typewriter by its shoulders, which was far from an easy or pleasant task, and set it on the floor of a closet. Out of sight, out of my mind, I thought, as I pulled myself into the shower, the very least I could do for my shortly arriving guest. It was only then, standing under the giddy pelting hot water, that the full weight of the last day and a half and all its strange, unplanned, and unwanted unusualness began to settle in on me.

The typewriter was only the beginning of what swirled around me like suds in the drain. Would I use it? Would I return it? Would I (could I?) burn it? Use it as a planter? Hit Charlie over the head with it as he jogged by next time, with that dazzling Cheshire Cat's smile that made him look as if he'd just murdered his seventeenth wife, hidden her in the closet, and was on his way to woo number eighteen?

I thought about Patsy and that drooling little pea of a baby face, and back to his louse of a father. To his father who cheated, lied, made love like a caged bandit, and came bearing typewriters and illicit dreams and causing new scars as well as disturbing the aggravating never-to-be-healed old ones.

I could feel my skin shrinking back into itself and my bones crumpling up as if they were foldable, collapsible. I had stood there in the hot downpour for so long it felt like forever, and yet not nearly long enough.

As I thought again about Charlie's unfaithfulness and his straying affections, I wondered if Patsy with the trusting gaze and the knockout knees had any inkling of what she had gotten herself into. And it suddenly grabbed me right there under that tireless, merciless showerhead that perhaps Charlie did actually mean for me to play the old game with him, but this time with me cast as the one to help him deceive wifey.

Was it possible, or was I just being melodramatic? Flattering myself, or insulting myself? And anyway, could he be serious about such an outrageous thing? And never mind about whether it was possible, more to the point was whether it was probable. I knew only too well that what went around usually came around (and Lord knows, he was certainly coming around a lot lately), but could he really have fashioned such a diabolical scheme? I remembered him telling me that Patsy wasn't jealous, but I had perhaps missed the kernel of what he had been trying to impress upon me, that maybe he wished she were. You never know, do you? I knew, from the cruel cut of personal experience, that the key element that could really put a damper on even the hottest, most sexually volcanic adulterous foray was a wife who truly did not give a damn. It dulled all excitement, subdued the illicitness, the sensual and psychological friction. What fun was it duping someone if you were entirely without guilt, and they didn't even care that you were doing it? What fun, indeed. I know at least that in Charlie's case this had always been so. Dolores, for instance, could not have cared a fig about his extramarital wanderings, and so in order to keep the fire and the pleasure of them alive for himself, he had had to replace Dolores.

An expert on this matter might be Flora Mastroianni, wife of the consummate Casanova of our century, who once said, quite coolly, that you had to '. . . understand the nature of the . . . male. He likes to wander, to feel potent and free. So you let him go, absolutely without strings – and sooner or later, he'll come back home.' When I read that one, I had to practically be wiped up off the floor. But that wasn't all. Flora, who must have an awful lot to say on the subject, continued, 'So when people ask me how I feel about Marcello coming home, I reply that he never left. This has always been his house, no? I've slammed the door a few times, but never kept it shut. Poor man, where else would he go?'

89

Now for all I know this is all pure public relations. Perhaps the high-heeled shoes and scalding pots of pasta go whizzing by, sailing by Marcello's sainted salt-and-pepper temple nightly, courtesy of Flora, but that is something we will never know.

As for myself, I had never opted for the role of the long-suffering wife, thank you very much. But an affair with *me*? To juggle the players and recast me as . . . the other woman? Could that be what Charlie wanted? I wondered as I dragged myself out of the shower. It astonished me, and yet it also made perfect sense. I got dressed and waited for my friend to appear with her additional baggage of assorted questions and theories.

'Anybody home?' I heard moments later as Mara came in through the kitchen door.

'I'm up here. Wait a second,' I called back.

'Don't worry, I'm not going anywhere. I hope you have good plums, Stevie,' she yelled up, which made me want to climb surreptitiously out my window like a cat, scale the side of the house, and crawl guiltily back to the city.

Instead, I crawled downstairs, and found Mara, with her marvelous flamingo legs, lying on one of my couches.

'Didn't you read what they said in the *New York Times* last week about eating too much fresh fruit?'

She sat up, curious.

'There's no such thing as eating too much fresh fruit, but what did they say?' she wanted to know. Now I was good and stuck.

I frowned. 'They said nothing about it. Nothing at all. They said they agreed with you.'

Mara was no moron, and certainly not about the really important things in life. She squinted purposefully. 'No fruit salad, huh?'

'Nope. You'll have to settle for tuna fish, or else we could go out somewhere.'

'It's too hot. I'm not budging. A little mercury poisoning never hurt anyone, right?' she joked, covering up, I was sure, her

90

deep feelings of devastation. We hugged in that East Hampton way, with nothing actually touching, and went into the kitchen.

Still, I felt compelled to defend myself.

'Believe it or not, I did try to get you your fruit, but the best-laid plans of mice and men often go astray when you run into Patsy Stamberg and a screaming baby in the Farmer's Market, and she decides to have a conversation.'

Mara never missed a beat. I knew I could count on her.

'Hmm. Very interesting. Best-laid plans and best-laid wives, eh? Hurry up and tell me everything.'

Where would I begin? Where did I begin? I don't know, I can't exactly remember. All I know is that once I started, it took an awfully long time to stop. I began with Charlie, with his visits, his innuendos, and with all of Mara's oohs, aahs, gasps, 'No! He didn't's, and picayune questions – 'What color T-shirt was he wearing? What color blue? What does he look like in blue?' – I came slowly, lazily, round the bend with Patsy and her question and the unexpected typewriter. When we finally paused a bit and managed to come up for air, I looked at the clock and half expected it to be midnight, but it was only three o'clock, and well past the time for lunch.

I opened the tuna, handed Mara her third glass of iced tea, which she drank with customary little guppy sips, as if it were hot soup, and at last began to get our lunch on the table.

'Some hostess I am,' I said. 'I invite you over for lunch, and it looks as if you'll be getting supper.'

But Mara, the worldly, sagacious one, waved away such triviality. 'Oh, never mind about that. This is a big day, and we've got lots of work to do.' She paused. 'You haven't got that new mayonnaise by any chance, have you?'

'Mayonnaise? Why?' I was puzzled. Mara was not from the school of Big Eaters.

'I was just reading about it, that's all. What is it called again? Giller's mayonnaise. You know, it costs about one hundred dollars a jar, has no preservatives, and no true Hamptonite can be seen without it. I mean, the tuna will jump right out of the bowl, Stevie. It'll feel underprivileged,' she laughed. She started rifling through all my shelves then, and sure enough, she produced a big barrel of a jar of Giller's all right, which I hadn't the faintest recollection of ever buying.

'You are a magician. I swear to God I've never seen that before.'

'Well, thank goodness it's here. Now I can sleep tonight.'

And then, all of a sudden it hit me. 'Beware of ex-husbands bringing typewriters and delicacies, my mother always taught me.'

'You're kidding. Charlie brought this over, too? What a prince. Let's see what else the scoundrel brought,' she purred, and with that she went tearing through my shelves and refrigerator again.

I, however, could tell already that I was headed for something of a sulk; I mean, she was supposed to be on my side.

'So what's the big deal about this stupid mayonnaise anyway?' I asked her, opening it up.

'I'm not sure. It's just extremely expensive, like a dollar for every minute it stays fresh without preservatives, which isn't many, and it's made by some couple in Grand Rapids – an Englishwoman and her husband, who raise Shetland sheepdogs, can you believe it?' Then she let out a yelp, my old friend Mara.

'Aah! Beluga! You know I love beluga. How could you hide this from me, you devil,' she whined, holding up a blue tin the size of a lunch box.

I shook my head, already starting to see the shape of the rest of my afternoon and not particularly liking it.

'Take it, be my guest. You *are* my guest,' I offered.

Well, in the next few minutes she not only turned up Scottish oatmeal, English anchovy paste, clotted cream, Spanish olives, and a tin of fragrantly oiled grape leaves flown all the way from some balmy little village outside Athens, all of Charlie's favorites, she also came up with a theory and an attitude that set every one of my teeth right on edge.

'The man is a god,' Mara announced, her mouth full of beluga. 'He always was. He just didn't know how to deal with you. I swear to God though, he must miss you terribly. He must be

92

crazy in love with you, dying to get you back. Think about it. I think it's incredibly romantic, the thought of you two getting back together. Pass the tuna fish,' she said, gesturing for the bowl, eating more in one sitting than I had seen her consume cumulatively in the past fifteen years. Having lost my appetite, I pushed all of the plates and platters of food down to her end of the table, muttering only, 'Watch out for Shetland sheepdog hairs.' Some hostess I was. What would Lady Mendl say now?

'Mara, you're supposed to be telling me what a selfish, egocentric psychopath the man is. You're supposed to be helping me ignore all of this nonsense. I can't believe you're actually encouraging all this. Falling for anchovy paste, for God's sake.'

I poured more iced tea for us as she gnawed her way through a couple more grape leaves, then looked over at me sadly.

'I'm sorry, maybe I'm not being sensitive,' she mumbled.

'You know him. He's bored and he's only playing with me.' I began to wring my hands.

'We don't know that for sure. Maybe you should give him a chance and see exactly what he's up to. I know I would.'

'Hah! You would, if it were your ex-husband –' I started.

'But that's just the thing, Stevie. It isn't. It's Charlie. I mean, God, maybe he's being sincere. What then?'

'I can't go through this again,' I whispered to her, plaintively.

'What if he's changed? What if he's more responsible?'

'Oh, please. How responsible is it to bring all this stuff over along with a typewriter when you're married to someone else?'

She thought about that for a moment.

'What if he's in love with you?'

'Charlie's in love with Charlie.'

'Well,' she started quietly, 'that just might make two of you.'

I got up and started clearing the table. As I went past her she grabbed one of my arms.

'What if he is?' she murmured, rhetorically.

'I just think he wants to have an affair with me. Maybe he's running out of new candidates and has to start repeating himself.'

'We just don't know,' she said solemnly. 'There's just no way of knowing.'

93

I couldn't keep the sarcasm out of my voice then; it blew right into my words just as if I'd left a window open.

'Well, what am I supposed to do in the meantime? Raise Shetland sheepdogs?'

'Take care of yourself. Look out for yourself. See what he's really after. If he loves you.'

'If he does, I'll eat this jar of mayonnaise, dog hairs and all.' I threw up my hands.

'And if he doesn't,' she continued, 'life will go on. Still, just remember how unpredictable the man is. You lived with him for almost thirteen years, and in all that time, the only thing you said you knew he'd do for sure was stand over you flossing his teeth whenever you wanted to practice the piano.'

'Don't remind me. Are you telling me, seriously, to go on with this thing? What if it were your ex-husband wooing you?'

Well, with that, her sunny sky of a face filled suddenly with darkness and clouds. If I listened carefully, I was sure I could hear distant thunder.

'Stevie, come on, we're comparing Pulitzer Prize-winning plays with quackless ducks. Don't do that to me,' she begged, and really, I couldn't blame her.

'First no plums, and then a reference to Matty. What did I ever do to you? Besides, it's irrelevant.'

And she was right. Any reference to Matty Marino, her shiftless ex-husband, was truly unforgivable. I'd never forget the first time I met Mara, the first time we were introduced at the agency and told we would work together. She was fresh from California and from the California divorce courts, and it was only a matter of minutes before she got up, closed the door, and spelled it all out for me in her elegant, spare, poetic style. By the end of the story, I looked up into her Persian cat's eyes, into that pale and lovely face, as frail-looking as Sèvres china, and knew that we'd not only be a cozy and formidable creative team, but that also, where friendship was concerned, we would probably come to mean a lot to each other. I wasn't wrong, and all it took was one hilarious story, about living in LA with an unemployed husband who had been an account man at an ad agency, to reveal this to me.

After bouncing around from place to place, Matty had cheerfully decided that he and the world of business were not cut out for each other, that he'd have to come up with some other plan. This plan, unbeknownst to Mara, was to snatch their last two thousand dollars out of a joint savings account and go into business with a friend. Their job? To begin to control the messy local problem of snails (the California counterpart to the New York cockroach) in an original and profitable way by selling people the ducks who loved eating them. But since ducks were so noisy, Matty had brought all of the one thousand they had purchased to the vet in order to have their quackers removed.

Now this was all a surprise to Mara, who slept that night blissfully unaware that her artist's studio, a tiny shed out back with an ill-fitting screen door, was that night filled with one thousand filthy, hungry, quackless ducks who paced and beat their wings as they waited to be sold at a roadside stand the next morning for $29.95 apiece. Unfortunately for Matty and his partner, for Mara, and for their empty savings account, a starving coyote or two found their treacherous way through that broken screen door that night, and all of them missed the ugly and macabre sight of a thousand doomed and voiceless ducks, tearing frantically out into the night in a vain attempt to escape their bloody persecution, leaving a trail of dried blood and feathers all the way from Paseo Miramar. Oh, lucky snails, but poor sweet Mara was all I could think, sitting there that first day with her as she spilled it all out to me so plainly and trustingly. As she explained it, that had been the duck that broke the camel's back, the end of California and of Matty for her. After that, whenever there was Peking Duck or Duck à l'Orange on a menu, we always had a good laugh.

And so, in answer to her question, it was not possible or fair to compare plays with quackless ducks, but to my mind, a snake in the grass was still a snake in the grass, even if it had won awards and slunk along the road in a silver Porsche, with or without grooved or tubular fangs.

95

'Still, if it were Charlie . . .' Mara trailed off. 'I just don't know what I would do. I wouldn't slam the door, Stevie, not before I took a good look at what was inside.'

The phone rang then, and my stomach began to curdle.

'What if it's him?' I asked her, already uneasy.

She laughed. 'Tell him that clotted cream by itself is a travesty. Ask him what happened to the scones.'

'I hope you still like beluga,' the voice spoke to me, stretching across an eternity.

'I like choosing my own foods, thank you. If I needed a professional shopper, I would go out and hire one.'

'Well, luckily you don't have to. How's the typewriter? You try it yet?' I stalled. I could have my pride or a decent typewriter to do my work on, but not both.

'No, and I'm not sure I will. I'm not sure I should.'

He paused. 'Of course you should. I thought about it, and I'm not sure you're ready for a word processor yet. I know the way you work and it'd take you time to learn, and you'd procrastinate, and –'

'We'll see, okay?'

'Of course we will. You remember that machine, don't you? It's the one I took to Forte dei Marmi with me when we spent that summer in Italy. If you look very closely, you'll see it runs on olive oil,' he laughed.

'I said we'll see.' I took a deep breath. 'By the way, I met your wife this morning. And your son.' Mara covered her face. Just where was I taking this?

'Well, well. So, what'd you think of Patsy?' he asked cheerfully, as if we were in a restaurant and he were quizzing me about the bouillabaisse. Were there enough clams? Was the broth seasoned to my liking?

I laughed nervously. 'Charlie, I'm not sure this conversation is entirely appropriate.'

'That's all right. I am. So what did you think?' he insisted.

'Well, you know, she's very –'

'Tall?' he supplied.

'Right. That's what I was going to say, tall.'

96

'What you were going to say was high-strung, overly talk-ative, and she sounds like a Mousketeer, and I wouldn't have disagreed with you –'

'I never would have said such a thing,' I protested, 'and you shouldn't either.'

'Oh, she has her moments, my Patsy; don't get me wrong. It's just that they're usually at about three or four in the morning and I generally miss them. The thing about marrying younger women –'

'Please stop this. I'm hanging up –'

He cut me off. 'The thing about marrying younger women is that men always think it'll make them feel younger, act younger, and look younger. But the truth is, all it does is make them feel like Methuselah, going on his nine hundred and seventieth year. Really, by now we all ought to know better,' he mused.

Well, I was speechless, but that was only one of us.

'So you talked to her?'

'Uh, yeah,' I hedged.

'She's very insecure and I do my best to keep her that way,' he joked. Some joke.

'Of course you know I'm only kidding,' he offered, but of course he knew I knew he wasn't.

'I have company, I have to go, Charlie.'

'Not a man, I hope. I didn't bring you over all that stuff for you to share it with some schlub, you know.'

'What did you bring it all over for?' I asked, hoping for something that might be in the same hemisphere as a coherent, truthful reply.

'Oh, just to let you know that I enjoy you. That I appreciate you. It's really very simple,' he said softly.

'Nothing is ever simple with you,' I countered. 'You ought to be put in jail.'

'I have news for you. They don't arrest people for caring about other people. Not yet, anyway. If I were you, I'd just relax and enjoy all this. Goethe once said, "Beginnings are always delight-ful. The threshold is the place to pause," and I'm inclined to agree with him.'

I laughed spitefully then. 'I don't think he was talking about us. I'm hanging up now,' I told him, meaning it.

'God, it's good to know you still love me,' he said, beating me to it. Click.

'You should see your face, it's as red as a McIntosh,' Mara observed, still with the fruit. 'He didn't proposition you or anything, did he?'

Soon after, Mara headed for home, but not before pausing to tell me at the back door as she left, 'God, Stevie, I know you're going to kill me for this, but I think this is just fabulous. I mean, no matter what happens, even if nothing happens, you haven't even stopped to think of the fact that right now, after so long, after so many years of feeling you never would, you've actually got the upper hand. You're holding all the cards. You should be thrilled, if even just for that alone. Think about it. Never mind his great ass and his cheekbones, his bank account and his idiotic dinners at the White House. Right now, you're the boss, and if that doesn't give you a feeling of ecstasy, nothing ever will.' She patted my cheek protectively, and loped through the door, a kind and generous wilted flamingo in search of ripe plums and peaches.

Which left me to hang around, sit around, pace around and ponder her words, as well as all of Charlie's, until they were all reduced in my mind to a big pot of mush, no longer making any sense whatsoever.

I walked out to my pool, and dangled my chalky-white, winter legs in the tepid water, and wondered what would happen next.

I could not know of course (and perhaps that was for the best) of the veritable bombardment, of the overwhelming rush, the deluge, the blizzard of activity that Charlie was plotting at that very moment where I was concerned, of the land and air troops that would be deployed in the blitzkrieg of my lifetime.

Sitting there that late afternoon at the pool as the sun began its descent in the sky, I worked with steely determination to remember why I had come there to the country for my time-out period – to rest, to rejuvenate myself, to refuel and to finish writing my play.

But all of this, the rest and the work, now seemed as remote as outer space. Goethe may indeed have been right about the threshold being the place to pause, but how long could one decently or reasonably remain there, pausing even at the threshold of thought? Not long enough to suit me, I'm afraid, for the opacity of Charlie's words and actions would soon, I feared, tug at me and pull me right over the edge; out of the frying pan and into the fire; across the threshold and into the thresher.

As I sat there, watching the sky fill up with the bold, slapdash, faraway crimson-pink stripes of a mournfully elegant sunset, I could only think of Charlie as I first knew him, before all the scars and baggage of wasted, painful, and dissatisfied time. As the man who had first swept me off my feet, and then for years had managed to keep me there. The man who had spirited me off to Italy after a good friend's sudden death from leukemia, taking time out from his own frantic, demanding schedule to love and care for me, to pamper and distract me.

And what a job he had done, taking five languid days, each one calculated to be filled with tenderness and closeness, as he cleverly devoted one day to each of my senses. The first was an eating tour of Florence. From there, we smelled our way through the perfumed countryside, ablaze with spring flowers. The three days remaining were each spent touching, hearing, and seeing, as we wound our way through towns and valleys in delicious, comfortable abandon. Even with all the splendor around us, to say nothing of the lovemaking and incessant shopping (aah, the smell and feel of Florentine leather; in that department, Charlie was no slouch either), I still found a way to grieve for my friend. Charlie did not try to prevent this, but instead made the hard road I had to travel a bit less so when paved with his kindness and company. He, and we, I've often thought, were at our very best then, and I could never forget it.

In fact, that evening out in East Hampton, I could think of him only as that brilliant, long-ago, dashing figure who shyly asked me out to dinner (before our series of shy, awkward lunches), which lasted seven hours, and left me at my door with a warm, urgent handshake with both of his hands, and an avuncular kiss over my right eyebrow that smelled of Gauloise and Korbel, and a husky 4.00 a.m. voice that whispered, 'I have a feeling you are the best-kept secret in New York, and I'm certainly not telling anyone. We will see each other again.' Well, of course, I was agog. Why wouldn't I have been? Two days later, without a word from the professor, I left for Paris with my parents for a little trip to celebrate their thirty-fifth anniversary. Why they wanted me along I never quite figured out, but the morning after our arrival I took off on my own and found my way by bus to Chartres Cathedral, where I promptly took three steps inside and, weakened by the threat of love or jet lag or both, fainted dead away on the cold, endless carpet of pale marble.

When I came to, I opened my eyes and looked up into the small faces, pinched with concern, of several priests, chattering away in their high-pitched, unintelligible, staccato French. Past them I saw the great walls of stained glass, beckoning to me with all the icy splendor of true French Gothic, and looking up and around me, not knowing precisely at that moment either who I was or where I was, I swore that I must be in heaven. In the next instant, when I reclaimed my self and proper surroundings, having spotted a fleet of Japanese tourists with cameras, I felt the raw bruise of a back not meant for a tumble onto a bed of chilly marble, and knew immediately that I must get home, as soon as possible, to New York.

I was in love, yes, but not just in love; I was in a sickness over love. I stayed in Paris for only two nights and two days, and never was I so besotted with love, so forlorn and aching with longing. I could not eat. I could not smell or sleep or laugh or think of anything but Charlie, and of that breeze of a feathery kiss over my eyebrow. I knew something was about to happen to me that would be absolutely monumental, and that it would begin just as soon as I got back home. Soon, impatient with my sullen demeanor and what they referred to as my morbid trances, and

100

fearing I might be ill, my parents agreed to pack me off and send me home.

On the return flight, as the stewardess dimmed the lights, and as I sat wrapped in itchy, fuzzy blankets, I felt I must be almost phosphorescent with love, that in the darkness I must be shimmering, blinding my fellow passengers with an unmistakable light. And so tuned in to my surge of blossoming feelings did I assume Charlie to be, that I was actually surprised that he was not standing there when I left the plane, meeting my flight. Now was this a crazy feeling? Most people would have said so, yet somehow to me it wasn't.

All of this had not been easy for me to stop and consider for many years, this particular pausing at the threshold, this temporary dawdling in the anteroom of optimism in our relationship, but now it was possible for me to think of it again without flinching, as a leg of a journey which was apparently unfinished after all. Perhaps Mara had been right about the power that I held over him finally, after so long, and my foolish reluctance at claiming and rejoicing in it.

What is it though, about the mind, that will not let us linger in the sunny spaces, that pulls us back down into the shade, the grayness, even the darkness? From there my restless thoughts propelled me, hopped, skipped, and jumped to about eight years after my dizzy epiphany in the Chartres Cathedral, to the time when things had already begun to turn, when for the first time I knew for certain that Charlie was fooling around, with his typist of all people, the girl known only as Chantal.

It's impossible to say why, but there I was, lost in the memory of his first known, indelible betrayal, which began, oddly enough, with his sudden, newfound, nightly faked craving for fruit, which would lead him out for roughly one hour every evening at precisely eight o'clock. If I had apples in the house, he'd be dying for a banana. If I had bananas, he'd be desperate for a tangerine. If I had crates of tangerines, it had to be a tangelo. There was no way to win, and shame on me, but it was a full ten days after it all began that I realized the grimy subplot of this particular drama, and became determined to outwit him.

It was a cold January day, I remember, that found me at my neighborhood fruit stand piling seven kinds of apples, oranges, grapefruits, and bananas into masses of shopping bags. I walked a few blocks north, stopping again, this time for different kinds of apples and oranges, and for as many pears and berries as my hands could hold. It was in a sweat and a fever that I then poured my bounty into the back of a cab and found my spirited way to Macy's, where to my astonished delight, I found pomegranates, Hawaiian papayas, persimmons, avocados, blueberries from Australia, kiwis from New Zealand, coconuts, pineapples, strawberries from Florida, grapes from California, and melons, plump and ripe, as well as not-so-ripe, also from the sun-drenched valleys of the land of snails and ducks that quacked. Then I tossed in some dates, figs, dried apples, apricots, and pineapples and some chocolate-covered strawberries for good luck.

From there I went home, with the cantaloupes and honey-dews, the Granny Smith and Red Delicious apples spilling out onto the floor of the taxi, onto the floor of my lobby and right into my elevator. It looked as if I had bought out the entire universe of fruit, had truly left no stone unturned. Oh, pomes, oh, berries, oh, drupes! Oh, the well-orchestrated plan that you execute with a hollow feeling of dread and partial shame at your own inventiveness, feeling it will all surely backfire and expose you and turn out to be, well, fruitless.

I unloaded my quarry and filled my refrigerator, as well as more than a dozen bowls which were positioned strategically throughout the apartment. I then made dinner and waited for my husband with a smug feeling of having swallowed a brace of canaries. We ate dinner in the kitchen that night rather than the dining room, where we occasionally sat when we were feeling the least bit grand. Halfway through dinner the phone rang. 'Is Sharlee there?' the tiny French voice wanted to know. I put him on. He spoke in a clipped, whispery, monosyllabic monotone, and then returned in a frazzled and preoccupied state to his wife and plate.

'That was, er, Chantal, my typist. She had a few questions

102

about Act One.' He spoke to the bread-basket, his eyes nowhere near mine. Anxiously awaiting his oncoming fruit derailment, I cared little about who called him then or for what reason. As I cleared the table, I noted the time, which was three minutes to eight. Soon he would yawn, I knew, put down his half-empty coffee cup, and stretch his arms high over his head, which would enable him, with just the slightest flick of his wrist, to snatch at the time with his quick, devil's eyes. All of this in one bold flourish, one shockingly graceful movement.

He yawned again, then took his coffee cup over to the sink and announced, with stunning predictability, 'I think I feel like a little fruit. I may just take a walk.'

My pulse was racing, I'm sure, but I was determined not to break any speed limits that night.

'I've got a few things here,' I told him, sweetly.

'Hmm, I think I'd like a grapefruit,' he went on.

'Pink or white? Florida or California?' I asked brightly, springing into action and opening the refrigerator.

He looked slightly taken aback then.

'On second thought, maybe an . . . orange,' he fumbled.

Again, I was ready.

'Navel? Temple? You name it.'

His eyes avoided mine.

'I hear that . . . the strawberries from Florida are very good these days,' he told the floor.

Aah, but it was nice being prepared.

I held some up for him.

'Would you prefer them straight or chocolate-covered. Luckily, we have both.'

He was starting to sulk, I could tell. He searched my face but found nothing there to explain why his kitchen had been miraculously transformed into a Korean fruit stand.

'You know, pomegranates are said to be good for the kidneys.'

Pomegranates? Was he kidding? He was not.

'They're in the bowl next to the toaster.' I pointed across the room.

103

Well, by now he was beginning to appear astonished. His face looked sallow, his eyes glazed. He was sweating.

'You know, now that I think of it, maybe it's not the night for fruit,' he muttered.

'Gee, what a pity,' I managed, somehow without sarcasm. 'Are you sure? Take a look. There must be something here you'd like.'

'I don't think so,' he almost whispered, reluctantly opening the door to the refrigerator.

I watched his face and almost laughed out loud, seeing his eyes grow big with horror and fascination.

'When,' he started miserably, 'did you get all this?' he asked, as a coconut rolled out and nearly cracked him on the foot. He picked it up, shaking his head. 'Really, Stevie. Coconuts?'

'I thought you might like a piña colada later on,' I offered.

'In January?' he almost shrieked.

'Is it really January . . . already?' I asked, loading the dishwasher. I turned on the water at the sink, and twice turned around to see him still standing there, shaking his head and examining the contents of the refrigerator in total, utter, terrified confusion. As one of his feet began tapping with frantic urgency, I looked once more into his face, now stunned with a glowering determination.

'I'm going out for a candy bar,' he mumbled.

'You're what?' I asked, raising my voice above the running water.

He actually barked at me then. Woof, woof.

'I'm going out for a goddamned candy bar,' he repeated, and in two seconds, he was gone.

I heard the front door slam, and then heard it slam again, only this time, I was the one who ran through it. Without a coat, without my keys, I flew down the fire steps to the lobby, on wings of fury and madness. Once outside, I hid in a doorway and waited for Charlie, who soon came barreling through the lobby doors as if he'd been shot out of a cannon. He looked, openly, at his watch several times, and then darted into a phone booth. He had just dropped a coin into the slot and was a breath away from dialing when I opened the door of the phone booth, put one shivering hand on his shoulder, and with the other cut off his connection. The dull, hollow thump of his coin returning was the only sound I heard as I looked into his startled, unhappy face. I didn't say a word and neither did he. We just stood there, crammed together in that phone booth, looking at each other with a stark, unrelenting, reproachful gaze. In a few more seconds, he pried my fingers from the phone, curled my hand into one of his, turned me around, and just muttered, 'Come on, it's cold out here.' Then he put his jacket over me and steered me back up into our apartment. Oh, I knew only too well that birds gotta fly and fish gotta swim, but husbands don't have to go out into the night chasing down cute French typists, and after that night, mine no longer did.

Which is not to say that after that little showdown, all was exactly right with the world again. When there is the tiniest crack in paradise, you are always on the verge of a complete structural collapse, and ours was surely no exception. Once it started to crumble, it usually kept on disintegrating. It just took a long time for my unfocused eyes to begin to see what they wished they didn't have to.

The next unwelcome saga, cataloged in my memory as the 'Superintendent Episode', came about two years after Charlie's sudden infatuation with fruit. Now that he was teaching again, after a two-year hiatus of working on a play, Charlie decided to bring his graduate seminar home with him for their weekly classes. Did he know I would object to this, or did he merely hope I would? I never could quite be sure. I knew only that after three of these classes were held in my living room, a towel was missing from the master bathroom, there was a cigarette burn the size of a bull mastiff on the piano, and two of my favorite lipsticks were found, uncapped, on my dressing table, with a cloud of crumpled, marijuana-smelling, red-smeared Kleenex next to them. Now, for all I know, Charlie had been the culprit, but at the time, I never even suspected such an outlandish thing. I

105

did, however, suggest quite another, and that was that he take a studio somewhere for his classes, which he did, with cheerful resignation.

Doris Lessing wrote, 'As soon as one has lived through something, it falls into a pattern. And the pattern of an affair, even one that has . . . been as close as a marriage, is seen in terms of what ends it. That's why all this is untrue. Because while living through something one doesn't think like that at all.' Doris, of course, is correct. Retrospect is almost completely shaded by the light of current, up-to-date insight and information, so perhaps all of this is untrue. I can and do look back and see Charlie as a scamp, a roué, a scavenger for women's flattery, catering to their amusement and erotic whims. I see it all now as a great, dark puff of a cloud that he pulled over everything, suffocating all that was contained within it, but maybe I am looking back with astigmatism rather than with a frozen, crystallized, clear-eyed awareness.

One Saturday, Charlie invited Mara and me to lunch in his studio, which was in a charming brownstone in the Village, a place just brimming with character and ambience. Arriving early, I knocked several times and rang the bell, but there was no response. Mara and I listened at the door but heard nothing. We stood around for a few more minutes, and then I decided to use the key Charlie had given me for emergencies. Did I think first about what I might find on the other side of the door? Certainly not. We were cold, we were hungry, and by now my fanatically punctual husband was sixteen minutes late.

I put the key in the door, but it wouldn't turn the lock. I tried three more times and then Mara tried too, but her luck was no better than my own. All of a sudden, I started getting worried, started panicking. What if Charlie was inside, sick, incapacitated? A woman I knew had come home from her therapist one night after work to find her husband of ten days slouched over the bathtub, dead of a stroke. By now, I was persuaded that I had somehow mistaken one key for another and had left the right one at home. I started banging on the door then and yelling for Charlie, even though Mara was laughing nervously, I thought, and telling me I was behaving like a madwoman. Just then the super came along, a greasy little man who smelled of onions and bad cigars and who greeted us cautiously, his eyes narrowing.

'Mr Stamberg gave me a key to use if he wasn't around, and it doesn't seem to be working. Do you have one?' I asked him, with enough anxiety in my tone to get me a choice room at Payne Whitney, with a river view and three meals a day.

He tried the key and muttered something to himself, and then to us.

'It looks like the right key. I don't know why it don't work. It usually does. It always works when Mrs Stamberg uses it. She don't have no problems.'

Mrs Stamberg? Charlie's mother and grandmother had been dead, both of them, before I was even born.

'Mrs Stamberg?' I managed to croak. 'Mr Stamberg's wife comes here?'

Well, with that he just about lost patience with the two idiotic fur-clad women who were keeping him from a beer at his local bar or from OTB. He waved us away, as if we were nothing but a nuisance.

'Of course she does. Who else do you think would be called Mrs Stamberg?'

I held on to Mara for support right there in the hallway, my legs were shaking so. I could not find my voice, and my entire body was suffused with a cold, wet bath of sticky perspiration. I thought I might faint, but I was not that lucky. When I regained some semblance of composure, I saw the super scampering away down the hall, and felt Mara clutching at my arm, pulling me down the steps.

'I can't believe it,' she kept whispering, echoing my own violent, incoherent thoughts, with a stab of real sorrow in her voice. I looked at her gray, perfect cat's eyes, and saw tears beginning to well in their corners.

'How horrible this is,' she repeated, over and over. 'How on earth could he do this to you?'

We were out in the street by then. I looked around, hoping to catch a glimpse of the man I married, the man I knew, who

107

would surely arrive with a plausible, comforting explanation for all this, but he was nowhere to be seen.

'I know what you need,' said my friend, patting me on the arm. 'You need a martini.'

I found my voice somewhere, lost among the ashes.

'I don't need a martini. I hate martinis.'

She took a deep breath. 'Well, then *I* need one,' she said, tugging me, in a gloomy, paralyzed trance, into a corner café.

Before I even sat down, I went to the pay phone and, with frozen fingers, tried to reach Charlie, at home and at the studio, but all I got were two recorded messages. The one at home was my own voice, cool and unruffled, before the cataclysmic revelation of the afternoon. I left messages on both answering machines, attempting to sound breezy rather than totally demolished (but was dubious about the strength of the breezes that blew across both).

When I found my way back to our table, Mara had ordered, despite my feverish protestations, two 'bone-dry' martinis, and they were put before us. After drinking them, we woodenly drank two more. If I hoped the full settling of alcohol would subdue my pain, I was sadly disappointed. Occasionally, my thoughts would drift back to the little man with the greasy fingers in Charlie's hallway, and to his words, and every time I thought of it, the laceration was as fresh as the first time, but why shouldn't it have been? Mara did her best to distract me, chattering with an astonishing velocity on a vast array of meaningless topics. But for all her singing and dancing, my miserable mind was rooted in its anger and sadness. Finally, I told her that it wasn't necessary to knock herself out, and we returned to the thing that hung in both our minds like a menacing scarecrow draped out over a fence in a cold field full of crows. In the lambent light of the café, the waiter eventually came around to see if we wanted more to drink, but I waved him away, saying, 'Please, I've already had tee martoonis,' and then I turned to the somber face of my friend. We shook our heads simultaneously.

'Did you notice anything lately?' she asked me then.

I cast about in my sozzled mind for suppressed bits of information that I might have hidden from myself, but could only come up with a fragment of one, long forgotten and seemingly unimportant at the time.

'One night when we were getting undressed, I noticed his underwear was inside out, but that's about it,' I told her flatly.

'Well, was it on that way when he got dressed in the morning?'

Suddenly, I was so tired. Each word needed its own longshoreman to carry it down from my mind to my mouth.

'Oh, God, how should I know? He could've gone to his gym.'

'Does he take his underwear off at the gym, Stevie? What the hell kind of gym is it?' she wanted to know, popping an olive into her mouth.

'He swims, he swims at the gym,' I explained, rubbing my eyes. 'I don't know. Please don't ask me anything else. I just don't know.'

Well, with that my friend knew enough to get me out of there and stuff me into a taxi. Before getting in, I tried Charlie again from a pay phone on the street, but there was no answer in either place.

'I think we'd better just ride around for a while, keep moving,' Mara announced with forced gaiety. She told the driver to take us to the Upper West Side, and then turned to me, and said in a low hush, 'What a spiteful thing, Stevie. I mean, for a woman not to tell him his underwear was on inside out.' She clucked her tongue meaningfully then, but by that time, my thinking was about 97 percent proof, and I was just floating away somewhere in a vapid, thoughtless haze. I looked at the divider in front of us where a line of graffiti was scrawled in thick, black Magic Marker in a wide, slanted script. DAWN-187-I'M WARM FOR YOUR FORM it said, and when I saw it, I began to laugh, to laugh so much that I could hardly stop laughing. Something just struck me about it, about how sex and the absurdity of sex was really the thread that held the world together, and once the silliness of it all clouded into my foggy, dizzy mind, I couldn't let it go.

It seemed to take ten years to reach Broadway and Ninety-sixth Street, and then Mara told the driver just to drive and to keep on driving, and so we rode in silence for a while, huddled against each other, trying to make sense of everything. Outside, the winter lights twinkled and people shivered against the wind, but inside I felt even colder.

On our third aimless foray up Central Park West, I finally got out of the cab, just a few blocks from our apartment. As I stepped onto the curb, a cold blast of air hit me, startling me and almost knocking me down. Mara offered to come upstairs, but I declined. I felt I had to face the music alone, no matter what the band happened to be playing. Inside-out underwear, my foot; my ass. As I stood in the wet gutter, I realized that Charlie's cheating had been every bit as predictable as halibut for a Catholic on a holy day, and that I had just refused to face up to it.

When I got upstairs, I found my husband sprawled on the couch, snoring, with a book of theater criticism open on the floor next to his shoes. I stood for a moment before waking him, just watching the face that was so angelic and guileless in sleep, searching out its secrets. One of them had been giving the key to his studio to a woman, but what else was there? Did one woman have the key, or did many? And what, if anything, was I to do about it? Should I just stand aside like Flora Mastroianni and silently watch the flood wash away everything most dear to me? Or confront him, put his back to the wall and pressure him into making choices? And anyway, would he tell me the truth, or silence me with the welcome pabulum of lies and verbal trickery? I knew from the ache of experience that pressuring Charlie about anything usually cost me more than I'd bargained for; he often kicked up his arrogant heels and acted out of pure spite and rebellion, cutting off his nose to spite his splendid face.

When he shifted position on the couch, I patted a sweatered shoulder gently and stirred him from sleep. He rubbed his eyes like a third grader and asked, in a voice still hoarse from dreaming, 'What time is it? I must have fallen asleep.' When I told him it was nearly seven, he whistled and announced that he must really have been exhausted. 'I just meant to close my eyes for a few minutes,' he grumbled. 'Now I'll be up all night.' He paused.

Still no mention of the lunch he'd invited Mara and me over for, the lunch he'd missed. 'What's for dinner?' he wanted to know. He put one hand on my neck and rubbed it, like a cat's. If he was waiting for me to purr, I didn't.

'That depends on what you had for lunch,' I started, slowly. 'I for one, had nothing,' I said, trying to keep the overflow of rancor from my voice.

And then, all of a sudden it hit him. Lights flashed. Bells clanged. Cymbals crashed.

'Our lunch date . . .' Yes, what about it? I nearly shrieked at the top of my sturdy lungs.

He slapped his forehead like a true bumpkin just off the Greyhound bus at the Port Authority, from someplace like, say, Manhattan, Kansas.

'I missed it, didn't I?' Alfalfa asked meekly, shaking his head, tossing it, as if it were a veritable salad of regret.

'Yes, old man, you certainly did.'

'How could I have forgotten? I was looking forward to it.' He scrunched up his mouth, to indicate sorriness. Oh, I'll bet you were, you dog, you.

'How could it have slipped my mind? I was going to cook for you both and everything.'

He kept asking questions like this and I kept not answering them. I know I was supposed to jump in at some point, the fearless deep-sea diver, and rescue him from this purely rhetorical masturbation, but I could not. I just left each and every question alone, let it lie there, humming with its own unanswerability, and gradually I felt as if the whole room had swelled with them.

'Where were you?' I finally asked, quietly.

He coughed nervously. 'How should I know? I was everywhere today,' he started.

'Everywhere but where you should've been, I guess.' I took a deep breath and tested the water with a toe or two.

'Look,' I pulled out of myself, 'what's going on?'

His eyes darted back and forth, Ping-Pong style. When they finally found their way back to me, his expression was of such

111

bewilderment and surprise, it suggested I had spoken to him in Bantu.

'With what? I went to bookstores. I bought a couple of shirts. The time just flew by. I came home to lie down, and . . .'

'Your super . . .' I proceeded, cautiously.

His face brightened then, the opposite of what I might have anticipated. It filled with light and relief and amusement. 'Well, you're not so bad yourself. Why don't you get dressed and . . .'

I cut him off. 'I am dressed. And by super, I mean superintendent. As in your building. He said that the key always worked when . . .' Whoosh! He chopped the rest of my words off in midair, like a Benihana chef. My eyes began smarting at his deftness, to say nothing of his smartness.

'That old baboon? Check him out closely next time, Stevie. He even has the same short tail and the doglike muzzle. He doesn't even know his own name, he's so reliable.' Charlie waved away all my protestations. 'I don't even want to know what he said to you. The guy has the mind of a minnow.' He stopped then, pausing to see if his words had had their desired effect.

I cleared my throat, lowered my wheels, turned on my lights, and prepared for landing.

'He said the key always worked when your wife used it.'

He glared at me then, closed his eyes and shook his head.

'Well, there you have it, then. The guy is a loony bird,' he finished with conviction, standing and changing the subject, swiftly and effortlessly, as if it were merely a tune on a jukebox.

'Let's just let it go, all right? Apologize to your friend, and I'll take you out to dinner. Never let it be said that my atonements do not have polish and flair.' He bowed a little.

Well, I was stupefied. Blocked once again, headed off at the pass.

'Getting dressed?' he asked, not unaware of his superb performance. 'Wear something nice and we'll go someplace special.'

'I'm really not very hungry,' I said wearily. 'I've got a bellyful of martinis and a splitting headache.'

'But *I'm* hungry,' he whined a little. 'And I've done nothing but dream my life away all afternoon on this couch,' he complained, as if it were my fault. The guy sure believed in pushing his luck.

I shook my head sadly. 'I really just can't believe you sometimes,' I told him.

'Maybe not, but what's your choice?' he countered. 'You're stuck with me.'

Well, after that I walked with the sorry heart and posture of Quasimodo into our bedroom, threw open the doors of my closet, concentrated on the words of Flora Mastroianni, and proceeded to dress myself and whip my mind back into something resembling normalcy. If Charlie could put on a show, well then, so could I. Wasn't our love of the theater one of the bonds that nurtured and fortified our connection? Oh boy, would I show him, I thought grandly, poised with my mascara at the bathroom mirror. And then I noticed that my hand was trembling like Pearl Harbor on December 7, 1941, and fell out of love with myself just a bit. Still, the show would go on. I would go on. Which meant, I supposed and hoped, more than a little frantically, that Charlie and I would go on. And on.

Little did I know as I dressed and readied myself for a few hours of determined gaiety and enforced ignorance and forgetfulness that the land that lies flat under perpetual anxiety must eventually rise, buckle, and trip you up when you least expect it. In my own case, this buckling was to occur that very night.

In fact, it was nothing less than a total collapse of things that evening. How dutifully I sat there at the snooty Italian restaurant we'd gone to, draped over the bar with my husband, so intent upon chattering up a guilty storm. I knew I was supposed to be impressed that he'd taken me there. I suppose I was unpolished, unchic, but the water that truffles swim in has never reminded me of ambrosia.

As I recall, the tablecloths were hot pink and seemed to be fashioned from spun sugar. Such sweetness, however, did not extend to the chorus line of faintly contemptuous waiters who, with chiseled noses pointed somewhere north of Uranus, breezed haughtily in and out of our smoke-filled line of vision.

If securing a dinner reservation (especially on short notice) was

113

not quite tantamount to winning the Nobel Prize, it was considered quite a coup. Almost anyone could sit at the bar, hoping all surrounding eyes supposed they'd gotten a reservation, but the real accomplishment was in actually being seated and served a meal, which was rumored to take months. The reservation, as it turned out, was just foreplay.

I had never been to this particular restaurant but I had been to others like it and always went home wondering what the big deal was. I often wanted to say that to Charlie, but I always held back a little, trying to be at least a bit gracious, waiting for Charlie to say it first, which he usually did. Of course, his name always opened such doors for him, always got his hand into the girl's sweater, but after that, it was always left to the whims of the gods, and never more so than on that night, when the end of my marriage was on the menu, in the form of an exotic-looking woman, with killer shoulders and a gold-plated perfume atomizer for a weapon.

We had been sitting, I can remember, at the bar, on brown suede barstools, long enough to qualify for squatter's rights when, peering across Charlie, I first spotted her. Was he raving that night about Shaw or Pirandello? That much I can't recall, but I can picture with appalling, neurotic clarity the French *pot à la crème* who kept lighting up cigarettes and who just couldn't keep her eyes off my husband. Her own, it seemed, was seated on her other side, but that failed to even faintly dim her pilot light. Wrapped up or poured into some gold sarong-type number, her steely shoulder blades seemed poised like a pair of attack dogs. Each of her ears boasted a gold earring big enough to bomb a Third World nation, and her skin gleamed like honey-coated copper. Oh, she was there, all right. There was certainly no doubt about that, and just like my husband, she was also chatting up a breathless hurricane, in that rat-a-tat French that always drives me bonkers, pausing furtively here and there for a quick dart of a look at him, just to see if it was all working, which, of course, it was. (He went for French women the way teenagers went for French fries.) My ears began a mournful ringing with the tintinnabulation of her words, spoken far too loudly, as she expertly directed the bluish trails of her cigarette smoke up and into my nostrils like a shepherd steering sheep.

Well, in spite of myself, I realized quite suddenly, incomprehensibly, that I was in love with her perfume. I had never in all my life smelled anything like it. It was spectacular. It tickled and stirred me just as she tickled and stirred Charlie. And so there we were; I was intoxicated with her perfume, while ballooning with the panic and despair that comprised our evening's subplot. The gray, unshaven face of Charlie's super kept swimming before me, so informed and so superior. How could I discount the words and conviction of a man with 'the mind of a minnow,' as Charlie had described him? Surely such a man was incapable of deceit or inventiveness. I knew my minnows, after all.

I kept hoping our table would be ready before breakfast, but I could only keep waiting and hoping, while Charlie and I and Frenchie and her husband kept two conversations going in different languages. All the while, of course, she was checking Charlie out, and he was checking her out, and Jean-Claude just sipped away at his vodka, ever so docilely, nodding occasionally to the French bombshell as I sat in a paranoid stupor. Was this all a setup? Did Charlie and she really know each other? Was she the keeper of the key? The 'wife' his super had explained about? Forcibly, I steered my beleaguered mind away from these thoughts with all the energy I could muster, and then again I became aware of her perfume. I sniffed and sniffed away at it but could not place it. Finally, even Charlie noticed that I was somewhat distracted.

'What is it? Do you want another drink? I think you've really had enough for one day,' he whispered to me. Well, at that, I could only laugh. If his playwriting career ever came to a crashing halt, he could always find work as an air traffic controller, so adept was he at directing and redirecting people, conversations, and motivations.

'I'd hardly call one glass of white wine with ice cubes a drunken sailor's holiday,' I whispered back.

'Well, what do you keep sniffing for?' he asked me then, beginning to sniff himself. 'Have you got a cold? Would

115

you like to go home?' he offered, a bit too brightly for my taste.

'Are you kidding? After waiting this long? I'm eating dinner if I have to go into the kitchen and make it myself.'

Just then, the maître d' presented himself with an obsequious wisp of a bow.

'Mr Stamberg, once again our apologies for keeping you waiting. Your table will be ready shortly,' he scraped, doing everything but leaning down and licking the dust from Charlie's brown leather shoes. He looked as if he were just about to. He gazed right through me as if I were utterly transparent, a Plexiglas replica of a would-be diner. I was tempted to trip him as he skated away on a veneer of self-important obnoxiousness, but I controlled myself. (If I had a dime for every restaurant person who'd treated me this way during our marriage, I could do more than just buy my own Italian restaurant, I could buy Italy itself.)

'Stop sniffling. Don't you have a Kleenex or something?' Charlie asked me then, still not taking his eyes off Sheba with the shoulders, who still hadn't taken her eyes off him.

And then I did just about the stupidest, least-thought-out thing in my whole life. 'It's her perfume,' I told him then, conspiratorially. 'It's terrific and I've never smelled it before. It's driving me crazy.'

His eyes now began to twinkle, as if with candles or with the sparks of comets.

'Ask her what it is,' he said then, with all the innocence of Klaus Barbie.

'I'm not doing that,' I gushed a bit. Why had I started this? But even then there was still time. I could still have saved myself. Why hadn't I?

It was then that the Pope of Obsequiousness sashayed back toward us, informing Charlie that our table was ready. As we slid off our stools and swerved to follow him, Charlie stopped right in front of Frenchie, told her that I was mad for her perfume, and asked her if it had a name. Well, in spite of his maddening predictability I was livid, flustered and livid all at once, so I broke in and spoke to her myself, as the room went spinning around me like a carousel.

'I can't place it, but it's absolutely delicious,' I told her, a bit too buoyantly, leaning right into the air of mystery I was inquiring about, filling up my lungs with enough of it to last for weeks.

Well, so stunned was she, I guess, that I had acknowledged her and her scent, that I had actually paid homage to those shoulder blades, that within seconds, she had whipped a gold-plated majestically carved perfume atomizer out of her purse, and whispered, breathlessly, into my face, 'Oh, tank you. I am mad about eet too, but you cannot buy eet except een France, you see. You cannot find eet here.' And with a few quick pushes of her finger, she sprayed the perfume right past Charlie, and right into my eyes. Directly into them. Purposely? I'll never know for sure, but that hardly mattered, even then. Of course, both she and Jean-Claude began shrieking their apologies, stuttering and stammering in two languages, while the bartender produced a cloth soaked with ice for me to hold over my burning eyes, but the truth was, I was blind, Tiresias stumbling along the side of the road, on the very brink of his sorry *éclaircissement*. Perfume from France is not meant for retinas, for pupils, for the vulnerability of mascara-dipped lashes. All around me was blackness, only blackness.

I started to cry and could not stop. Into the sightless abyss I plunged, right into the heart of darkness, and all the horror, the horror. But I will never forget the last blurred vision I saw. In her feverish, emotional chaos of an apology to me, the copper-coated *pot à la crème* had toppled her drink and dropped the evil atomizer to the floor. And as I kept screaming that I could not see, I can still picture Charlie, bent over on all fours, ass high in the air, with a lone bald spot I'd never noticed before winking up at me as he scrounged about on the floor helping her to locate her perfume.

It was exactly at that moment, in the grip of a black denouement that I imagined felt something like eclampsia, that I suddenly kissed the whole wretched show good-bye. In that blind fraction of a second, I knew for certain that the ball game was over, that my marriage was over, all because of some crummy atomizer and an unreliable minnow-brain of a super. Who can say why what was enough yesterday is suddenly too much to tolerate today? I cannot, could not. I only saw that the ship had sailed, and sailed without me. And how utterly strange it was, I always thought after that, that it had taken blindness for me to suddenly be able to see. That had been it, the end for us. Charlie's ass may have been up in the air, but my feet were on the ground, solidly planted and awaiting the journey, the path of unsure footsteps that I now clearly understood were to lead me far and away from him. Amazing grace, oh stupendous, earth-shattering grace. I was blind but then I saw, and oh boy, what I saw.

When the phone rang, startling me back from my poolside reverie, and it was Calvin, it did not strike me as such a bad thing, although it did surprise me. But then, there was very little about him that did not throw me as off balance as snow flurries in July. Calvin was not like anybody else. He was the man my mother had asked me about on the phone, Mr Illness, a man she knew I saw off and on.

A sudden, out-of-the-blue call from Calvin required no explanation. With him, there was never any explanation for erratic, inconsistent behaviour. I have never traveled to Poland, but I imagine a trip there is rather like a romantic relationship with Calvin Persky. You do not travel there for the geographical beauty, for the shopping, for the world-renowned cuisine and luxurious accommodations. You expect a certain degree of discomfort and a punishing grimness. It goes beyond the drippy faucet in your bathroom or the runny toilet. And yet people do journey to Poland. It's a trade-off, and so would be even an on-again, off-again rapport with Calvin.

He was an investment banker from a wealthy Canadian family, and I had met him almost two years earlier at an office Christmas party, where he'd come with an old, boyhood friend. Crinkling up his nose at the trays of hors d'oeuvres with an expression of revulsion and disgust, he knocked back the Diet Cokes faster than I could count them. And as he looked down my dress while cleverly, intelligently, and humorously discussing the national deficit, I was strangely charmed and could not believe my luck when he asked if he could call me. He seemed not only refined, debonair, and smart as a whip, but also quite funny, in a cozy, comfortable way that seemed, in those days, the aftermath of my postdivorce trauma, to be in even shorter supply than caviar or truffles in the bedraggled markets of Warsaw.

When a bunch of slightly sloshed art directors and copywriters at this party brought some noisemakers out of their coat pockets and began using them, Calvin, this reedy vagabond of the diet wars, took a giant slurp of soda to fortify himself and said, in a voice full of patronizing contempt, 'Enough with the Purim gragers!' I threw back my head and clapped my hands and roared with laughter, the kind I had not enjoyed since my divorce. Silently, I thanked God and marveled at my sudden good fortune, my early gift from Santa Claus.

Yes, Calvin, I came to learn, could be adorable and endearing. He was also incredibly attractive. The whole package seemed tidy and full of promise at first, even with the rigid rock of determination that was his foundation, the proud, prominent jaw, even with the nerves that jangled like telephones or a pocketful of loose change.

It is said that female cowbirds send romantic signals to males without ever making a sound, indicating what songs they like with body language, by lifting their wings to indicate approval or disapproval. Apparently, such nonverbal communication is positively rife in the bird kingdom, and explains how male cowbirds learn songs that please females.

This is not hard to believe for a nonbird person, even if it seems controversial to those who really know about that kind of stuff. After all, don't we do just about the same? That night, as the Purim gragers spun and cracked, I lifted my glass and my wing to Calvin, and we were off and running.

Did I happen also to think of Charlie? Of course. After so many holidays spent together, how could I fail to? True, a full nine months had elapsed since our divorce, since I had clung to those Ralph Lauren pillows at the edge of my tub and just lost it, lost everything. But it was Christmas, our first one apart and now those nine months felt like seconds; all of the pain suddenly felt fresh again, even as I tried to escape it.

When I met Calvin, I didn't think about the word 'rebound.' I assumed he would mark a new beginning for me, rather than just intermingle with the shadows of the past, but of course that is far easier said than done, and besides, Calvin had his own problems. Trouble was ahead.

Our first dinner together should have tipped me off, but things are never quite so clear-cut where gridlock of the heart and mind are concerned, and perhaps never less so than at holiday time when we are all fending off an aloneness so chilly and so potent that it nearly breaks us into pieces.

If I had aptly observed the silent language of cowbirds that first evening when we walked into a cozy, neat little restaurant on Amsterdam Avenue that had pigs on the coffee mugs, home-made cakes and pies, and good, hearty American down-to-earth cooking in gargantuan portions; if I had kept a watchful eye on my companion, shivering there in the doorway as we came in from the piercing cold, I might have spared myself an awful lot of needless nonsense, instead of just shutting my eyes to the obvious and throwing back my head, as stupid as a turkey in the rain. Fooled again, Ace, Charlie might have gloated.

As he took off his elegant cashmere coat and moved ahead of me to our table, I noticed the stern, solitary way Calvin walked, with straight, heavy, weighted strides, as rigid as the slices of a scissor. The thin, shivery shoulders were a little boy's shoulders, with big, bony blades that gave up midway across his back and caved in at the center. It looked as if a single, callous gust of wind off the Central Park reservoir could topple him, his fine clothes on windless days making him something of an optical illusion.

Sitting at the table, I first noticed the sweat on his upper lip, a refined kind of dampness, and I saw his hands beginning to fidget

120

and pick at each other. We were certainly chatting easily enough, but down deep somewhere in the marrow of my hungry bones, I knew something was terribly wrong. I could see it in the dry, cool glitter of his eyes that seemed suddenly so full of panic, like those of a frantic animal who might have to chew his own leg off in order to free himself from a trap. That was how Calvin looked to me there in the cozy candlelight of the restaurant, as the waiter brought us our menus.

I watched wordlessly as Calvin accepted his menu with a shaking hand, and scanned it quickly for something steamed, for salad, for pallid vegetables with no flavor, for calories that he could deftly swirl about his plate, for a dish that could save him, anything, please, help.

But there was no hope for him that night. He could not chew off his leg, any more than he could order from a menu that boasted of such rich, calorie-drenched dishes as pork loin with a sweet sauce of prunes and apples, steak with oysters swimming, butterfly-stroking their way across the plate, or Duck à l'Orange drowning in Courvoisier and orange marmalade. Very big were they, I can remember, on this fruit and liqueur thing. I myself had no problem with it; going into a diabetic, overpriced coma these days was par for the course on Amsterdam Avenue. I was game.

Calvin, however, looked as if he were about to go into cardiac arrest as he clenched his menu so tightly it could have shrieked from suffocation. He loosened his tie and began hyperventilating. 'There's so much to choose from,' he muttered with a sickly smile, opening his shirt. I nodded, thinking he was kidding, putting on a little histrionic playlet for my benefit. See what a restaurant I've brought you to, I thought he was saying. Look at how agonizing it is to choose from this menu of such magnificent opportunities.

'Do you mind very much if we go?' he asked, finally, looking away from me with veiled, unemotional embarrassment, and quickly spilling money onto the table before he heard my more than astonished reply.

'Was it something I said?' I tried to joke (already starting to feel emotionally attached to the slab of pork loin I'd wanted to order).

121

Before I knew it, we were back in the street, after a swirl of activity, and after a befuddled maître d' had retrieved our coats. Then we were left only to ourselves and the bitter January winds. Calvin smoothed his hair back with a nervous, still-shaking hand and mumbled, 'I'm sorry but I just couldn't breathe in that place. I wanted tonight to be special. I wanted you to like it . . .' He stared down at the pavement, and indeed, I could see his breathing had slowed down, paced itself. 'Let's look for someplace else, okay?' I nodded dumbly. Silently we headed uptown and ended up settling for a neighborhood Chinese restaurant, both of us a little ashamed of the other, I for having witnessed his panicked behavior, and he for the same reason.

'I owe you an explanation, but let's order first,' he offered, disappearing behind his menu. Luckily, the only fruit he could react to, if that was his problem, was kumquats, placed quite unthreateningly in the little postage-stamp-sized column in a lower corner of dessert listings, like a second-class afterthought.

When our food came, so did the explanation. As I ate my dinner, Calvin knotted, twisted, and turned his paper napkin into about a thousand tiny, tortured little balls. He was anorectic, he explained patiently. Or had been, the result of a conscientious, graduate-school-initiated diet from long ago gone haywire. It was over, oh, of course, it was over, he stressed again and again, as he ordered Diet Coke after Diet Coke, and pushed his egg roll around his plate. It was the only thing he'd ordered.

'It took me a long time to realize it, but I had just bitten off more than I could chew with graduate school. Not everyone's cut out to be a genius, a mogul. I was just pushing myself too hard. But not anymore.' He smiled faintly, searching my face for some small sign of acceptance. The crazy thing was, he found it. 'I've lived with a pretty full plate ever since,' he announced, chewing a mouthful of ice into smithereens with his little teeth, seemingly oblivious to the irony of his own words.

So there I sat, with the warning signs flashing all around me, still hoping for some sign that all would be well. We left the Chinese restaurant soon after and went somewhere else for coffee. As soon as we strayed from the subject of his illness, I

122

began to relax and enjoy myself. I felt the little alarm bells inside my heart recede as we wound up the evening laughing, sharing secrets, telling old stories and beginning to make new ones.

Calvin seemed kind to me, pure and honest. And how could I object to a little asceticism? Here was a man who could be faithful and true, I thought; who needed nurturing, polishing, fine tuning. Whereas Charlie had been a self-reliant, finished product when I'd met him, Calvin struck me as a work still in progress, still rough around the edges, and in need of a lot of love. To me, this business of his past eating disorder seemed trivial, almost irrelevant. He'd said he'd been cured, after all.

The truth was he wasn't even as cured as a baked ham, but I wanted to think he was, and for a long while, that seemed to be the case.

But little by little in our year together his highly obsessive, compulsive traits began to reveal themselves. Never mind the fourteen rolls of unwrapped toilet paper lined up on his bathroom shelf like toy soldiers. Never mind the jogging, sometimes before dawn, in the bleak winter darkness. Never mind the laundry that had to be done daily, sometimes even twice daily. And never mind the sturdy supply of Diet Coke he poured steadily down his throat during practically every waking moment. Or his midnight snacks (which were practically all he ate all day), the big, mushy, Tupperware tubs full of Sugar Frosted Flakes that he'd beaten together and mashed with the contents of several chocolate-flavored Frozen Danny cups.

No, what we're talking about here is sex. If I had known I was meant to spend my life in the missionary position, I'd have joined the Peace Corps. Sex with Calvin was annoyingly empty but occasionally somehow palatable, like a made-for-TV movie that seldom falls short of your expectations because, of course, those expectations fall so impossibly low themselves. More often than not, I looked up into that face that was all jaw and tension, that wore so clearly the marks of his quintessential anal compulsiveness; I looked right up into that rigid face with clenched teeth, and wondered what on earth we were playing at, just what sort of peculiar romance was this anyway? The word *pleasure* was so

123

clearly not a part of his vocabulary. And yet, we did have our moments together, times when a delicate sort of tenderness, an eerily hungry vulnerability would show through the denseness of clouds and fog, when sex freed him of his restrained self-imprisonment, if only briefly, and he could laugh and show affection, move a bit ahead and overtake himself, forget to stand watch and allow himself to actually feel things.

At times, he'd exhibit a boundless, nearly unstoppable flood of tenderness and unselfishness, like the time I had my wisdom teeth extracted and he refused to leave my side. Missing work for two days, he sat with me in bed, plying me with Tylenol and codeine, reading me Winnie the Pooh stories, even changing his voice for all the different voices, jumping on the bed, wielding his Diet Coke, giggling and purring in the voices of bears, pigs, tigers, and kangaroos; changing the gauze that kept refilling with blood in my mouth like a real trouper, with not a single complaint, a nasty, weary crack, or a hint of uneasiness or disgruntlement. He even served me tea and toast when I was ready for it, laboriously cutting up the toast into minuscule, microscopic bits that wouldn't require chewing.

For all these highs and lows, he was a 'project,' all right. But for a time he was my project, through thick and thin, through Diet Cokes and Tupperware tubs, through sex that he sometimes anesthetized himself to, as if his penis had been dipped in novocaine, through evenings of laughter, through weekend outings where we were riveted to each other; for a time things were going well in my workshop.

The trouble was, I came to understand, that in his capacity to be intimate and to display affection – which I believe he sincerely felt toward me – he was actually a revolving door, meaning that just as you were on your way in with him, you were on your way out, gaining no ground whatsoever in terms of feelings or commitment. Still, I just kept plugging away at it. Whatever needs I had at that time, he was fulfilling, and it is not a credit to myself to realize in retrospect that if I'd spent even half the time trying to identify and puzzle out my own problems that I did working so slavishly on his, I might have come out of it with a bit

124

more to show for myself. I even read books about Calvin's problems, about anorexia. Searching them out in libraries and in esoteric little bookstores, I always got a second glance; people always looked me over with disbelief, as if to say, 'Who's kidding who? You're not anorectic,' and by God, they were right. Being with Calvin had certainly not diminished my own appetite. In fact his self-denial, so pronounced and aggressive, often stimulated mine, and had proved to be quite fattening for me.

And yet for all his strangeness he seemed to somehow manage in the world and seemed not to notice that something was awry. My mother, however, was another story. Oddly enough, it had been his idea to meet her. I was beyond asking for too much by that time; my arms were already starting to ache from the futility of holding them outstretched, waiting to be handed something that would never be forthcoming.

As we approached the restaurant where we had arranged to meet, a quaint little fish place in the Village that smelled of roses and cloves, I watched his steely nerves beginning to harden. 'Please let go of me,' he said anxiously, embarrassed, dropping my arm, as he opened the door of the restaurant. 'She shouldn't see this.'

Even after that inauspicious beginning, though, I thought the evening went very well. For dinner, Calvin ordered a pallid little heel of Dover sole and he even cleaned his plate, although I knew it must've been a monumental task. The conversation was surprisingly normal. Over coffee, when I told my mother I'd been having bad sinus problems, an eternal complaint, she turned to Calvin conspiratorially and whispered, 'What do you think? Is she a . . . kleptomaniac?' And then, realizing her flamboyantly amusing malaprop, the three of us laughed and laughed.

I left the restaurant feeling a great sense of relief and gratitude to Calvin for having made such an effort. We ended the evening as we ended many of the sporadic Saturday evenings we spent together, cruising by Zabar's, giggling at all the Cadillacs piled up outside, all the Jersey plates, and Connecticut BMWs, and going inside to listen to the shrill-voiced ladies, many of them poured into their designer jeans like hot paraffin into candle molds, screaming for their nova to be sliced 'Very thin, did you hear me? Very thin.' Indeed, those joyous little treks to Zabar's represented some of Calvin's and my best moments together. Somehow there, in the face of so much food denied, he became his very purest, most lovable and loving self. This was what kept me hanging in there, the flip side to Dr Jekyll and Mr Snide. It was there in those turbulent Saturday night crowds, among the acres of breads and meats and cheeses, the smoked fishes and creamed herrings, that we were bountifully welded together in some fine, silent, almost spiritual bond.

As he clutched my hand, his dark eyes warmly, sweetly alive with kindness and laughter, we would push our way through the exit on more Saturday nights than I can remember. Often he'd pull me close to him in one long, exquisite, prodigal gesture, murmuring to my neck, 'God, I love you,' or some such wonderment, his eyes still shining, triumphantly proud of the fifty thousand and one edible temptations he'd just deprived himself of. At such moments, I could not help but love him with a special extravagance, even as my mouth watered and my belly growled.

From there, we'd push our way back out to the street, buy two Sunday *Times*es (we both did the puzzle), and race home to Calvin's apartment, where he'd make a quick dive for the wedding announcements (he always seemed to know someone who was getting married) and I went right for the recipes, which I generally ripped out if it was anything at all interesting, and which I tucked away in a book somewhere and eventually forgot about.

On this particular Saturday though, my heart was full of joy after our dinner, mistakenly thinking it had been an unqualified success. The next morning, my mother called me at home and left a message on my machine. 'Boy oh boy, a nervous wreck who hates to eat! I would just like to know where you found this bargain, and wherever it was, will they take him back?' Imagine, I hadn't even told her about his anorexia, and he had finished his food, but this lady, like I've said, was no dummy.

★

It was after that that I began my pilgrimages to several doctors specializing in anorexia. By then I had reluctantly realized I was not equipped to help him. Sitting in the doctors' waiting rooms, leafing through the obligatory magazines spread out on chrome and glass coffee tables festooned with nameless, faceless plants growing out of baskets with seemingly little light, air, care, or attention, I could not help but be amused as I turned past one food ad and recipe page after another. It was almost but not quite as perverse as having a liquor cabinet fully stocked at AA, with its mahogany doors thrown wide open to incite maximum temptation.

At any rate, these doctors, with their couches and yellowing diplomas, would glaze over like frosty windshields at my terribly predictable first sentence, which was always 'I am here about a friend,' and would scan my face for honesty or duplicity, perhaps picturing me with a finger down my own throat after mealtimes. A friend, indeed. But once they realized I was sincere, and not only that, but talking about a male anorectic, and a middle-aged one at that, they positively sprang to life. Leaning forward in their seats, abandoning their pads and pencils, they would drink in my words as if they would die without them, often buzzing their nurses or secretaries in the anteroom, saying 'Hold all calls,' and then, returning to me, proceed to treat me like visiting royalty.

It seemed, they explained to me, that Calvin was a special case, indeed. Male anorectics were almost unheard of, and their illness was much more serious than that of their female counterparts. Also, they unanimously agreed, the later in life it developed, the more serious and incurable it was. No wonder they seized upon my every word as I talked about Calvin, my voice climbing higher, the words spilling out faster, as I gathered speed and got farther along. In each instance, I waited for them to exhibit shock or disbelief, to remove their glasses and say to me, head at a slant, 'Come, Mrs Stamberg, aren't we gilding the lily a bit here?' but they never did.

More than once they asked if they could use my story, with no names, of course, in the papers or books they were in the process of writing or compiling. That was the good news. They believed me. They seemed even compassionate. But the bad news was much more bad than the good news was good, and that was that there was little hope of ever leading this poor, lost little moth back out into the path of light.

Food, they explained to me, was the circle of fire Calvin had drawn around himself to separate him from everyone else, to keep them away and to control them, as well as to keep himself special, and different. Rather than abandon myself to a losing proposition, they went on, I'd do better to further examine my own reasons for prolonging something so futile and unrewarding as staying too long on a road so paved with vexation and inevitable disappointment.

The thing was, I regarded them as I suppose some people regard fortune-tellers or tarot readers; if they tell you what you want to hear they are reliable. If not, they are nothing but charlatans, quacks, and their words and the implications of their words are tossed away with all the casualness of yesterday's newspaper. Therefore, did I believe their words? It was pretty unavoidable. But did I also incorporate them into my wayward dreams, into my actions and my prognosis for how things would turn out for me and Calvin? For the longest time, I did not. There was just no reaching me. Not by land, by sea, or I suspected, even with electroshock treatments. Like any illness, it had its own private trajectory, had to run its course, and I felt powerless to either hurry or impede it. I was willing to settle for the few moments of happiness with Calvin, scattered in between the madness and frustration until that bleak and sorry final curtain. But what *would* it take? I used to wonder. Just how much could I, would I, stand, and why?

I considered these questions with the help of a decent psychiatrist, a white-haired French doctor with a trace of a lisp. The only thing I can remember about my sessions with the sweet-voiced Dr La Pierre was a green-eyed black cat, an evil-looking little thing that used to wrap itself around my leg, even though I had told Dr La Pierre on more than one occasion that I didn't particularly care for cats. In fact, when she used to ask me if there had been any dreams I could remember, I always sprinkled in a few malevolent cat images; cats burning, cats being strangled, cats being run over on Columbus Avenue by moving vans, but nothing seemed to get through to her. Often, she would leave me at the door with the words, 'Well, let's play it by ear, shall we?', which always sent me back out onto Riverside Drive just absolutely furious. Play it by ear? At those prices?

Nevertheless, as if I were reliving some morbid dream, I made no changes. I let Calvin take over where Charlie had left off, even though I knew the life lived directly under someone else's thumb was a dangerous one, indeed.

This was never more apparent than when I took my train trip to Chicago. That was the day my patience finally ran out, and something at last snapped in my complacent, masochistic little mind, the day I finally faced the fact that I would tolerate no more of this catatonic enslavement. There had been no perfume sprayed into my eyes this time, giving me the power of super sight, but luckily I hadn't needed it.

Calvin was in Chicago for several weeks working on a business deal and had invited me to come out for a couple of days. Waylaid by an ear infection that was just about gone but not quite, I rejected air travel in favor of a nice, quaint, leisurely train ride. In my mind, I pictured a dining car with gentle-faced porters in crisp, starched uniforms, and vases of fresh-cut flowers on each table. I thought the whole idea was extremely romantic, even traveling alone, through the snowy vistas of Pennsylvania and Indiana, all decorated for Christmas, as each hour of the rhythm and rumble of the train pulled me closer and closer to the man I loved.

I packed enough Barbara Pym novels for a twelve-year cruise around the universe, threw in my pain-killers in case my ear should start hammering away again, tossed in my most shimmery lingerie, and left Penn Station with all the clamor and frenzy of Christmas overflowing in my own hopeful heart. I had reserved a bedroom, a necessity for an eighteen-hour journey, but the word *bedroom* did not begin to describe the cramped, dimly lit box Amtrak proffered at no small expense. When the bed came down, you could not use the toilet, which sat directly underneath it. After I crammed my bags in, full of Calvin's many Christmas presents, I found that precious little room was left in the compartment for me. Did I picture afternoon tea being served from a silver platter in my cozy compartment? Not quite. What I got instead was a vacuum-sealed Styrofoam plate, onto which had been piled crackers, Laughing Cow cheese, beef jerky, and stale pretzels, all of which tasted like wilted celery. The Orient-Express, it was not.

When the train stopped suddenly and the lights went out in Harrisburg for forty-five minutes, I took it as an omen. Unfortunately, as it turned out, I was right.

True, the trip was not without a certain homey quaintness, like a sturdy, faded old quilt that's been in the family for years. There were the snowy graveyards in Indiana, all laden with Christmas wreaths. Very Thornton Wilder, I thought, but a bit monotonous after about the thirty-seventh one. (Did everybody just die in Indiana? Didn't anybody live there?) There were all the churches, more than I could count, all strung with colored lights in Ohio. There were the spiny trees that grazed the windows of the train, blowing out against a slate sky. And then there was the airplane food in the dining car, the plastic that had replaced my fantasies of silver cutlery and china and spanking white tablecloths. I dragged along poor Barbara Pym to sit with me over a measly little slab of watery chicken. With broken memories of long-ago overnight train trips to Florida on the *Silver Meteor* to see my grandparents, I had barely returned with a steely heart to my compartment, when the ice pick of pain began its attack on my bad ear.

And there you have it. The rest of the night was spent in agony, tossing back my painkillers with flat ginger ale, wondering why, oh, why, I had ever embarked on such a joyless, ill-fated mission. In the morning, the heat broke down in my room and my ear felt the size of a baseball. I sat at my chilly window with a paper cup of lukewarm tea, and watched the terrain glide by in a hungover, foggy haze of Tylenol with Codeine #4 and no sleep, trying very hard to drum up in myself

130

again the passion and optimism of our first Christmas together that had originally propelled me to board this Amtrak machine in the first place.

I kept telling myself it *would* be a great time with Calvin, *wouldn't* it, as the icy tracks whizzed by. He'd act like a real lover, wouldn't he? With affection, with love, with consistency, wouldn't he? After all, he had invited me and had sounded so excited when I had phoned him the previous morning to tell him which train to meet, hadn't he? Perhaps this chunk of time spent so comfortably together would be enough to convince him that being together was far better than being apart, that there was nothing to be afraid of.

I wondered about all this and more that blustery morning as my ear begged for amputation and I felt the vicious morning wind of Valparaiso, Indiana, blow right through me. Great clouds of white smoke billowed out of giant smokestacks, and then we pulled gently past the green and white colors of Comisky Park, visible through the now heavily falling snow, and I knew it was just minutes until I'd see Calvin's great, warm, cockeyed grin on the platform, as he wrapped me up in those cashmere-covered white-bony arms of his and ushered me into the caverns of his strange, perversely intriguing world.

But of course, when I left the train there was no Calvin. I stood about for a while not quite believing my bloodshot eyes, but still there was no Calvin. Perhaps I had misunderstood, I thought to myself in a real panic now. Maybe he had said he'd meet me upstairs at the taxis. I was pretty sure he hadn't, but I scrambled up there anyway, and there again he was nowhere to be seen. Had he gotten the date or the train number wrong? It wasn't possible, but then again, with him anything was. At last I thought to call his hotel room. To my horror and surprise, he answered after about twelve rings.

'Well, I'm here. Where are you?' I asked, trying not to sound too accusatory or pathetic.

'You're where?' he asked, yawning, sounding bored, sleepy, or thoroughly preoccupied.

My ear began hammering again, like a judge's gavel. I shifted

131

my weight onto my other foot. 'Union Station, where I'm supposed to be. Where are you supposed to be?'

He didn't say anything right away. He just let me stand there, poised at the abyss of catastrophe.

'You're not serious,' he pronounced then, absolutely seriously, pausing between each word for the blood in my heart to turn to ice. 'I can't believe it. You didn't really go and do such a thing.' He clucked his tongue.

'I am coming', I started slowly, on wobbly legs, 'to your hotel. What is your room number?'

Silence. Then: 'You can't be serious,' he kept repeating, as if dazed with a blow from a baseball bat, which would've been too good for him.

'I have to go now,' he announced. 'This is all too much for me.'

'What', I whispered furiously, harshly, 'is your room number?' Again, no answer. My time was up then, and I had no more change to my name.

I took a cab to his hotel, where I once again phoned him, from the lobby.

He began with a chuckle. 'I guess you really mean this thing, eh?'

'Calvin,' I said, starting to cry a little bit now. 'I came out here because of you. You asked me to. You invited me.'

'Was that your impression?' he asked, incredulously.

'What is your –'

'Four twenty-two,' he said snippily, and slammed down the receiver.

Walking into his room was like gazing ever so briefly into the burning recesses of hell.

The devil, you see, was in his jogging outfit, buried deep in his financial papers, and all around him, on the table, as if he had spent the night with a Shriners' convention of dippy anorectics, were boxes of Sugar Frosted Flakes, Tupperware containers, and empty Diet Coke cans.

On the television were cartoons, Winnie the Pooh I think, and when I asked him to turn it down, he would not. Nor would he come out from behind his wall of papers.

'Did you or did you not ask me to come out here to see you? Which one of us is crazy?'

No answer. After I had demanded an answer to my question for the fifth time, I ripped the papers from out of his steely, gripped claws and I looked into a face so frozen with fury that it stemmed my own. He finally answered.

'I'm crazy. I am crazier than crazy. Crazier than you will ever know or guess. Now that we've settled that, will you please go, or do I have to shoot you to get rid of you?'

He did not. The next thing I remember is waking up in a different room at the same hotel, with the hotel doctor standing over me. I do not remember how or when I got there. I had a fever of about 102° and my ear was in very bad shape. And so there I was, stranded in a strange city at Christmastime, with only the numbness of shock to comfort me. Calvin, it seems, had checked out almost immediately afterward, had fled to another hotel in a different part of Chicago, leaving for me only a note, scribbled hastily on a flap torn off a cereal box. It said: 'Sorry about the mixup. Let's hope there are better days around the corner for us both together. See you back in NY.' See you in hell, buddy, was more to my way of thinking at the time, feeling quite sure he'd be there one day. As for myself, I felt I had already arrived.

I spent three more days as a refugee in Chicago, and during that time I made a concerted, if half-hearted, effort to try to be very good to myself: bubble baths, room service (I'm talking seventeen-dollar lobster bisque, *foie gras*, and caviar), an unabashedly hedonistic shopping spree, and a leisurely stroll through the Art Institute. I was home free.

When my ear was somewhat better, when I had exhausted the city's supply of overpriced French lingerie, when the kitchen at my hotel had run clear out of the Armagnac to lace my lobster bisque, when I had had enough R&R to graduate from this temporary camp for the mentally and emotionally and sexually

133

deprived and abused, I picked myself up, packed everything up (leaving behind all of Calvin's holiday presents for the hotel personnel), and took the same train back home; it broke down once again outside Harrisburg, right on cue.

I arrived home frazzled and dazed at the outcome of things, but with more than a trace of relief. A friend of mine had said about Calvin many, many months ago that it was time to 'throw that toy back', and now, thrown back he was.

And that was where we had left it. There was no follow-up to that time, no high-pitched, passionate reconciliation in a candlelit restaurant where he could gaze longingly into my eyes, and I could nervously gaze at him while he moved the dreaded bits of food around his plate as if they were studded with arsenic. I did not call him, and he did not call me. And now, seven months later, there was this call from him, right out of nowhere, which, I had learned from bitter experience, was right back where it, and he, would go.

Of course, nothing could have startled me more, and I could not have been less prepared.

'Hey, remember me?' he began, which was for me the second most maddening way to start a conversation, after 'Guess who this is.'

My stomach dropped forty floors in an elevator.

The seconds ticked by. He said nothing else.

'Unfortunately . . . yes,' I mumbled. I hate silent conversations.

'I was thinking about you, Stevie. I've been having kind of a hard time, you know.' I could hear his mind fidgeting about. 'I need to talk to you.' I also heard him lift the top off a soda can. Some things never change.

'Need! Now there's a laugh. I know what you need! A Diet Coke! Toilet paper! Fab detergent!'

'Everything's just awful without you. I mean it,' he grumbled quite miserably. 'Nothing works. Nothing's fun.'

'It wasn't too much fun either, as I recall, when you ran out on me in Chicago.'

'Oh, well, that,' he laughed, forcing it out of himself

with tremendous effort. 'That was all just a gigantic mis-understanding.'

'I didn't see it that way. I'm still recovering.'

'Look, Stevie, I need to see you. I'm coming out there to see my sister. She's out at her house recuperating from Lyme disease.'

Again I was quiet, astonished, suddenly feeling very black. And very blue.

He giggled nervously, slurping at his soda.

'Lisa's gained so much weight with this thing, I call it Key Lime Disease.'

Why was this happening to me? How had my vacation turned into a summer rerun of *This Is Your Life*?

'I'm driving out tomorrow, and I'd like to take you to dinner.'

'You don't eat dinner,' I snapped.

'But you do,' he pushed.

'You really hurt me, you know,' I blurted out, and instantly regretted I'd said it. There was surely no point.

'Well, I know all about that. And I want to talk to you about it. I have a lot to say. Please hear me out, Stevie. Come on,' he begged.

'I don't owe it to you. I don't owe you anything, you know,' I told him angrily.

'But I owe it to you,' he said simply. And he was right. He owed me plenty, but bankrupt institutions are not required to settle accounts, and he was about as Chapter 11 as one could get. How well I knew that deep down inside, and yet, I found, not for the first time in the last couple of days, that I felt powerless to refuse.

'You dumped me,' I threw in, just to keep him dancing before I finally acquiesced, which I already knew I would.

'So how about the Fireplace Inn tomorrow night at eight?' Silence again. I stumbled. And fell.

'Seven-thirty would be better.'

'I already made the reservation for eight. But I'll change it if you want. How about if I come by your house first? Give me the directions,' he went on, which I finally did, wondering as I was

135

speaking just what in the world I was getting into now. First Charlie and now this, and I had come out there in search of a quiet little vacation, or so I had thought. There was just this thing in me that always wanted to follow something to its conclusion. I was forever asking 'What's going to happen?' to the point that it exasperated people beyond belief, and I really couldn't blame them. At a cocktail party I'd attended with Charlie in the better days of our marriage, a marine biologist with an annoying postnasal drip commented to me about having just been told about my quirk by my loyal and faithful husband, who at the time had found my ravenous curiosity endearing.

Dr Sinusitis seemed concerned. 'Mmm. Do you read the ends of books first?'

I thought about it. 'Sometimes.'

He dripped away like melting icicles. 'Do you ask friends about the ends of movies before you've seen them?'

'That's you, babe,' Charlie chimed in, sidling up to me.

Dr Ocean Spray just clucked his tongue sympathetically, talking to Charlie, not to me.

'And she's always possessed by the thought of what will happen? Of cutting to the chase?'

'Possessed?' Charlie laughed. 'That's like saying Hitler was possessed by patriotism.'

'Just remember, dear,' the doctor began slowly, for effect, turning from Charlie to look at a passing woman's derrière. 'Pursuing things to their conclusion can be very dangerous, "just to see what happens". You could sleep on a park bench one night or put your arm in a crocodile's mouth just to see what happens, and then where would you be?'

And here I was, in the crocodile's mouth, asleep in the Sheep Meadow, just as he warned. And how well I knew it. Just to see what would happen, as if I didn't already know. As if it weren't every bit as tediously predictable as cramps every month or indecently warm weather for the Jewish holidays. Still, the Fireplace Inn it would be.

The following morning, I went about my business, eating breakfast, taking a swim, reading the paper, and working on my

136

play with the new typewriter (how could I, really, look such a gift horse in the mouth), which I must say did seem like driving a BMW instead of a 1962 Volkswagen Bug, and in general managed to blot out the thought that for me, the world was on the brink of just exploding and self-destructing all in one single, calamitous, unguarded moment.

As I've said before though, this sense of enforced relaxation wasn't just the calm before the storm, for Charlie's calculated assault on all my defenses was just in its beginning stages. It was time-released, like the capsule you take for a cold, and its effects could not be gauged by examining just a moment or an hour. You had to stand back and see it in its entirety.

That day, the calls began coming. Not for me, but for Charlie. Theatrical agents were looking for him, bookies, a barber, his tailor from the city. Asked why all these people were calling my house rather than his, they each responded with the answer that mine was the number they had been given. I tried calling Charlie's house to rectify this, but no one was home. And the calls, like a telethon, just kept pouring in, flooding the switchboard.

And then the packages began arriving. One from Federal Express, which I flatly refused to sign for, and which elicited some nasty curses from the Cro-Magnon courier who wouldn't leave until I threatened to drench him with my garden hose. An A&P delivery boy was next, bearing an order large enough to feed Congress for an entire presidential term, and then from a video store came the delivery of a new camera for Charlie. It was the desk lamp from Bloomingdale's that did it, though. It wasn't even four o'clock and I'd already had more calls and deliveries than the Pope on Christmas Day. Oh, this was some vacation, all right. True, I managed to send everything back, but you can imagine all the friends I made and the fun I had doing it. Then, by seven o'clock, I still hadn't been able to reach Charlie, and it was time to start getting ready for my dinner with Norman Bates.

137

Between the two of them, I felt so violated and invaded that I was positively wild.

Opening the medicine chest in my bathroom upstairs only heightened my rage. Lodged between the Kaopectate and the Q-Tips was a thin, pale-green booklet folded in half, entitled 'The Nobel Prize in Literature,' written by Lars Gyllensten. I sat on the edge of my bed, and my hair stood up like a class in an auditorium reciting the Pledge of Allegiance as I turned to page ten, which had been folded back, and read the paragraph under-lined in green pen:

> *Immediately after the final voting in the Academy the decision is announced and the prizewinner is informed, usually by telegram. At the same time the Academy issues a brief citation, which is later embossed on the Nobel diploma which the laureate receives from the King at the ceremony on 10th December. The Nobel Foundation is given special information about the prize decision and thereafter is responsible for the invitation to the prizewinner, and usually his family.*

Herr Gyllensten continued: 'The Academy, however, is usually host at a lunch or a dinner for the prizewinner and at the so-called Nobel lecture, which is normally given by him or her.'

My head swam and my blood was on fire as I read the singled-out passages. I heard a knock at the back door, but I ignored it, thinking it must be the butcher, the baker, the Armani suit-maker, making yet another preposterous delivery to the illustrious playwright Stamberg. Oh, he was going to hear from me.

As I began dressing for dinner I realized that whoever had been at my door had not gone away but was moving about down below in my kitchen.

'Who's there?' I called out twice, finally receiving the ominous reply.

'Oh, good! Milanos are my favorite!' referring to a bag of Pepperidge Farm cookies lying untouched in the bread box.

'Who is it?' I yelled down, full of fear and misapprehension,

138

knowing full well that it couldn't possibly be Calvin since he'd no more eat a cookie than I would a clock.

I threw on some clothes, piled all the makeup I was to put on into a bag, and went downstairs to find Charlie, in a ratty, orange-striped Korean kimono over jeans and a white shirt, seated at my kitchen table, with the cookies and a glass of milk, dabbing away very theatrically at his nose with a paper towel.

Before I could say a word, he held up both arms to me, warding off the certain barrage of vituperative daggers he knew was headed his way, and said softly, 'Please, Stevie, take pity on a sick man.'

I glared at him in disbelief.

'I wouldn't take pity on you if you were a dead man,' I snapped, and went over to the kitchen door, opening it. 'Out. Now. Hear me? I want you out now.'

'I don't think I could move if my life depended on it, Stevie,' he whined, rubbing at his nose furiously.

'But you don't understand,' I began, in a harsh whisper. 'It does.'

He went a little pale then, still managing to pop a cookie into his mouth as he fielded my wrath. 'And stop getting things sent to you here. And stop having people call you here.' The phone began to ring and just kept ringing. 'I don't know what you're doing, but it won't work. Do you understand me? Do you?' I turned my back to him, walking over to the door, hoping to shovel him out somehow, and as I did, he answered the phone. 'No, she's not here. Nah,' he sniffled ceremoniously. 'She won't be back.' I grabbed the phone from him then, and listened to Calvin explaining how he was running late, literally, that is, and how he'd prefer to meet me at the restaurant, which was just fine with me.

'You wouldn't treat me this way if only you knew how sick I am, what a high fever I have,' Charlie moaned to me as I hung up the phone.

'What's your temperature?' I barked at him then, more a rabid Doberman than a placid beagle pup.

'At least one hundred and three,' he whispered, biting into yet another Milano.

I felt his forehead. It was as cool as the milk he was pouring down his throat with my cookies.

I appealed to him plainly then.

'Look, I have to be somewhere. I haven't got time for this. Jesus Christ, why aren't you home?'

'You're a better nurse than she is,' he answered petulantly.

'You're missing the point, assuming there is one. This behavior is . . . inappropriate. You . . . all this business of being here, sending things . . . it's *inappropriate*.'

To that he just smiled sweetly. He wasn't sick, but he was going to make damned sure I was.

'Why can't you act . . . appropriately?' I screeched now, loud enough for my mother in Miami to hear me and be horrified. I gave up hope then, at that very moment. He was no more going to get up and move himself than Lefrak City was. My life was over.

'I am acting appropriately sick,' he insisted.

I retreated to the little bathroom off the kitchen and began putting on my makeup. On with the show, and all that, you see.

I could hear him slobbering and sniffling.

'I felt your forehead and you have no fever,' I yelled out at him.

'I washed my face before I left the house, that's why,' he called back. 'I have a terrible cold. One of the worst I can ever remember.'

I stood before him again. 'Are you sneezing and coughing?' I demanded.

He shrugged his shoulders in that pitiful, hideous kimono. 'No, I just feel queasy.'

'Then you have no cold,' I threw at him, returning to my makeup.

'Well, it's some kind of nasal virus,' he implored.

'A nasal virus? A nasal virus?' I kept repeating. Just how far would he take this thing?

'You have no fever!' I bellowed then, ready to string him up by his thumbs and his awful kimono.

140

'No,' he finally admitted, 'but I'm going to. I can always tell, Stevie.' He smiled placidly, a serpent's smile.

'You are driving me crazy!' I wailed from the bathroom, deftly putting my mascara on the bridge of my nose, painting my lipstick across my chin.

'Oh, well,' he sighed contentedly. '*Forsan et haec olim meminisse juvabit*, I always say.'

I circled him like a ravenous buzzard.

'What does that mean?' I hissed. 'Who said that?'

He grinned. '*I* said that. It means perhaps this too will be a pleasure to look back on someday.'

I went to the phone. 'I am calling your wife and telling her to come get you. I just can't take any more of this. I don't know what else to do.' I began dialing.

'She can't take care of me,' he groaned. 'You haven't understood anything I've said.'

'Look, I have a date, and I don't care about anything you've said.' I finished dialing.

Well, at that, he was up like a shot. He slammed down the phone and said with incredible audacity, 'A date? How can you do that to me? That's not in my plan at all. How can you betray me like that? What about us?'

It was my turn to laugh then. I put on my earrings and made for the door. 'You'd be amazed at how easy it is.'

'My skin is clammy,' he whispered.

'That comes with high fevers . . . and nasal . . . viruses. Why don't you just go home?' I pleaded. 'I'm sure Patsy is very worried about you.'

He waved away her invisible presence. 'You've got to cancel this date, Stevie. You can't *date* anymore. We're getting back together,' he stated plainly. 'You're coming to Sweden with me in December to the Nobel ceremony. Didn't you read what I left for you?' His eyes glinted mischievously.

'We're not getting back together, and I'm not coming to Sweden with you. This whole Nobel thing is just ridiculous. Every year you get yourself hopelessly worked up over nothing. I remember. Look, I have to go.'

He blocked the door. 'I love you, Stevie,' he whispered hoarsely.

I felt as if a huge hurricane had lifted me up and whipped me around with tremendous force.

'If that's true,' I wobbled, in a shaky whisper, 'then it's too little and too late.'

I looked at him but he looked far from defeated, crestfallen, or, I might add, sick with a nasal virus or any virus. On the contrary, he looked radiant, as splendid as I had ever seen him.

'I will win,' he began triumphantly, 'and you will come with me.'

I leaned into his face, close enough to lick a few lone Milano crumbs from the corner of his mouth.

'Well, even if you do, just remember what you used to tell me, "Awards are like hemorrhoids; in the end, every asshole gets one." I forget who said that,' I finished, very proud of myself.

'But only the very best assholes get the Nobel,' he tossed back, and as I went out the screen door, he yelled after me, 'What do you think about that?'

What did I think, indeed? Soon I was away from him, speeding from one time bomb to another. I looked in my rearview mirror after a few moments and was startled to see Charlie following me in his car, taking the turns when I took them, tailing me in the opposite direction from his house. At one point I pulled aside and waved him past me, but he would not budge, to the great consternation of all the honking drivers he was detaining on the Montauk Highway. When I pulled into the Fireplace Inn, he was right behind me, leaving his car with the valet just as I had done. I turned around once and tried to wither him with a potent glare, but he was impervious. Just what he was up to, I couldn't imagine, but I shifted my concerns elsewhere. After all, I was about to jump out of the frying pan into the great Chicago fire. The only difference was, where Mrs O'Leary's cow was said to have kicked over a lamp, I was in the sort of mood to kick myself.

Stepping into the inner foyer of the Fireplace Inn, I was

142

warmly greeted by the proprietress, Ginny, who steered me to my table. Quite understandably, she appeared to be a bit astonished at the sight of my ex-husband following right behind me, but somehow retained her spectacular composure. 'Do you have a reservation, Mr Stamberg?' she inquired of him, just as I left for my table, not glancing backward. The table she scared up for him was directly across from mine and Calvin's. In fact, it was the next worst thing to having Charlie sitting right with us.

I sat down, determined to remain unflustered, but when Charlie did the same, raising his water glass to me with a ceremonious bow of his head, I nearly screamed.

Luckily, it was just about then that my dinner companion joined me at my table so that my attention was deflected, if only temporarily, from the grinning fool in the ridiculous orange kimono who had parked himself across from us.

Looking up, I did not at first see Calvin. Instead, I saw a lavish bunch of luscious, deep-pink peonies, my very favorite. They smelled and looked so magnificent that when Ginny took them into the kitchen to put them in the refrigerator, I actually missed them. I peered over at Charlie, who looked completely unruffled as he buried himself in his menu.

Once Calvin sat down, I could finally get a good look at him, and crazily enough, I once again liked what I saw.

'Don't look now, but your ex-husband is sitting over there,' he whispered.

'I know,' I whispered back, pleased in spite of it all at the sheer silliness of what was happening.

'What's with the kimono?' he went on. 'Does he think he's in *M. Butterfly* or something?' he asked me, turning to order his first Diet Coke of the evening.

I thanked him for the flowers, and we made some polite, uncomfortable small talk. 'You look wonderful,' he said, his eyes misting over. 'You have no idea how much I've missed you.'

'You've got an awfully funny way of not showing it, Mister. My back still hurts from the train ride home from Chicago where I was carrying all that misery.'

143

'I'd like to start over . . . make a new beginning . . . if you'll let me,' he stated quietly. 'I care about you very much. In my own way.'

Again, I couldn't help but look quickly over at Charlie, who was tearing into a piece of bread and drinking a glass of white wine. He lifted his glass to me and pursed his lips, as if to kiss me from across the room.

'I think part of our problem is with language. People get so lost in it sometimes. Well, you know that, you're a writer. Again and again, people misunderstand each other, and the course of their lives changes. And it's all because of language, the fault of words.'

Well, by now, he had lost me in his own. We considered the menu and made our choices. I looked over and studied him for the first time, after not having seen him for months.

He was thinner than I remembered, thin and birdlike. I could see more clearly now, especially in his casual summer clothes instead of his boxy, big man's suits, that he was truly just a stick of a man, as fragile and flimsy-looking as a goddamned Saltine cracker.

'This thing I'm trying to say about language,' he persisted, 'well, I was in this coffee shop last week in Boston, about ready to leave for my flight home, and I stopped in for . . . I said specifically no dressing on my salad,' he harshly admonished the waiter, who had erred on the side of humanness, bringing him a normal person's salad. Turning back to me, he continued about this Boston thing, making me wish I were there instead of at the wonderful Fireplace Inn. 'So anyway, I stopped in for a diet soda . . .' No kidding, I couldn't help but think to myself. I thought it'd be for a banana split. 'So this guy's in there ordering breakfast, only he's not from this country, and he doesn't speak English very well.'

'Where was he from?'

'That is irrelevant to the story,' he pronounced with great finality, diving into his salad, which was as dry as the Gobi Desert. 'This point is, he ordered two eggs facing the sun, a pair of toast, bacon parallel, and a cup of beans, and that's exactly what the waiter brought him. They understood each other.' He beamed at me and at his leafy rabbit's food. I snuck a peek over at Charlie, who was engrossed in his lamb chops but not too engrossed to grin at me and roll his eyes twice at the ceiling.

'It *is* possible for people to communicate and understand one another. They just have to work hard at listening, at making sure that what they say is what the other person hears.' He paused seriously, wiping his mouth. 'I never said I didn't love you, Stevie, I never said to go away. That may be what you heard, but that wasn't at all what I said.'

Well, just then our friend the waiter was back, telling Calvin he had a phone call, and so I was suddenly left there for a few moments, considering my fate, which seemed strangely comical, although, in truth, amusement was not part of the guaranteed package as you steered your boat through Scylla and the deadly maelstrom of Charybdis. Thinking about this, I looked up to find my ex-husband standing at my table.

'I ordered ice cream, but it didn't come yet,' he explained feebly. To that, I said nothing, hoping I could just will him away.

'You know, Nero used to put ice and snow into his fruit juices and wine in the first century AD. Ice cream goes back a long time.'

I glared up at him.

'*We* go back a long time, but I guess not as far back as when Nero fiddled and Rome burned,' he sighed.

'Get back to your table,' I whispered at him furiously, 'and stop talking to me about your role model.'

'Well, I will if you'll just tell me one thing. Who's the neb with the diet soda?' Even his eyes were laughing.

'The *what*?' I asked, looking behind me to see if Calvin was coming back. He wasn't.

'Does he ever stop whining?'

'Oh, stop it! Go away, please,' I begged.

He laughed insolently. 'I'll tell you one thing, he gives new meaning to the phrase "wining and dining." Why does he hate food so much?'

'God, why are you suddenly everywhere I go?' I groaned for all the world to hear.

145

'I came to rescue you, Slim. You certainly look as if you need rescuing.'

'I most certainly do not.'

'Not much you don't. The guy looks like every day is Yom Kippur.' His eyes were dancing now, but he could see Calvin making his way back to our table, so he talked faster.

'By the way, about that "pair of toast" bit. I bet he's never eaten a whole pair of toast in his life,' he finished, slinking back to his table where his ice cream and coffee were waiting. I could just hear the fiddle playing, as he winked at me and began demolishing the scoops of vanilla and chocolate.

'I hope nothing's wrong,' I said to Calvin.

'Turned out it was a mistake. There was no one there when I got to the phone.'

I looked over at Charlie, who winked at me again, and then I understood why.

'Kind of ruined my appetite,' he mumbled, pushing away his fish and vegetables, and once again I was reminded about how it felt to eat out with Calvin, which is to say, to eat out more or less alone. Still, we got through the dinner, not really deciding anything, with me wondering if our finest moments were indeed behind us.

Then, over coffee, Calvin looked at his watch and announced, apropos of nothing, I guess, except the position of the stars and interstellar matter in the Milky Way, that he thought we should 'take things slowly this time around, do things carefully. Not make the same old mistakes.'

Well, I couldn't help wondering what mistakes I had made, but apparently he seemed sincere about meeting me at least halfway.

'I guess what I'm saying is that I don't think we should sleep together yet,' he finished.

Quickly, I looked over at Charlie, hoping he hadn't heard, but he'd already finished his dinner and left.

'Yet?' I stammered.

'Right. Let's just go very slowly this time and be very good to each other. No bacon parallel, or any of that, okay?' He finished

146

signing for the meal and then called Ginny over and asked her to retrieve my peonies, which had been languishing in the refrigerator. But when she reappeared, it was with a look of panic and confusion. Even before she spoke, I knew what she would say.

'They're gone,' she kept repeating, her face quite pale and deflated. 'I just don't understand it. I put them in there myself, and now they're gone. I can't imagine what happened,' she kept saying, all flustered and apologetic. 'Please allow me to compensate you for this, Mrs Stamberg, I mean . . .' I shook my head and assured her that it was indeed no crisis, that there were plenty of flowers to be found in the Hamptons in July, ones as large, as bountifully beautiful, and as fragrant. To this, Calvin looked somewhat peeved, but that was just too bad. The flowers were gone, and I knew who had taken them.

And I wasn't wrong. As we got into our respective cars out in the driveway after a brief kiss and a hug (that can best be described as semi-urgent), I spotted Charlie under the perfect circle of light from a street lamp, kneeling at the far side of the East Hampton pond, floating each flower into the water. He was hard to miss, crouching down in the tightly manicured grass, in that rumpled orange rag. I stared at him for a few moments without his seeing me, thinking I might go over and confront him, but knew there was no point. I was between Scylla and Charybdis, all right, and there was a lot more to lose here than just a bunch of ill-fated peonies.

I drove home without the flowers, but with a reinforced, resurgent feeling of strength and determination.

The harsh light of day, however, did not support me in my crusade. Before I had even come downstairs for the morning paper, I heard Charlie in my kitchen, typing away on the new machine.

'I already made the coffee,' he said dully, facing me with a baffling serenity I imagined serial killers displayed moments before their execution.

Recalling my resolve of the night before, I lectured him,

scolded and threatened him, but he remained impervious, staring at me as if my tirade had been in Punjabi, in Telugu, or in broken Amoy-Swatow Chinese.

'My computer's acting up at home and I promised Clovis these rewrites by next week. Sorry, Slim,' he told me lamely.

Clovis Dill (a name that always conjured up a nauseating mixture of baked ham and potpourri) was his theatrical agent, a bitchy, imperious Englishwoman whose speaking voice gave new meaning to the word *nasal*. Clovis had never been on my Top Ten list of people to evacuate in the event of a nuclear holocaust, since she'd always spoken to me as if I were Charlie's secretary, and not a very good one at that, rather than his wife.

'I need him to call me today, have you got that?' her voice would scrape and crackle over the phone, as it scrambled up octaves the way a squirrel climbs trees. 'Can you write that down please, dear?' she'd say. She was, and had been for many years, a good friend of Dolores, the deposed Contessa Stamberg; indeed, they were drinking and gossiping buddies, so I always put on a great front of cheerfulness and efficiency for her, no matter what was going on behind the scenes. Katharine Gibbs herself would've busted her buttons at my impeccable display of unerring professionalism.

'I have no sympathy for you or your deadline, and certainly even less for that repulsive English toad who gets your money for you,' I barked.

'You're not using the word *repulsive* right, Stevo. Writers should be more careful.' He clucked his tongue and blithely went on typing. Click, click, click went those keys as he kept hammering away.

Finally, I just pulled the page out of the machine and ripped it up into tiny pieces. At that, he finally seemed daunted and went home, but I did not delude myself into thinking that I had in any way effected a permanent solution. Indeed, I felt shakier than before about it all, and as it turned out, I was right. All through the remainder of my vacation, the great presence of Charlie, of Charlie past and Charlie present, both in the flesh and in the form of phone calls, flowers and gifts for me and deliveries for himself, swirled up over my head like swarming bees, gathering steam, loudly pullulating into a great tornado of such force and magnitude that I felt truly powerless to escape it. Oh, I tried, of course, again and again, but nothing I did seemed to make the slightest difference. At several points I actually considered cutting short my vacation and fleeing back to the city, but in the end I couldn't let him drive me away, even if I couldn't manage to quite do the same with him.

Midway through my vacation, just as I felt I was beginning to edge my little boat out of those goddamned Straits of Messina, I decided a little harmless distraction was called for, and so I invited my younger sister, Leslie, to come out for a few days. If people were paid vast sums of money just for having outrageous yet intelligent philosophies, my sister would be a billionaire. (Although I could never quite forget those long-ago years, back when we were children, growing up on Riverside Drive, when Leslie was so steadfastly opposed to being properly toilet trained. Even then, she had her own ideas about how things ought to be done. For some strange reason, her bowel movements always took place in my mother's closet, into which she would waddle on her shaky, dimpled baby's legs, but not before announcing to whoever was present, in defiant, coquettish tones, 'Good-bye, everyone, I'm going to Jackson Heights!' We never understood why Jackson Heights, and my mother never understood why *her* – certainly with the advent of Leslie's toilet training, my mother's almost world-renowned shoe collection was never the same again. And neither was my mother.)

But in a world that still basically values mediocrity and safe thinking, Leslie was forced to make a living by working for the New York City Transit Authority, in the Human Resources Department, for which she had prepared herself by getting a postgraduate degree in management at the New School. Now, *management* was an especially amusing word when applied to Leslie. Given the disorganized mishmash she had made of her life, mismanagement would've been more like it.

149

One of my favorite things about her had always been her guileless confession that she possessed absolutely no taste. (How many people recognize and admit this in themselves?) So, for as far back as I can remember, she and I would put together wardrobes for her by using a pack of index cards and a bit of ingenuity on my part, which is to say that when the seasons changed, I took her shopping. After that, we'd go into a quiet place for lunch where I'd put the outfits together for her on cards, like flash cards (which she'd then use and place at the back of the pack so she could revolve them). The thing was, she attached absolutely no shame whatsoever to this enterprise, was glad of my help, humble even, and enjoyed the whole thing almost as much as I did.

Leslie had never been married, but had lived with a string of men over the years. It would be oversimplifying it, but not by much, to say she used and rotated them just like the index cards of her designer wardrobe; still, the comparison is an alluring one. Her feeling was that a woman should always keep a supply of different men on hand to suit her varying needs. The key, to her, was in having backups, and not only that, but backups for her backups. The last of her prominent players had been a former college English teacher of hers, whom she had run into at the drugstore several months ago and who had recently bumped her from his romantic agenda.

Seated now by my pool under an umbrella, with a broken-backed copy of an Alison Lurie novel spread over her stomach, she told me how she had run into him, how friendly and warm he had been. I looked over at her as she spoke to me, envying her her small, shapely, compact body, her healthy, rosy cheeks and the masses of dark curls that rounded out the whole perfect, adorable picture, and I ached a little for her low expectations, for the calluses of bitterness that were beginning to form at the edges of her experiences, and yet, who was I to argue with her? What proof or hope could I hold out to her for a sunnier scenario? All I could do was listen and try to temper her disillusion somehow. There was no one who could turn a silk purse into a sow's ear the way Leslie could.

150

Come to think of it, the only man who had overwhelmingly bowled her over in the last millennium had been Charlie. As far as she was concerned, the sun rose and set with him. He could do no wrong, and this had been the source of many arguments between us over the years.

I could remember once, about eight years ago, when she had first gone to work for the Transit Authority (which had always made me laugh. I mean, this striking, independent, soft-spoken Jewish girl from Riverside Drive becoming Ralph Kramden?), I met her at her office one pretty April afternoon and took a trip to Brooklyn with her, to what she called 'the field.' At the time, she was writing a report on changing the titles of subway mechanics, and she had to investigate for herself just how the men worked at the various 'barns' where the cars were overhauled and repaired.

Well, once we were on our way it took her no time to arrive at her favorite subject, which always seemed to be my husband. He was Leslie's blind spot, her Achilles heel. As we entered the barn, and I saw all the men in helmets and jumpsuits, with wrenches and welding tools, I hoped this would be the end of our discussion, which we could never settle because Leslie was so impossibly insistent that everything was always my fault. As we climbed down into the pit with one of the men she was to speak to, she was still yammering at me, not giving up, whispering at me behind the man's back as he spoke to us about the car equipment, telling me how lucky I was to have Charlie, and how unsupportive I was of him. Just then, the man turned around, pausing in his diatribe, and said to Leslie, 'Now remember, in your report, don't say "motorman". You gotta make it bisexual.' Well, after that, I just took a seat on the sidelines and watched her ask the men questions, writing their answers down in a little blue spiraled book she carried with her. After spiriting me back to the F train, she picked up, almost in mid-sentence, her impassioned plea for Charlie. Like I said, this was one cause she was committed to, in fact, I'd say, almost committable about. You couldn't take a bone away from this scrappy little pit bull. You were crazy to even try.

So it really didn't surprise me to hear her views about Charlie that day in East Hampton, over a late-afternoon pitcher of overripe, oversweet banana daiquiris, as the mournful tones of Dietrich singing 'Falling in Love Again' drifted out to us from the house. She was all for him, still the pit bull.

That night we both went to bed with splitting headaches, from the sun, from the drinks and no dinner, and from the heated debate about Spike Church's Bastille Day party which I'd told her about and which was the following day, and which Leslie insisted I attend. With her, of course.

'We're going, all right, we have to. You have to do this for me, Stevie,' she implored. 'I'm running out of men.' To which I just kept telling her no, until I couldn't even say the word anymore.

'Is Charlie paying you?' I finally asked, to shut her up. 'I mean, are you in on all this? Did he hire you? What on earth makes either of you think I'd want to attend a party with his wife and friends? How perverse are both of you, anyway?' By now my voice was rising. Oh, what a little daiquiri can do.

Well, with that, she seemed to give up on the party. At least that's what I thought that night, until the next morning when Charlie showed up for his coffee, and after giving Leslie a big hug and kiss, informed us that he had a terrible toothache which was going to prevent him from going anywhere that day except to the dentist.

'The coast is clear, my little chickadees. I just came over to tell both of you to go and have a good time. Give everyone my regards, will you?' he rambled on, holding his cheek, which did look a bit swollen.

'Are you sure?' I asked him cagily. 'Are you telling me the absolute truth?'

Leslie clapped her hands. 'We can go! We can go!' she exulted, but I still wasn't completely convinced.

'Look at this cheek,' he asked me, removing his hand. 'Is this swollen or is this swollen?' he asked pitifully, pronouncing *swollen* 'schwollen'.

'It's schwollen!' cried Leslie gleefully. 'We can go!'

Charlie headed for the door then, certain that his mission had been accomplished.

152

'I'd love to hang around but I've got to get home and take something for this,' he apologized, quite unnecessarily.

'What time is Spike's party?' I asked him.

'It starts at seven.'

'When is your dentist's appointment?'

'It starts at six,' he answered, *starts* being 'schtarts'.

Then he was gone.

'God, he looks good' was the first thing my blood-related little Judas said to me the instant he was out the door. 'What will I wear?' was the second. 'We can go, can't we?' she bubbled over. 'My God, the lobsters, the fireworks –'

'We'll go for a little while,' I finally relented, having wanted to go all along. 'But just for a little while.'

'What do you think it'll be like?' my man-crazy sister, dolled up and looking like a dream, asked me in a feverish whisper, dabbing at her lipstick in the fold-down mirror in the car that night as we made our way over to Spike's.

'I have no idea, really. Remember, I haven't been to this in years,' I answered, seriously beginning to wonder myself.

The first thing we saw when we drove up were two huge moving vans parked out in front. These, I remembered from experience, were used to get all of Spike's furniture out of the house for the party. Since the surrounding streets were so backed up with parked cars, looking like the parking lots at Jones Beach, we left the car several streets over and walked, stepping gingerly over manicured lawns in pinching, open sandals.

Once at the door, decorated with French flags, I had to stop and take a deep breath, before immersing myself in this social Cuisinart. I remembered from past experience that before morning at least two extramarital assignations would be arranged, at least five marital fights would be sparked, people would be caught flirting, fibbing, bragging, getting drunk, humiliating their spouses, causing new hurts, bringing up old ones. Over coffee the morning after, at least four couples would look across the table at their mates with new eyes, with bitter sad eyes

153

reflecting new knowledge that would now lead them down the sorry road to parting. Whether it took two weeks or two years, the journey had begun.

For Leslie and me, however, there were no such meaty verdicts hanging in the balance. We were just there to dress up, to watch people, drink a little champagne, eat a little lobster, and get some juicy dirt to roll around in our paws for the next few days (about this one's hairline, that one's hemline). Even if we had a bad time, which was highly unlikely, the evening promised to be entertaining.

The front door was open so we just stepped inside, and happily for me, the first person I encountered was Spike's housekeeper, Dinitra, an elderly but saucy black woman who had been with him since before time began. Dinitra was too busy holding the leashes of Spike's two English sheepdogs, Serpico I and II, which were circling her legs and trying to make a getaway, and also miraculously puffing away on a cigarette during all this, to notice me, but I went right up to her, gave her a big hug for old time's sake, and introduced her to my sister. Taking a huge drag on her Lucky Strike, Dinitra broke into a broad grin. Gripping the dogs' leashes tighter, she explained that they were supposed to be locked up in the laundry room, but had almost broken the door down, so she was now in charge of them. 'Big miserable beasts,' she muttered. 'Now how am I supposed to have any fun at this thing when I'm a lousy dogkeeper?' She shook her head. 'Mister Church is sure gonna get it from me,' she warned, and I didn't doubt it.

'Where is Spike?' I finally asked, looking around but not spotting him, as Serpico II began coming in for the kill on my right leg.

'Oh, he's in back at the roulette table, probably. You can't miss him. He's the one in the tuxedo, with no shoes,' she mumbled wearily, then shoved off with her animals in tow, nudging them forward with her gold-sequined shoe. What a night it promised to be.

Leslie and I began making our way through the rooms, all done up in elaborate red, white, and blue bunting. There must

154

have been thirty people just to serve the lobsters and the great groaning platters of clams, oyster, steamers, shrimp, and crab-meat. The noise level was almost deafening. It required a tremendous effort to be heard, especially since, in the living room, a jazz band was going at full throttle. Outside colored lights were strung up in all the trees as if it were Christmas, making quite a picture as the sun went down in a pink summer sky and the balmy darkness rose over Spike and his three hundred and fifty guests.

We finally found our host bent over the blackjack table in a giant exercise room-cum-sauna, where there were also tables for craps, baccarat, and roulette. Raffle tickets were being given away for dinners for two at La Cremaillere in Banksville, in honor of Bastille Day, and in addition to a huge, crowded bar at the back of the house, enough champagne flowed to fill the oceans of several continents several times over.

After kisses and hugs and introductions all around, I ended up chatting for a while with Lucky, Spike's current lady friend, a hard-drinking, hard-speaking Irish redhead, who was a good deal more colorful than the women I'd usually seen around Spike. Draped all over him like an asp on someone's arm, she made Leslie and me the reluctant vessels into which she began to empty her spleen as Spike puffed away on a great cigar and turned back to his blackjack. Here and there I saw men, women, couples that I knew, and heard snippets of conversations about Lyme disease and real estate prices, but there was no one I was terrifically anxious to talk to, so I just stood there, picking at bits of lobster as it passed me occasionally, and listening to this tipsy, hostile Irish rose pour out her heart.

'I've been with Spike for over a year now, you know, and practically since the beginning, I've been begging the fuckin' guy to marry me, you know, give me a ring, give me a ring, blah blah. Right, Spike?' she asked him. 'Right, Lucky,' he answered dully, without looking up. I looked at her with her hennaed hair falling like great daggers about her face and, recalling Spike's cavalcade of failed romances, suddenly felt sorry for her.

'So last Christmas, after I've been begging the son of a bitch

155

bastard for a shiny goddamned something to stick on my fucking ring finger . . .' she went on, conspiratorially, just as Spike cut in.

'Do you believe she eats with that mouth?' he asked me then, shaking his head, throwing down some cards.

'. . . So he gives me a diamond, but not in a setting, you know what I mean. Just a lonely, fucking diamond,' she continued, draining yet another glass of champagne, and reaching to pull one more from a passing tray. I looked around for Leslie to come to my rescue, but she was dancing to 'Body and Soul' with a croupier (who was wearing a rhinestone crucifix earring, and incorporating a great deal of both).

'So I just took the cocksucking stone, you know, and swallowed it.' She looked at me for a reaction, but my shock didn't reveal itself quite so quickly.

'I washed it down with a martini, and it was gone. That'll show him, I thought. And it did, didn't it, Spike?' She poked him in the rib, her eyes shining brightly.

'Oh, it sure showed me a lot, Lucky. Before you had nothing. Then you had a diamond. Then you had nothing again. But you sure taught me a lesson,' he cackled.

'You're damn straight I did,' she started again, grabbing my arm for emphasis.

'I really do have to go and say hello to some people,' I told her plainly, recovering my arm.

'You know, he loves anal sex so much, I have to confine him to national holidays.'

'That's enough, Lucky,' Spike told her, looking up for the first time.

'He likes to think he's so genteel,' she continued. 'His idea of having sex is like a couple of goddamned ice cubes clinking together in a cocktail glass. I –'

'It was nice meeting you,' I cut her off then, plotting my escape through the heavy throng that hung in my path. It wouldn't be easy, but neither would staying there with her.

I looked up and saw a woman I used to work with hanging over the Jacuzzi in a miniskirt that made her look like a crisp

156

breadstick with tough, leathery skin. If only I could get to her. The woman next to me, sleek as a panther in pink Valentino, with a black velvet headband, was speaking to a friend about her husband's recent death. 'And it was a good thing I remembered at the last minute to tell them about his pacemaker before the cremation. They told me afterward that it would've just exploded,' she told the woman in a fierce shocked whisper.

In the meantime, Lucky seemed to be getting more unlucky by the minute, as she prattled on, trying to impress me and to bait Spike at the same time, a theatrical, depressing combination of Ethel Merman and Ethel Barrymore.

Locked there in party purgatory, I listened to only one more of her shrieky anti-Spike tirades before Dinitra approached, the dogs whipping around her legs, inviting the revelers outdoors for the next portion of the evening's program.

'Your husband sure looks fine,' she whispered to me, breathlessly, moving away with her huge, slobbering monsters, as if on roller skates. 'Get ready for the fireworks,' she called. My husband? My husband? I kept thinking to myself. Had she guzzled down just a bit too much bubbly? I had no husband, and looking around at the women who did, it was a strangely consoling thought. Scanning the room for my sister, I found she had disappeared with her dance partner. Instead there were many women, mostly in white, a lot of them with what was said to be the year's rage, red hair that looked like little fires that needed to be put out everywhere, standing talking to men in tennis sneakers or sockless loafers. Many of them were fidgeting and seemed spectacularly bored, while discussing things like the RJR Nabisco takeover, the perils of insider trading, and other earth-shattering situations that they were all, of course, intimately involved with.

And then, as the music slowed, and the roulette wheel was abandoned, the great crowds of boozy, over-lobstered masses began moving out, trampling across the lawns for the fireworks display. Putting my champagne glass down in the kitchen, I saw out of the corner of my eye just a tiny slice of gold, a knee in silk

157

pants, and before I could see more, I knew exactly who the knee belonged to. And also who the wife with the knee belonged to. Charlie Stamberg. Oh, Dinitra Buchanan, you sly old fox, I thought to myself, the day your mind gets rusty or you miss a beat is the day I'll gladly shoot myself, if I don't do it first, here tonight, that is.

I was about to head outside, to lose myself anonymously in all the people, when I heard Charlie speak my name and in my white-hot fury and horror, I couldn't move any more than a butterfly pinned to a corkboard. In my mind, kettles were whistling, pots were boiling over. It was a tasty night for a murder.

Charlie's champagne glass, I could tell, had already runneth over that evening, and his feet were sort of shuffling along at a slant. Dutifully holding the cheek with the supposed ailing tooth, he zeroed in on me, putting both arms up beside me against the wall, so I could not escape.

'I love you in white linen, you know that,' he began slowly, sleepily, those green eyes breaking right through me like atom smashers.

'Charlie, let's go, the fireworks are starting,' Patsy whined at him then, coming into the room and trying to drag him away. I looked from him to her, knew I'd had enough, and yelled at her, 'Get your goddamned husband away from me!' shrilly enough to shatter all the empty glasses in the kitchen. She looked around desperately, not knowing what to do. Outside, I could hear the fireworks starting, the rockets' red glare, the bombs bursting in air. It was at that moment that Charlie climbed up onto the dishwasher and, swaying as if he were standing in a docked rowboat, holding his offended cheek, began his mighty oration – an oration so impassioned and full of sound and fury, signifying nothing, that throngs of people began spilling back into the house, willing to forgo the splendor of the Grucci brothers for the fireworks within. After all, how often in a lifetime did you get to witness the spectacle of a falling-down-drunk Pulitzer Prize-winning playwright, perched high above someone's dishwasher (which was running, I might add), proceeding articulately, I'll give him that, to tear his marriage and his entire life to shreds.

'I did not go to the dentist today as I should have,' he informed his audience loudly but melodically.

'Hey, everybody, there's fireworks outside,' said a nervous, worried Spike, who had just come into the kitchen to see what was holding everything up. Just then, Serpico I and II broke free from Dinitra's leashes and tore into the kitchen, too, barking wildly and circling like rabid whirling dervishes.

'I was in pain, there was no doubt,' Charlie went on melodramatically, 'but I had already succumbed to an even greater, more searing pain, you see. The pain in my heart. The pain over my wife,' he droned on drunkenly. At this, all eyes sympathetically searched for and found poor Patsy, who was now huddled in a corner, holding her face in her hands. A great hush rippled through the crowd. Outside the neglected fireworks detonated with earthshaking reports. Inside the barking dogs quieted. There was no mistaking it. He had a great house for his performance that night. They were positively enthralled.

Spike cleared his throat; his forehead was covered with the filmy sweat of panic and despair. 'Come on now, Stambie. Time for the fireworks.' He moved to the dishwasher and tried to pull Charlie down, but he wasn't about to cooperate. 'Stambie' wasn't anywhere near finished. In fact, he hadn't even gotten started.

'There is some pain that one cannot hope to dull with Tylenol or codeine, not even when taken in dosages more fit for a herd of elephants and washed down with excellent champagne,' his voice thundered. He ran a hand through his hair, paused, and then, having gathered his rambling thoughts, proceeded.

'Oscar Wilde once said that "bigamy is having one wife too many. Monogamy is the same", but I'll tell you people, he never met my wife.' His eyes shone with the threat of impending tears as he dimmed his voice. 'She has been the only true light of my life, you see. The tiny beacon that pulled me home through the cloud of hopelessness, loneliness, and bitterness in the dark, murky, foggy stillness of dawn,' he ranted, as we all heard the

159

sudden whoosh of Serpico I peeing copiously all over Spike's kitchen floor. Still, nobody moved, spoke, or even breathed. I glanced over at Patsy, who was smiling somewhat smugly at the turn things were taking. (After all, a public tribute to her replete with fireworks and peeing dogs? How many women could boast of such things?) My stomach suddenly felt as if the lobster I'd eaten had been studded with thumbtacks. I began to move, to push my way to the door, startling and annoying everyone around me, just as the words began poking their way through the air again.

'Until I met her, until I met Stevie,' his voice resounded, freezing me dead in my tracks as all eyes turned on me with bloodless surprise. As Patsy began to whimper, he continued, 'I all but agreed with Coleridge, who said, "The most happy marriage I can picture . . . would be the union of a deaf man to a blind woman."' Then he paused and yawned. Serpico II started up barking again, and Dinitra shouted at him, 'Oh Lord, will you shut up!', at which Charlie took great offense, thinking she was admonishing him.

'Madam, kindly do not interrupt my words here tonight. I am here to pay tribute to a great lady – to my muse, my backbone, my divine inspiration.' His voice faltered with half-choked sobs and then his tears brimmed over, just as the machine gyrating loudly beneath him switched over from washing to drying the dishes, changing to a low, whirring hum. Charlie actually reached out a long arm and pointed to me then, just in case by some sheer miracle I had escaped anyone's notice, just as I saw Patsy take one long and regal deep breath, and drawing herself up by her shoulders, propel herself out of there and into the night, in great, wobbly strides, like a pony on new, unsteady legs.

'There she is,' said Charlie, pointing to me, his eyes ablaze with the effects of codeine, Tylenol, and champagne, as a loud, astonished gasp fell over his rapt and willing audience.

Again, Spike reached up ceremoniously and tried to grab him down, but again to no avail. Then, just as Charlie stretched both arms out to me, like Evita to Argentina (and we all know where that ended up), and whispered, his eyes closed, 'She is my life,

160

my life, my life,' he passed out, just swooned dead away on those watery legs. He had swayed once too often with the leaden weight of his blustering, weepy histrionics, just as the long-forgotten grand finale of fireworks illuminated the sky in an elaborately shocking pageantry of colors. Utterly lost on all inside, they dripped down and disappeared into the darkened ocean's horizon; glittering, crashing and booming, thundering, to an audience of no one.

Part Three

So foul a sky clears not without a storm.
—SHAKESPEARE

I f, out of the rubble of the French Revolution and the storming of the Bastille, a new republic had been forged, the same could certainly not be said for my own Bastille Day, the aftereffects of which I could still feel in sweaty, shivery tremors.

In the harsh morning light of July 15, which I faced with a scarlet-red, reverberating memory and an unrelenting headache, I had woken up late and had woken up scared. Before Leslie was even up (champagne had steered her, too, deep into the Land of Nod), I had packed half my things, spilled all the milk down the kitchen sink, made several calls canceling engagements for the next few days, and begun packing up the car, eager to flee back to the precious anonymity of the steamy July streets of New York City. I knew enough to know that I'd been beaten, that there was just no earthly way I'd be able to salvage what was left of my vacation. I looked glumly over at the roses climbing like lazy caterpillars up and around my garage, and bid them good riddance. You can just bloom without me this year, I cursed them, as silently as I knew how, suddenly resenting them for their beauty, which was so careless and fleeting.

I was just about to hurl two badly packed suitcases into the trunk and go wake my sister when I saw Charlie jogging up my driveway, just as he had done so nonchalantly the week before, only this time he looked a bit green, a bit shaky, and thankfully, now his runner's stride looked more than a bit tentative.

'What's the matter, Scarlett, are the Yankees coming?' he

laughed, testing the waters cautiously, gently. I just stared angrily at him. What else could I do?

He took a deep breath. 'Well, Patsy's leaving me, taking the baby and going back to Kansas, if you can imagine such a thing,' he said distastefully.

I glared at him. 'Oh, I can imagine it, all right.'

'I really just came over to apologize, Stevie. I really lost it last night.'

'You certainly did,' I butted in, but he was too quick for me.

'The thing is, not a word I said was untrue.' He held out his open palms to me.

'You threw away your whole marriage, you idiot. You have a son now, you know. Life's not just a square dance for you anymore. You have real responsibilities.' My voice rose. He rubbed at his eyes and pulled his hand over his whole face, distorting it, making it look like a rubber mask.

'The thing you don't seem to see is that it's all for the best. I just wasn't into this family and picket-fence deal.'

'What?' I nearly shrieked.

'It didn't suit me,' he said tonelessly, as if talking about a pair of shoes he'd tried on at Brooks Brothers.

'Well, that's just perfect, that's just ducky.' I shook my head at him, once again marveling at his nerve.

He shifted to one foot, looking a bit sheepish then, and spoke barely above a whisper.

'Like I said, I just wanted to come over and say I was sorry if I embarrassed you last night.' He paused, waiting for me to speak, but I said nothing.

'I won't . . . bother you anymore if you don't want me to. I'll back off,' he offered, testing me again.

'Hey, both of you. I'm making scrambled eggs,' Leslie yelled from the kitchen window, totally oblivious to our arabesque.

'I mean it, I'll leave you alone. Just say the word. I love you very much, but I don't want to be a burden to you anymore. Really,' he said, the self-pity swelling in his voice like a tidal wave.

'Consider it said, then,' I told him haughtily. I turned my back

166

to him and was ready to return to the house when I heard him say, 'There's just one other thing I have to say to you and then I'll go.' He seemed to take a deep breath before going on. The dramatist had not planned for his plot to veer off course quite this way.

'I know I shouldn't have, but I read your play.'

'You *what?*'

'You know, *Glad Tidings.* The day I brought over the new typewriter, I read it. It's wonderful, Slim. I'm really proud of you.'

'You bastard!' I thundered at him. 'You had no right to do that! Who gave you permission?'

'But I *loved* it,' he protested. I was nonplussed.

'That has nothing to do with it,' I fumed. 'That's no excuse for you to act like such an unbelievable shit,' I told him, my voice shaking.

Well, at this he actually smiled.

'But I didn't *need* an excuse. God, I loved it,' he explained, with a deranged, immutable logic only he could fathom. 'And I told you, I'm proud of you.'

'Well, I'm ashamed of you,' I sneered, starting to feel a bit wobbly there with him in the sticky morning sun.

'It's really . . . really . . . excellent. I mean it. It's almost there.'

'Almost where?' I asked, reluctantly curious now. Aah, the fish had almost gotten away, but now I could feel the hook so close to me again, I could nearly shiver from its coldness.

'You know, ready to be shown to someone. It just needs a bit of restructuring, but it's no big deal.'

'Oh, come on,' I waved at him. 'Who's kidding who? Now what are you after?'

Insulted, he gave me his best dirty look and said, defiantly, 'I don't kid about the theater and you know it.' Thinking about it, I remembered that that was true.

'What do you suggest I do, then?'

'Well, for one thing, take me out of it. It's not an accurate depiction of me at all,' he said flatly.

'The eggs are ready!' shouted Leslie.

167

'You are not,' I spoke slowly, emphatically, 'in my play. I don't know where you'd get such an outrageous idea,' I said. 'It's about two people in a *happy* marriage, for starters!' I started to laugh for the first time that awful morning.

'See, what'd I tell you?' he asked, triumphantly.

'You really are the most miserable, self-centered creature.'

'Ouch,' Charlie groaned, holding a hand up to his heart.

I shook my head wearily. 'It's not you, you crackpot,' I told him, lying through my teeth. 'The man in my play is madly in love with his wife. His *wife*, do you hear me!' My voice was rising along with my blood pressure.

'Well, can I help you with it? Can I help you with the play, Stevie?'

'You mean your autobiography? Help me, how?'

'Well, now that I seem to be single . . . again' – he grinned, a bit crookedly – 'I'll probably have some time on my hands. Maybe we could have dinner in the city or something. I really believe in it. I'd just like to see you go as far as you can with this thing.'

'Oh, please. I'll see you in a dress with earrings on first. Now get out of here,' I told him. And with that I turned without a word and went back into the house.

To my surprise, he actually left then, backing slowly up my driveway, humbled, I thought, defeated, I hoped.

Leslie and I had our eggs, and then I finished packing up and dragged her, kicking and screaming, back to the city. My vacation, which in truth had never really begun, was finally over, and not a moment too soon, as far as I was concerned.

I went back to work, to the office, tranquilizing myself with the old-fashioned sedative of hard work.

Charlie called a couple of times, leaving messages on my machine, but I was in no way prepared to deal with him, and hoped I never would be. In the meantime, bolstered by his words, in my spare time I worked feverishly away at my play. If there was even a grain of truth to his ranting and raving, I owed it to myself to hone and polish it until my knuckles came off, and that was just what I intended to do.

I also heard from Calvin soon after I got back to town, and managed somehow to spend a few easy, comfortable evenings with him, without a surfeit of Sturm & Drang, the couple we usually double-dated with. True to his word, and much to my liking, we were taking everything slowly, so slowly it was as if everything were taking place underwater. I expected nothing, and always came up feeling overindulged.

Calvin for the most part now behaved with me like a prisoner ten breaths shy of parole. He was model-perfect, considerate, warm and affectionate; even sexually, when we finally got around to that, he made a few bold, if hesitant and unpracticed gestures that were meant to show me that he was aware that he wasn't the only person in the room.

The problem was that even when he was on his best behavior, as if on probation, I was not so filled with emotion for Calvin that my feeling for Charlie, the insidiously seductive Charlie, couldn't begin to creep in through the cracks. And so more and more I felt that Calvin had begun to serve a less than totally honorable purpose for me, namely, as my protective bulwark against Charlie. As long as Calvin was in my life, Tupperware tubs and awkward, edgy intimacy and all, Charlie couldn't really present a substantial threat, could he?

I allowed myself the luxury of my delusions until one night in late September. By then the pile of unreturned phone messages from Charlie was taller than a windmill and I had almost – but not quite – stopped thinking about him (meaning that I no longer lifted up the phone twelve times a day, pressed the first three numbers for him, and then hung up).

Stepping out of a cab and into my lobby that evening, I was presented with a large, cumbersome, oddly shaped bundle from Federal Express, which turned out to be, lo and behold, an olive branch wrapped in what can best be described as a white flag. And not just some shabby, shallow poke at corny symbolism – this was the real thing, sent to me by, of course, my ex-husband, via Fausto Palladino, a dear friend of ours far away in Italy. Full of wary astonishment I sat down in my foyer with my coat still on and read the card. 'This olive branch and white flag come to you as a sincere and heartfelt offer for everything they stand for. What do you say?' he had scribbled, adding, 'By the way, as you know, olives are terrific in martinis. Let's go somewhere soon and have some. Please call me.'

Shoving this package into the garbage that night, I couldn't help but marvel at Charlie's cleverness, but then I worked hard to push it out of my mind, determined not to be too impressed.

It almost worked too, except that the following night the doorman handed me another package, this time containing a little hatchet from the Museum of the American Indian, with a note inside about how we should bury it together.

The night after that I was greeted with a huge lemon-meringue pie from some swanky Upper East Side patisserie, wrapped with about a thousand different-colored curling ribbons, and a card about Charlie eating humble pie.

Another night it was an engraved silver whistle on a chain (which required no note), and then thirty Ralph Lauren bath towels, with a note that said he'd never, ever throw in the towel where I was concerned.

Night after night in spite of myself, I came to half dread and half hope the doorman would feed me a new and different prize, and then, once upstairs, I'd sit with it in my foyer, handling whatever it happened to be as gingerly as if it were a bomb waiting to go off. In my mind, perhaps it was.

Still, through all of this, I never responded in any way to Charlie. I never returned his calls, his packages, acknowledged the flowers that appeared regularly and sat like orphaned, neglected children atop my piano. I put them there but I refused to look at them or take any pleasure in them.

I put up a good fight with myself, all right, and was just about to think I'd won the war when one night the elevator man rang my bell and presented me with a box of three kittens, all with big red ribbons around their necks and a card that said, 'After all this, not so much as a *word* from you? I'm having kittens.' Well, with that I threw up my hands, started cursing out loud (my poor elevator man!) and in a flash got Charlie on the phone.

'I want these out of here now,' I seethed.

'Stevie?'

'Yes, it's Stevie. I want you to come over and pick up these poor little babies and get them as far away as possible. I'm calling the police,' I threatened.

'The police?' he teased. 'They don't even show up if you're being *murdered*; you think they're going to break their necks getting there over a couple of kittens?'

I wasn't amused.

'Are you going to take them away or not?'

'It's your fault, you know. You forced me into this. After all, you never called me back and I've been trying to reach you for weeks. I had to do something drastic,' he explained.

'Are you picking them up, or not?' I breathed desperately, with fire in my voice.

'I'll be right over,' he answered, a little too eagerly.

'Just hold on a second. I'll leave them downstairs with the doorman. I don't want to see you.'

'Why not?' he sulked.

'Because you're vile. You're the devil. I can't believe you could do such a thing. Take three poor, innocent kittens . . .'

'Well, what else was I supposed to do?' he yelled at me then, with a real edge in his voice. 'I love you. How the hell else was I supposed to get your attention? Don't get all hysterical. I'll come pick them up. I'll get them out of your way. Just calm down and forget about it.' He sounded so weary then, all of a sudden. I peered at the box with the three little balls of fur tumbling over each other with their red bows all off center, and suddenly felt quite weary and depressed myself.

'Well, what will you do with them?'

'I said not to worry about it. Just forget it.'

'I can't forget it,' I said softly, looking over at the box once again. 'I want to make sure they'll be okay.'

'They'll be fine. I may keep them myself,' he said defiantly.

171

'You?' I nearly laughed.

'Yeah, maybe I will. What's wrong with that?'

'What on earth would you do with three helpless little creatures?'

'Maybe they'd be my friends. Maybe I need friends right now. Maybe I'm lonely, and in love with a woman who'd gladly put cyanide in my mouthwash. You know, I only did all this because I miss you. Because I'd like us at least to be friends. I'd do anything in the world if I could earn the right to be your friend again. And then, of course, there's your play . . .' he veered off, quite unexpectedly.

'My *play*?' I nearly hollered.

'That's right. You've got a goddamned brilliant hit on your hands, and you don't even know it. All it needs is just a little work –'

Well, in spite of myself, I felt as if the ice in my heart was beginning to thaw, turning right to slush in that very instant. All of a sudden the kittens receded, and Charlie's voice, sounding disjointed and disembodied, seemed to rise and travel away as if on a cloud, leaving me with words like 'talent,' 'gift,' and 'potential' to stun and flatter me, sweep me off my feet, break through to me where olive branches, flags, pies, whistles, towels, and adorable kittens could not, paralyzing my anger and leeriness.

The next thing I knew, we were discussing my play as easily and as unemotionally as if there had never been any bad blood or animosity between us, let alone the three kittens sitting in a box on my floor. As a friend, he pleaded with me to let him help me get the play finished and ready to be 'seen by someone', an agent or a producer. It was then that I really started listening to him and taking seriously what he was proposing. And right then and there I went for it. After all, I told myself, the boy knew his stuff. He more than knew it, he'd invented most of it. Would it be so terrible to cash in on his terrific nest egg of knowledge? After all the years I'd put in, breaking my back with *his* plays, would a little reciprocity now really be so reprehensible? I thought about it and honestly didn't think so. After all the years I had put in with

172

him, why shouldn't I pick *his* brain, use him, even milk him shamelessly?

Even so, afloat in all of this professional mutual admiration, I still managed somehow to keep one foot on the ground, because I set out some pretty stringent rules for myself and managed to keep to them.

Right from the beginning, I told Charlie I didn't want to work with him in person, that all contact must be limited to other avenues. As long as we didn't see each other, I rationalized, he could help me without my risking anything. (It never occurred to me that I'd given the kittens back but still might be going to the dogs where Charlie was concerned.)

In the meantime, for the next few weeks we kept the messages flying, the Federal Express trucks moving, the fax machines (from my office to Charlie's studio) burning up with activity. Not a day went by that we didn't speak about this project, that we didn't send some fragment of the play to each other. Not a night went by that we didn't pass at least a half hour on the phone together, ostensibly talking about the play, but often not a bit about the play. Several times Charlie asked if we could meet for a drink, for dinner, a movie, or a ballet, but I never wavered. I stuck to my guns and he didn't push.

And through it all there was always crazy, unreliable Calvin, still wooing me in his own eccentric, inimitable fashion, still buzzing the roofs of intimacy and commitment, but never quite landing; distracting me with his own enduring, endearing, affec-tionate peculiarity, but even more importantly, I realized, in moments of exemplary clarity, protecting me from a further involvement with Charlie. Which is why the news that he'd be traveling to France, Italy, and Switzerland shortly on an im-portant, extended business trip (announced one evening to me mid-Tupperware) unsettled me, left me feeling painfully vulnerable.

'You might want to meet me somewhere,' he said.

I held up my hands and shook my head wildly. 'I haven't recovered yet from meeting you in Chicago,' I couldn't help but tell him, meaning it.

'Again, Chicago!' he muttered with annoyance. 'Maybe I'd like to make that up to you; did that ever occur to you?' It hadn't, and I wasn't even sure it should have.

'I can't just pick up and go to Europe, but give me a copy of your itinerary in case Amtrak decides to go to Italy.'

'You're some piece of work.' He shook his head, working the spoon in his Tupperware mush.

The truth was, though, that at first I was far less cavalier about his going away than I appeared. After all, with him gone and Charlie and me speaking again, who would catch me if I fell? But then I steadied myself and calmed down somehow.

A few weeks passed and the threat seemed to recede. I was really overloaded at the office, so I had little time to either work at or worry about my play or my newfound alliance with my ex-husband, who, I'd recently read in the *Times*, was once again legally separated (although he hadn't mentioned it). Calvin left for Europe, sending me his itinerary as promised, and everything just slowed down, like a movie in slow motion. I hurled myself into my work at the office the way a seagull might throw itself at an unmarked glass window. By early November, the machine was humming along, working again. The train was back on track.

But such serenity, even when accompanied by hard work, early meetings, and late nights, is usually short-lived, and Lord knows it certainly was in my case, when I received the cable from Venice informing me that Fausto Palladino had died.

Santa Scuderi, Fausto's wife, was an old friend of ours, a somewhat faded former Sicilian opera singer, married to one of Charlie's oldest friends. Fausto Palladino, her husband, was a wealthy Venetian and the arts critic for the local conservative paper, *Il Gazzettino*, a man so intent on having a good time in life, he'd willingly dive for pearls in his own toilet bowl. For years, his marriage to Santa had been on the rocks, just like the Cinzano and soda he kept pouring down the throats of the local

174

Venetian girls he kept after with a vigorous appetite and appreciation known and respected all the way to Trieste.

Santa, in her turn, retaliated by losing herself in her children, and in a friendship established long ago, when her voice still filled La Scala with the clean peal of church bells, with the handsome, brooding straight-as-asparagus local priest, Don Giona. For years now, they had sat together in the damp twilight outside Fausto's farmhouse in Passariano, like a pair of old married people, drinking Chivas and playing poker. She gave him money, lots of money for the church, and he fed the coffers of her lonely imagination. Fausto, of course, welcomed with open arms this faithful, hardworking appendage to his family; a friend and confidant to his wife, a chaste and circumspect companion for her, who would perhaps fuel the fires of love, but never stand near enough to feel the heat of its flames. Over the years, both Santa and Fausto had spoken often of Don Giona on their frequent trips to New York, but I had never actually met him until one day about eight years ago, when Charlie and I had traveled to Rome on a publicity trip, and had stopped over in Venice for several days to spend some time with the Palladinos.

Now, in case there is any doubt in your mind, all is definitely right with the world when you are seated with two old and cherished friends and an Italian priest with unquestionable charisma, who really could've given Mona Lisa something to smile about. Especially on the breezy, sun-dappled terrace of the Danieli Hotel in Venice, where you have walked over from your own hotel to have lunch overlooking a bright splash of sailboats out for a day's pleasure on the Grand Canal. The waiters bowed and scraped for the flashy journalist in his suit of silk, the famous American playwright, and their wives. Perhaps if the sun and the stars were aligned in auspicious symmetry, and if Fausto drank enough wine and was pleased with the service, he might favor them later with a tip on a horse running in Agnano, or with an expensive cigar.

Whenever I thought of Santa, one of the greatest lyric sopranos of our time, I always thought of the pale, elongated face, very Anna Magnani, so steep you'd need a staircase to climb it, and

175

also, somehow, of her feet. I could never quite forget them: long, flat, and narrow, like two lonely canoes. Feet that had stepped in for an ailing Renata Tebaldi's Mimì one night in Parma so many springs ago, and had won over the unyielding Italian operatic community, virtually overnight, including a young, hot, and somewhat arrogant critic, Fausto Palladino. The papers sang her praises the next morning almost as ebulliently as she herself had poured out 'Mi Chiamano Mimì' the night before, citing the fullness, the sweetness, the roundness and liquidity of her extravagant voice.

Several years of Mimìs later, however, the critics and her voice maliciously got the better of her and accused her of overachieving. Stepping onto the stage of La Scala one drizzly Saturday afternoon, in the part of Liù in *Turandot*, all at once she knew her luck had left her, just traveled away, like a faithless flock of geese. After all the years of training and hard work, it took her only an instant to realize the fickleness of her own instrument. Each and every note came out as she had rehearsed it and yet not a single note was right. It was the very last time her flat, canoe feet would take her onto an Italian stage – or any stage.

Santa wasn't a quitter, but she was a realist. Is it fair to say that the light went out of her eyes that night just as the crystal chandeliers at La Scala did after the performance, and never came on again? Perhaps. I only know that that afternoon in Venice, as Don Giona was led to our table, I held my breath and could not help but think, 'Come to Mama.' Was I attracted? Only about as much as a pyromaniac is to a match shop. And then, afterward, as we all sat so easily together over wine, a creamy risotto flecked with shrimp as plump as a baby's fist, conversation, laughter, and the kind of quiet creaks and pauses that pieces of old furniture share when they have stood together for a long time in the same room, I saw the light go on again in Santa's eyes, and it was blinding. But who could blame her? Man of the cloth, indeed. He hadn't even taken his first sip of wine, and I was dressing him in cloth, all right: Armani, Versace, Missoni. Before we even ordered, I knew what I wanted was not on any menu and never would be.

He didn't need a voice that was a dry, throaty crackle, which suggested he'd gargled with glass, or eyes with lashes as thick as cat's paws, but he had them, and they weren't wasted. The main thing, though, was the way he looked right through you, as if you were a thin sheet of mica, instantly making you feel he knew you better than you knew yourself. And then there was the kind, reassuring way he spoke to you, as only a man with no true use for a woman could.

No wonder Santa watched him as she did, her eyes bathing him in a warm glow, all but oblivious to the animated disagreement Fausto was having with my husband about sailing.

Although Santa and I had deftly skirted the issue for years, watching her watching him I knew that she had gotten lost more than once in those lashes and the lonely tunnel of his voice, as did, I'm sure, half the women in Venice, even as he stood among them on a Sunday, reading tonelessly from a letter from Paul to the Colossians. Parched as she was from so many years of self-deflection, as well as from turning the other cheek so often to Fausto's fleeting peccadillos that she'd retained a kind of permanent whiplash, I had found her constant barrage of Don Giona talk, over the phone, in person, and in her letters, always unsettling. Had Santa at last found religion? I worried. Nah, I saw with a tremendous relief that settled over me as cozily as drinking afternoon wine in the Venetian sun, she had only found Don Giona. And any woman who wasn't exhilarated at such a discovery would require the medical attention of Aesculapius himself. Over a sleepy espresso and the last runny corner of Charlie's *tiramisù*, I yawned happily and watched as the afternoon's pastel sailboats glided off into the sunset.

Listening to Santa talk to Don Giona about a church benefit they were planning for the following September, I sat and prayed to the pale blue skies above that Santa was not earning a Ph.D. in Yearning and Unfulfillment at the Academy of Perpetual Longing. After she had played so many tragic roles, I hoped her greatest one, the role of a lifetime, would not turn out to be the role of her life. Puccini may indeed have been the supreme master of passion, tragedy, and melodrama, but I suspected he was no match for the sumptuously craving Santa. Her unrequited longings were wrapped around her like bandages, and peering through their many layers, I was left to draw my own perturbing conclusions, all of which went down as bitterly as the bucketfuls of paregoric I slugged down when we got back to our hotel room.

And then, later that night as I slept and my stomach rebounded from a day of divinely orchestrated overindulgence, I dreamed that Don Giona and I made love in a muddy chicken coop on Torcello. His breath smelled faintly of oranges and his thick, dark hair was full of feathers. Afterward, he leaned over and whispered to me, '*Te Deum*', his kind face all ablaze with amusement. But I didn't get it. *Te Deum?* I thought, worried in my dream. Was that the Venetian or priestly way of referring to . . . tedium? After all, what on earth did I know about Catholicism? I was Jewish, and the bulk of my religious training had taken place at the delicacy counter at Zabar's. Instinctively, I pulled away from him, like a cake that pulls away from the sides of its pan as it cools. And this dream was so real to me that when Charlie reached across the bed to me in the morning, I pushed him away, recoiling from and mistaking him for the hot-blooded matinee idol with the Rossano Brazzi accent, and the strong arms that could crush you like dried rose petals, the man who had just scalded my ego.

Imagine my astonishment then, when fresh from my sleep-induced frolic in a chicken coop, I awoke with a mouth and face full of feathers, the result of a pillow with a poorly sewn seam. My shock and disorientation were so great, I was sure my spurned husband had looked into my face, plastered with guilt and feathers, and had known the man who breathed the hot perfume of oranges had stolen into our bed and raided my fantasies. Thinking of Santa again, I wondered how many mornings over the years she had awakened just this way, slapping Fausto's feverish affections away like a fly, at the mercy of her own misguided dream-life. Long ago I had read somewhere that 'Unrequited love is like a question without an answer,' which seemed chilly, bloodless to me. (A question without an answer is, after all, its own dreaded answer.) To me, it was more like being trapped in a purgatory of endless heart surgery without any hope of anesthesia.

Just what is it about unrequited love objects or about forbidden fruit that makes its promise so sweet that you wouldn't mind choking on a couple of pits, while Persephone stands in the shadows laughing at you? Don't ask me. And don't ask poor Santa, with her feckless fluency in pining. I'd have you ask Dolores, instead, that sly and stealthy demon, a wolf in wolf's clothing if ever there was one; a woman who wouldn't know a moral or an ethic if it reared up and bit her on her breast. Just leave it to her to find a way to weave a newly sober minister into her sticky matrimonial web. Marrying him was small potatoes to Dolores, the mink eel; a creature with the collective conscience of Attila the Hun and Benito Mussolini. Such a crafty devil was our Dolores, she could, I had no doubt, leave a museum with goddamned *Guernica* tucked away in her handbag and never get caught.

It was supremely hard for me to believe that the same glorious, sun-kissed spot in the universe that had produced Dolores's ancestors (the Neapolitan Longos, and hence Dolores) had also given us da Vinci, the Medicis, and Tintoretto (to say nothing of a good, steaming bowl of linguine all'amatriciana, or a nice, frothy zabaglione). To say nothing of dear Fausto Palladino, who had meant so much more to me than all of them.

This was why the telegram conveying the sad news about Fausto had thrown me so off balance, had wounded and upset me as if it had been a member of my own family.

I called Santa in Venice right away, but when I reached her, her voice, or rather the tone of her voice, was not what I had expected.

'Santa,' I started quietly, afraid I would cry, trying hard not to. 'I'm so sorry. What happened?'

'The worm finally got cut into pieces and couldn't move anymore,' she snorted angrily.

'What do you mean?' I asked her, suddenly more horrified than sad. 'What happened to him?' I asked her again gently.

179

'I told him not to see her again! I told him one more time with that bitch Flavia and God would get him, and see, I was right!' she hissed, her poison sizzling right through the wires. I could tell there was no hope of getting any answers from her in her current state, so I just asked her if she wanted me there, and she said yes.

'Charlie is coming too. I hope that is no problem,' she warned.

'Don't you worry yourself about anything like that,' I told her. 'I'll leave tonight and I'll see you there tomorrow,' I told her, hanging up.

Next, I called Charlie at his studio, where he was now living, but I couldn't locate him, so I made my own plans to go to Italy. As an afterthought that afternoon, I called Calvin (whose itinerary told me he was in Milan) and told him the unhappy news, and that I'd be in Venice the following day.

'I could meet you there if you like,' he stated flatly, offering no condolences for my dear, old friend. 'Just leave me out of all the death stuff, okay?'

After arranging for some days off from work, I called Charlie a few more times, but he was nowhere to be found. I assumed he'd already left, and late that night I boarded an Alitalia jet, and did the same myself.

Arriving the next morning in the chilly November gloom of Venice, I thought about how there is no such thing as a day with good weather when you are mourning someone you love. If the weather is bad, if it is dark, dim, or rainy, it only compounds the grimness in your heart. And if it is instead a sunny day, you only feel that the day is mocking you. There is no way to win, and as I approached my hotel in a little blue boat, I looked out over the tangled mélange of cramped, stubby buildings, the pink brick and yellow limestone all awash against a gray, murky sky. I held my head low, and hoped that the man who drove my boat didn't see my tears, but didn't really care if he did. What was a little more water in Venice? There were 117 islets, 400 bridges, and 150 canals. That morning I could easily have wept into all of them, and it was really none of his business.

180

The usually bolstering sight of the lobby of the Gritti Palace in all its regal splendor, with the pale ghosts of Maria Callas, Charlie Chaplin, Charles de Gaulle, Ernest Hemingway, Somerset Maugham, Winston Churchill, and the Aga Khan hovering just beneath the ceilings, like delicate balloons, did little to cheer me. At the desk, I asked whether Charlie Stamberg had checked in yet, as I knew he surely would. The concierge told me he was expected later in the day. Mr Persky, however, had already registered and was up in his room, so my baggage was brought upstairs to my room as I went to say hello to Calvin in his.

Once we were alone, I went over to him. He was on the phone, sitting at a desk near the window, entrenched in diet-soda cans and tangled up in phone lines; pads and pencils were everywhere, a portable computer terminal was set up on the bed, and there were three briefcases open and spilling out onto the floor. I looked around me. The rooms were just as I remembered them from four years before when I had last come to Venice; the ceilings were just as high, the damask couches as sumptuous, the antique tables and chests as polished and pristine, the parquet floors as elaborate, the Venetian mirrors as intricate and awe-inspiring, the marble bathroom as befitting of royalty as when it had been the residence of Venetian nobility during the Renaissance. Looking over at the bed, I knew the down pillows would be eight feet deep, the linen crisp enough to slice my skin. I was suddenly overwhelmed with fatigue, but knew I should phone Santa before even contemplating getting any kind of rest.

'Sorry about your friend,' Calvin said to me when he was finally off the phone. I drew nearer and kissed him, in the fragrant cloud of freshly washed laundry that trailed him everywhere, apparently even across oceans. He had deep rings around his eyes and I could see one of his knees jiggling nervously beneath the desk. 'I know you loved him very much, for a long time,' he offered quietly, giving me his own version of a hug, one-armed, and lasting but a few seconds.

I sat down wearily and called Santa. The phone rang many

times, and then Don Giona finally answered. In hushed tones, he began to explain to me what had happened to Fausto, saying that Santa was under medication, was not herself, was lying down because she needed her rest.

'It was the women again,' he began, clucking his tongue. 'With him, you know, it was always the women,' he continued cryptically, not telling me anything I didn't already know.

'Did he . . . have a heart attack?' I inquired delicately.

At this he laughed, a bit ruefully. 'Oh, no, he was out in the boat, in the sailboat. He always liked to take them out in the sea . . . impress them.'

'It was a sailing accident?'

'Oh, yes, a bad one. He was with the girl, the new girl, Flavia. Off the coast of Yugoslavia. Santa begged him not to go,' he sighed.

'Then what?' I pushed impatiently, beginning to fear that he might never get the whole story out.

'The weather was fine when they left, but when they were below, he was . . . I guess . . . distracted. It began to rain and thunder, but still he didn't notice. Then the winds came up and it was a squall, very bad. When he finally came up to lower his sails it was too late. The winds were very strong. The mast was struck by lightning and the boom was whipping around. It hit him in the head and he was . . . just finished, you know. It was very sad, very sad,' he said glumly. 'The girl, luckily, was okay, but very scared. When the Water Patrol found them a few hours later she was delirious.'

'How is Santa?' I wanted to know now, more than anything else.

'Santa is . . . not herself.' He spoke cautiously. 'She is very angry.' He laughed nervously, self-consciously. 'Well, more than angry. She fought with him the night before about this Flavia. She didn't want him to take her out on the boat. She is in a fury, Signora Stamberg. None of us knows quite what to do with her,' he whispered feebly. 'The children are here and the relatives, but all she does is scream and curse him. She is inconsolable, you see,' he finished, a bit frantically.

Telling him I'd be there later in the day, I hung up, my head spinning with the weight of all this new knowledge.

While Calvin busied himself on the phone again, wheeling and dealing, burning up the wires, I found my way to my room and unpacked my clothes, sank down into a cavernous bathtub of pink marble and bubbles, and let the story about Fausto fill my mind.

It was all so typical, of course, so mournfully predictable. Fausto would never have come to his end quietly, uneventfully, without some woman or other around, for there had never been a man more born to please women or to have women please him than Fausto. He had a vigor for women and for sex that was said to replenish itself half-hourly. There was no such thing as a woman who couldn't be had or who wasn't worth having, including married women, who Fausto claimed were just 'playing hard to get' by being married. Everything about him was sensual, almost shamefully so, but not to him. I could remember easily the eyes, so icy blue, that burned right through a woman's clothes; the tall, lean, muscular physique, the chest hair like soft, shiny fur. Even the way he held and smoked a cigarette, resting it between his second and third fingers, holding them at the side of his forehead with his thumb to his cheek, like a professor or a dictator, was undeniably intense, as was the way he stirred a drink with his pinkie, his eyes crinkling with laughter.

With me, however, I must say that he never even edged his way toward the precipice of impropriety. Every kiss I had ever gotten from him over the years had been positively brotherly; and if he had had other kinds of thoughts, as I'm sure he'd had all right, he was classy enough to keep them to himself.

And his classiness didn't end there. When Charlie and I split up, he'd been one of the few friends we'd had who was loyal and true enough to insist on remaining close to us both. He had never let me down, although I gave him plenty of opportunities. He just wouldn't have it any other way, although I never knew what was in it for him.

After the divorce, when my mother came up from Florida to stay with me for the longest week of my life, I remember Fausto

183

had come to New York on business, for his paper, *Il Gazzettino*. He was gracious enough to take us to lunch at the Four Seasons, where my mother had never been.

After recovering from the breathless charm of this palace of rosewood, from how well her drink had been made, and from the copper-corded drapes that rippled like magical waters, she turned her attention to our handsome host, who after kissing us both several times, had kissed the waitress's hand (as well as that of the woman who had led us to our table) and had finally settled back to sip his drink.

'Fausto, you must love oral sex,' she announced to him.

Well, nothing fazed him, ever, nothing a woman could say to him on any subject, even this one. He put down his drink and turned to her, delighted, his eyes twinkling. I, however, was blushing down to my kneecaps. What was she talking about?

'Well, yes, I do,' he told her, clearly amused. 'Do you?'

'Of course I do. I think kissing is a lot of fun, myself.'

'Kissing?' he inquired, by now utterly charmed.

'You know, oral sex, kissing.' She looked at me, at my face, which was a portrait in shock and relief.

'You mean kissing isn't oral sex, Mr Palladino?' she wanted to know.

'Well, not exclusively,' he said tactfully, and left it at that. It had often been the source of many jokes between us afterward. The realization that there would be no more such moments shared between us made me cry for a long, long time into that bubbly cave of a bathtub.

When I finally emerged, all dried and dressed, I called Calvin and asked if he'd like to go out for a little while and let me show him Venice, where he had never been before. (Calvin never traveled for pleasure, and if a place was not in his business orbit, it didn't exist.)

I could hear him cringe a bit. I imagined him passing a hand over his tired-looking face, smoothing back the electrified barbed-wire curtain of hair.

'I think I'll pass' was what he answered.

'I could use the company,' I tried, appealing to his compassion.

'There's a lot of work I should do, Stevie.'

'Can't it wait a few hours? Jesus Christ,' I pleaded, losing patience. 'Do you really want to stay cooped up in here? Don't you want to get out and see things?' I asked, talking about our rooms, our hotel, as if they were the Augean stables.

'I just have a feeling Venice is not my city, okay?' he said defiantly.

'And how can you tell that, Anne Frank? Just what exactly is that based on, I'd like to know,' I countered petulantly, not really wanting to fight with him, but angry at the world nonetheless. My friend was dead.

'I base it on the fact that what I *have* seen is dark, damp, and depressing,' he said, sounding as if he were gritting and grinding his teeth down to sawdust.

'Then why did you come?' I shouted into the phone, much too shabbily for the Gritti Palace.

'To make you happy!' he screamed back miserably, incomprehensibly.

After that, I got out of there as quickly as possible for a breath of fresh, uncomplicated air. As I wandered the streets, I was entranced by the gray, placid murkiness of the nearly empty city. In contrast to the other times I had spent in Venice, I was not mercilessly baked by the relentless sun, nor was I pushed around senselessly by mobs of people at the landing stages for the vaporettos, at the Doge's Palace, or even in the huge expanse of San Marco Square, usually swelled beyond capacity with tourists and pigeons.

That day I roamed quite freely through narrowed, mostly deserted streets, listening only to the hollow echo of my shoes hitting the pavement, breathing deeply for the first time in twenty-four hours. Finally, when I had walked enough and seen enough, I took myself over to Harry's, which always felt like coming home to me. It had gotten quite chilly outside, and the chilly dampness in my bones could stand a Tiepolo or two. I knew I'd welcome the spectacle of the waiters who would prance

185

and leap, darting between the tables as agilely as any ballet dancer I'd ever seen.

From there, I picked myself up and found my way to Santa's, to her house, which was so jammed with people it felt more like a wedding than a wake. Everywhere I looked, there were relatives, friends, people from her days in the opera, and newspapermen from Fausto's paper as well as from others.

When I finally reached her through the sea of faces, she put her arms around me and we held each other for a long time. Drawing back to look at her, I saw a stony countenance ravaged by grief and, perhaps, by a few too many Valium. The magnificent steep face, twenty stories high, was pale and green, the eyes red-ringed.

'Santa,' I started, my voice shaking.

'Stop,' she said, interrupting me, pulling me close again and whispering into my hair. 'Stop. He was a monster. We all knew he was a monster.' She spoke dully, in a drugged, leaden voice, without emotion.

I pulled back from her in fear. Who was this woman? Did she know what she was saying? In life, she had worshiped her husband above all others. How could she turn on him in death? 'Come with me,' she said, taking my hand and leading me to the back of her apartment, into her bedroom, where we were finally alone. We sat on her bed and I waited for her to speak. She rubbed her eyes, and raked a bony, pale hand through her thick, neglected hair.

'Why lie? He was a beast,' she began in a low, flat voice, as if she were telling me yesterday's soccer scores. 'That Flavia . . .' she sneered. 'I had had it with the women, Stevie. I couldn't take it anymore. I told him, you take her out on the boat, lightning will strike you both. I was only half right,' she went on, a flicker of mad Ophelia passing over her face like a glimmer of candle-light.

'Santa,' I had to say, I had to interject then, 'you are just overcome. You don't know what you're saying.' She held up a hand to silence me.

'He just had to go with her. You knew him, he couldn't stop

186

himself. Why? Because she was young? Because her nipples were dark the way he liked them? Because she had a light moustache, like peach fuzz, the kind that drove him crazy? You know, I had to go to get his body in Trieste, I had to ride back here on the train with him and Don Giona, and I just kept thinking to myself, you snake, you worm, you have fucked your last woman behind my back, and it made me happy.' She was smiling crazily and laughing spitefully when there was a knock at the door. 'Jesus,' she moaned, 'can't I have some peace?' I patted her hand and went to the door. I was glad of the intrusion. Like Don Giona, I didn't know what to do for her. Her ravings, I was sure, were just temporary, the result of the tremendous shock. She had lost the great love of her life; how could she be expected to behave rationally? How, indeed.

I opened the door and there stood Charlie, and at that moment I was never so glad to see anybody in my life. He was a sight for sore eyes, all decked out in a charcoal silk suit, wearing a tie shot through with about seventy shades of purple and gray. I grabbed on to him for support and wouldn't let go. I felt dizzy, lifeless, as drained of life as anyone there, I was sure, except Fausto. I took a good look at Charlie, who, despite the immaculate presentation, looked like hell. I hadn't, after all, actually seen him since that sunny, breezy morning of July 15, when he'd been tan, perky-eyed, bouncing with energy and mischief. Now he had, after all, lost his best friend in the world, and even in lesser crises I had seen him go to pieces. In fact, I had seen more than one widow comforting Charlie at her own husband's funeral, and I hoped he wouldn't be relying on Santa's services in the same capacity, given her present state of mind. I stood outside the door while Charlie went inside to be with her. When they came out, she asked us both if we would like to see Fausto. 'Come, I'll take you to him,' she told us, before we could answer.

I could see Charlie steeling himself, imagining the great vats of *grappa* he'd find solace with later on to extinguish the indelible sight of Fausto in death.

We were taken to a room lit with candles, draped in black bunting. As we approached the open casket, Charlie reached for my hand and I reached for his. It was no time to turn away from each other. I felt the years apart suddenly sink away from us, I felt the distance evaporate as we both stood over our departed friend. Just then Santa let out a low, vengeful laugh from behind us. 'Notice anything different about him?' she wanted to know.

To our mutual horror, we couldn't help but notice what she was referring to, namely, the total absence of one of Fausto's eyebrows. We stared at him, dumbfounded, then at each other.

'Was it . . . the accident?' Charlie asked her, tenderly.

'Oh, no, I shaved it off when he was sleeping the night before he left. I *told* him not to go out on the boat with her, and I meant it.'

Well, I almost laughed at the dark absurdity of it all, but this was not a day for laughing. Soon after that, Santa was put back to bed for more rest. Charlie and I stayed for a while, talking to her children and to Don Giona, who seemed to have neatly taken charge of everything except for Santa's wild, bitter outbursts. Then we set out into the night, so overcome with sadness, jet lag, and bewilderment at Santa's unexpected state of mind that we barely spoke.

In the lobby of the Gritti, Charlie asked if I'd like to get a late-night drink, but I declined. Suddenly, after many hours of not thinking about it, I remembered the strange and dour-looking man upstairs in my hotel, who was, presumably, waiting for me.

'I hate to think of you all alone in a big hotel at a time like this,' Charlie said gently, I think honestly meaning it. 'Or maybe I'm talking more about myself,' he added grimly.

Calvin hadn't asked, not thinking to, I suppose, whether or not Charlie was coming to Venice, and I hadn't told him. It was really none of his concern, all walled up there in paradise as he was, with his phones, his reports, and his diet sodas. On that particular day, at that particular moment, I must say I found both him and his illness not the least bit alluring.

I didn't tell Charlie about Calvin being there any more than I'd told Calvin about him. Even in the depths of my grief, somewhere in myself I was holding back, watching. There had been many times in the past when Charlie and I had stayed in hotels, and then, afterward, I found out that he'd had some woman stashed in another room the entire time. Now I saw how easy it was just not to mention it. We said goodnight, making arrangements to meet the following morning at the boat landing that would take us to the island of San Michele, to Fausto's funeral. 'I love you, Stevo,' he whispered to me wistfully before taking himself off to the Gritti bar. I watched his gray silken back disappear through the lobby.

Upstairs, I didn't get much of a greeting from my skinny, clean-laundry-smelling friend, who was sitting in his room engrossed in a news broadcast which more than likely he did not understand. If I expected anything, some words of compassion, I came away empty-handed. I sat with him a few moments as he babbled about how sleazy the newscasters looked, and then I'd had enough. Shocking me as he always did, with the brazen inappropriateness and poor timing of his cold, selfish sexual stirrings, he asked me, his eyes still glued to the screen, if I might like to spend the night with him. Realizing then and there that I'd done my last missionary work and there was no place on earth I'd less like to be, I made a joke about the high price of my room, and slipped away.

Once I was alone there, I sank into the deepest sleep I could ever remember. I took a good, long look at Calvin in my mind, and kissed him good-bye.

The next morning, when I awoke, I found a note from him pushed under my door saying he was out jogging, and was skipping breakfast. Breakfast? Jogging? I had to laugh. The streets were so narrow and chopped up with tiny bridges, only a cricket could have succeeded at something like jogging. Leave it to him though, jog he would. Fausto would be buried, Santa would hopefully return to her senses, and the world would go on turning, in spite of itself. I ordered coffee and rolls, ate quickly, and got dressed in a hurry, being late as usual. As I hurried out of the lobby, I nearly slammed into Calvin, all sweaty and puffing for breath. 'What news on the Rialto?' I hissed at him. Leaving him there, I headed for the boat landing at a quick trot in a pair of tight, clacking heels.

I arrived at the landing too late, just as the three gold and black funeral gondolas with their flower-decked biers started their misty, melancholy journey down the Laguna Morta. In my pathetic, limping Italian, I gleaned from strangers that I needed to catch the Vaporetto No. 5, which left every fifteen minutes from the Victor Emmanuel Monument. So I went running like a wild woman along the Riva degli Schiavoni, running in front of the *piazzetta* leading into San Marco Square. Having just missed a boat, I sat down to wait for another. Once aboard, it took about twelve minutes on the water until the grim sight of San Michele appeared, floating in the lagoon like some mighty, forgotten fortress.

I hurried along to the gleaming white church, the oldest Renaissance church in all of Venice, and got there just as Don Giona had finished the mass for Fausto, just as the sprawling, sniffling crowd was spilling outside and trudging along to the burial ground. I looked vainly around for Charlie, but couldn't locate him.

I followed the long line of people past the great cypress groves to the acres of woods dotted with crosses and headstones, where lavish domed mausoleums built of precious marble loomed behind forbidding, wrought-iron gates. This is where my departed friend would be laid to rest, his wealth and prominence securing for him a fate in contrast to most who were buried on this island. Usually interred in marble drawers, his fellow Venetians were allowed to remain for no more than a dozen years. Thereafter their relatives would have to ante up a steep renewal fee, have the bones consolidated to make room for later family members, or let them be taken to a remote part of the island, to a common grave.

Passing by the endless rows and tiers of these drawers, I had to shudder at the crassness of it all, knowing Fausto would never settle for anything less than his own imposing marble monument. These humble terraced boxes would simply not do, each

190

with its own minuscule bottle of plastic flowers, a battery-run votive light, and a photograph of the dead set into the wall just above it. Presumably, the lower tiers, easier to reach than the higher ones, were more expensive real estate, but still, none of this would be nearly grand enough for a Palladino.

As Don Giona began speaking at the grave, I looked over at Santa, who still moved as if in a dream. Her two tall sons stood at her sides, grasping her hands. I heard running behind us, and turned around to see my ex-husband, all out of breath, and barely shaven, coming to stand next to me.

'*Requiem aeternam dona, Domine,*' Don Giona began in a low, sonorous Latin, his head bowed. '*Et lux perpetua luceat eis,*' he went on, his radiant face etched with sadness.

'How's Santa?' Charlie whispered, causing several heads to turn.

'I don't know yet,' I answered quietly, as the heads swiveled toward us again.

'You'll never guess who I thought I saw jog right past me in San Marco Square this morning,' he dangled, baiting me.

'*Pater Noster, qui es in caelis,*' intoned Don Giona, moving right along.

'*Stronzi!*' the crowd heard Santa cry then, under her breath, as she pointed to the casket. '*Stronzi!*'

'*Sanctificetur nomen tuum,*' Don Giona pushed ahead, ignoring her. The man had a job to do.

'That nebbish from the Fireplace Inn,' Charlie kept fishing. 'The one with the dead flowers and the diet sodas. It was the strangest thing. I guess I must've imagined it, eh?' he finished, looking me straight in the eye.

'*Stronzi! Che Dio ti maledica!*' cried Santa then, in a blood-curdling shriek, as her two sons led her reluctantly away.

'. . . *Adveniat regnum tuum . . .*' droned on Don Giona as efficiently as possible, with a light rain beginning to fall everywhere and the wind whipping up around us.

Once the service was over, I thought of taking a walk around this island graveyard. I thought of looking for the graves of Stravinsky, Ezra Pound, and Diaghilev, but abandoned the idea,

191

deciding to return to Venice in the company of the other mourners. From the boat, I looked down into the murky green water and saw two dead cats, all swollen and glassy-eyed, floating beside a Coke bottle, and started to cry quietly, even as Charlie kept up his gentle ribbing about the nebbish in the restaurant. It was a strange thing, but the more he pushed me, the less I wanted him to know that he had really seen Calvin, as he knew he had. Suddenly I had a secret, two of them in fact, like two jewels hidden away in a safe, and I was not about to forfeit them.

'Fausto's gone,' Charlie said then on the boat, quietly, his voice cracking. He reached for my hand, and squeezed it tightly.

As we made our way back to the landing in Venice in the strange cloying light, I looked into the patrician palaces we passed, at the pastel chandeliers and the high ceilings and the deep, crashing water that swerved up to meet the doorways, and it all made me even sadder. What a place, this Venice. What a place for death, in November. People needed order, security, permanence. More than a muddy, shifting track of posts and piles in the changing waters. At least I knew I did.

In fact, it made me recall a story I had heard from Fausto many years before, about a boatman, a Venetian vaporetto driver at the turn of the century whose boat made a daily path around the islands, including San Michele. His course was set by the campanile in San Marco Square, which was visible at that time from all parts of the lagoon. On July 14, 1902, after the campanile had collapsed during an earthquake, he turned his boat toward Venice as he had every day before that, but there was no longer a bell tower, and it was said that the man had gone mad.

This, for me, was especially easy to understand particularly on a day so rooted in everything transient, even the bones of the dead.

Had Santa lost her bell tower? Would she go mad?

Had Charlie been my own bell tower? I turned to look over at his face, now lost in thought and melancholy. Would I go mad?

Our party wended its way to the grand Antico Martini for a funeral lunch, where I was seated between Charlie and Santa's small-boned, devoutly religious mother, who mostly sat in

192

silence. I watched her fill and refill her wine glass, as Don Giona, with his splendid, charismatic personality, attempted to hold forth on a variety of innocuous topics in order, I supposed, to distract us from the real reason we were there.

The food arrived, and between the clatter of cutlery and the buzz of conversation, the room became extremely noisy.

'My friend Romano Levi is famous for his *grappa*,' Don Giona was explaining to Charlie. 'He is in the village of Neive. He's very eccentric, very shy. People call him "*il grappaiol'angelico*", an angelic *grappa* maker.' Don Giona beamed, lifting a spoon of thick, dark soup to his full lips.

As he continued with his story, I wondered again, as I had for so long, just what his relationship to Santa had been, was now. Was she in love with him? Did he know? Did he care? Was the sentiment returned, even in part? What would happen between them now, now that Fausto was gone, or had he never made a difference?

'He works in an old farmhouse, with not even a telephone. It looks like it's from the nineteenth century, dark, with cobwebs, a sloping floor,' Don Giona went on, tearing off big hunks from a loaf of bread at his elbow, and floating them in his soup bowl. 'Unlike anyone else, he doesn't boil his *vinaccia*-and-water solution in a *bain-marie* sort of arrangement. Instead, Levi boils his over direct heat, from blocks of dried post-*grappa vinaccia* from the previous year's production.' Charlie kept nodding, but it was here they lost me. 'When the *grappa*'s ready, Levi bottles it himself, with one-of-a-kind, hand-sketched labels of angels and strange-looking women, and wildflowers, and always with a cryptic message.'

Charlie, in a trance of wine and sorrow, repeated Don Giona's words, mumbling them, '. . . always a cryptic message.'

'Yes, for instance, "*In Sogno, Ho Sognat*," "In a dream, I dreamed,"' he finished, taking a large sip of wine.

'In a dream, I dreamed,' echoed Charlie.

Later, during coffee, as I finished mine and prepared to go, a very strange thing happened, one that none of us would ever have anticipated. Charlie, entirely unprovoked, turned to me, chuckling and blushing suddenly. 'Stevie, stop it. Not here,' he had murmured to me, not once but three times, in a low, embarrassed, throaty warble, to which I responded, each time, with 'I'm not doing anything.'

Finally, he whispered to me, still chuckling, 'Get your hand off me! Stop rubbing my foot!' It was then that we both peeked under the table to find it was Don Giona's foot, without its shoe, that caressed Charlie's. And it was Don Giona's hand that rested naughtily in Charlie's lap. Utterly amazed, Charlie threw his balled napkin down on the table and pushed back his chair, just as Don Giona leaned over and nervously began to whisper in Charlie's ear. All I could make out was Charlie's voice, incredulous, saying over and over, 'You've got to be kidding,' as he just kept shaking his head. 'These are times when people can become . . . closer,' Don Giona whispered to Charlie, almost pleadingly, at which Charlie stood up and in a voice that was low, stern, and urgent, replied, 'You ever try that again, my friend, and the only thing you'll be close to is a night in jail.'

The great playwright was not immune to overacting or overreacting himself.

Well, soon after that, we left together, and found our way to Florian's for a rum punch or two, wanting to forget ourselves for a while in the red velvet, in the rich paneling and painting, and in the crowd of noisy Venetians, who were huddled together in the coffee-fragrant bar. I knew that Calvin must be waiting for me back at the hotel, but in the grand scheme that meant very little to me.

Settling in at our table, Charlie was still incredulous about Don Giona, as was I.

'Well, I guess that settles all our questions about him and Santa,' he laughed.

'It certainly does,' I had to agree, putting the thought to rest, as Fausto had been put to rest, once and for all.

Then, as we lost ourselves a bit in the rum and in the circumstances, pressed so closely together, I could just have kissed him then and there. Charlie began to reminisce about trips we had taken to Italy together in the past, and I let him.

'Remember that summer when I was rewriting *Master Planner* for the production in Rome?'

How could I forget? 'Forte dei Marmi for an entire summer,' I recalled, deliciously, remembering him rubbing suntan lotion on my back at the beach, stroking my neck, spilling white wine on me and licking it off.

'Remember the candy-cane-striped beach tents? The smell everywhere of mimosa and eucalyptus?' I nodded and nodded, and suddenly it was as near to me as yesterday. I leaned back and closed my eyes. This all couldn't, shouldn't, really be happening, and yet it was and really didn't feel that bad.

After his third rum punch, and more than a handful of endearing recollections of Fausto, he suddenly turned to me and said, 'In a dream, I dreamed. *Jag ä iskar dig.*'

I held my breath. 'Uh, oh. That sounds perilously like Swedish to me.'

'That's right, it is,' he said, apparently pleased at my alertness.

'About the Nobel,' he pushed ahead.

I held up a hand.

'Puleese don't start in on that old song again. I beg you.' He had come perilously close to spoiling the moment. 'As if there were even a chance,' I moaned, but he cut me off.

'That's what I'm trying to tell you,' he plunged on loudly, above the chattering Venetians. 'There is. There's a good chance. I spoke to my friend in Stockholm yesterday. You remember him, don't you, Stefan Andersson? He told me there's really a very good chance this year,' he insisted.

I shook my head and looked up at the ceiling.

'But he's not on the committee, and even the committee doesn't know yet, Charlie. Why do you put yourself through this every year, over and over again?'

'This year's different. You'll see,' he threatened happily.

'Oh, because some old pal of yours who's marginally connected with the committee said so?' I asked petulantly, remembering Stefan only too well from the time he had stayed with us years ago in New York. He was, predictably, tall, lean, blond, and bloodless; sexually ambivalent, and as cool as a passing cloud, with his lips planted solidly on my husband's buttocks the entire time.

'We'll see,' Charlie sang again several times, for effect.

Well, it was immediately after that that the fog of rum and memory began to part for me, letting in, at last, some light and fresh air. And that was precisely when the panic in me began to rise again, to bubble up and grab at me.

I looked over at the elegant man next to me, casually leaning over his empty glass, his curling eyelashes cast down, fluttering as if with wings, and I suddenly knew I had to get out of there, away from him. I knew I was being pulled, with strong fingers, down, back, into the past, and it was all happening too quickly. I needed to get away.

'And we'll have dinner tonight?' Charlie was asking me then, his hand on my wrist. I told him yes, sure, anything so that I could leave. My mind was on fire.

'I just need to go back to the hotel now to take a nap,' I told him without looking at him. 'I have a terrible headache,' which was truer than just true.

'Okay,' he said, summoning our waiter for the bill and paying it. 'Rest period. Then what about Harry's, about eight?' he asked, eager to please, clearly thrilled at the most recent turn of events. 'I'm going to take a good, long walk. I'll meet you over there at seven-forty-five.'

On the way back to the hotel, as he rambled on about Stefan, I decided that I would catch an early evening train to Florence and spend the weekend there, leaving no forwarding address at the Gritti, of course.

After we had said good-bye, I went up to my room to find that Calvin had left me a note telling me to meet him at eight o'clock at Harry's Bar. I called his room hoping to head off a meeting between Charlie and Calvin, but his phone rang and rang, and finally I thought, oh, the hell with it, I'm getting out of here. I made arrangements with the front desk for my train trip and my

196

hotel in Florence and began packing, quietly and quickly, and as stealthily as a thief.

I got to the railway station with just enough time to telephone Santa, whom I was feeling very guilty about abandoning, and was told she was lying down but feeling very much better, 'A lot more herself,' her younger son, Olivo, told me. Leaving her made me feel just awful, but I was sure that later on, once I'd spoken to her, she would understand.

On the train to Florence, I felt strangely superhuman, as if I had jumped from the top of a skyscraper and somehow landed without a scratch, or had leaped from a building in flames, unburned. (Cowardice, when successfully executed and gotten away with, can be an intoxicating, exhilarating experience.) Instead of shrinking away in shame with my tail between my legs, unable to face the music no matter what the tune, I was foolish enough to feel bold, fearless, and idiotically invincible. Now I could properly replenish myself, restore my bankrupt resources of emotion and will, and what better setting for this restoration could I have chosen than Florence, which had rebuilt *itself* twice in this century, after two catastrophes?

In 1944, every bridge spanning the Arno, except the Ponte Vecchio, had been blown to bits by the Nazis, but the minute the last black, polished boot had retreated, the refurbishing had begun. Then twenty years later, floodwaters that reached a height of twenty-three feet had covered the historic center of the city with an onslaught of 600,000 tons of oil, muddy slime, and debris. Fifteen hundred works of art, two million valuable books, and countless homes were damaged. The people of Florence, with help from all over the world, rose to the challenge of rebuilding, the instant the floodwaters began to recede.

In the face of such undaunted spirit, how could I help but be encouraged? Inspired? Emboldened?

I did not know just what I'd do in Florence, I told myself on that train, but whatever it was, I determined to leave Calvin and my crisis, my ambivalence, my unsettling and incongruous thoughts of Charlie behind me, like those dead, puffy cats floating in the canal.

197

Pulling into the chaotic station in Florence, I began to plan what I'd do with myself over the next several days. First, I knew I'd sink my bones, numb with the damp chill of several centuries, into my soft hotel bed at the Lungarno, a hotel on the quieter, more untraditional side of the Arno.

Later, I might walk over to Alderisio's, that famous little China-lacquered, black and red jewel of a jazz club, which was right down the street from my hotel. But maybe not.

And then tomorrow, losing myself in the watercolor of calming, neutral shades all around me, in the browns and blacks, the whites and beiges, with just a splash of bottle green, I might take myself to the Duomo, to the Boboli Gardens, to the Bargello Museum and its gallery of murderers that always intrigued me: Donatello's *David*, Cellini's model for *Perseus*, Verrochio's *David*, and Michelangelo's *Brutus*.

Later on, I might well wander into Cocco Lezzone (the restaurant described by one guidebook I'd read years ago as looking like a 'public rest room'), with its sign outside that said 'smelly cook,' and its good, hearty Tuscan food. I knew from experience, from the mad, frantic, peppy pace of the place, that they wouldn't allow me to linger, but still, I might push my luck and hang around after my meal just long enough for a slice of winter chestnut cake, and perhaps a glass of Aleatica, from Elba. Or I might not.

The main thing was that no matter what I did, or where I went, all thoughts of Charlie (and certainly Calvin) would be locked as far away from me as the bones of Ferdinand I. Or so I thought.

My first day there, right after breakfast, even before I could cross the Ponte Vecchio I saw, in a fraction of a second, or at least I could swear I saw, the somber profile of Patsy Stamberg, now a long way from Manhattan, Kansas, poised over a cameo, picking it up to examine it in the light, inside a small, dimly lit jeweler's shop. I took a few disjointed, flabbergasted steps forward, but then I could not move. I retraced my steps to verify that I had seen her. But when I did, she was gone. A flood about twenty-three feet deep of panic, uncertainty, and paranoia swept over me during the next two days, as I turned Florence upside down, inside out searching for her. But I came up empty-handed, and the upshot was that when I finally got back to New York, with all of my plans once again shot to hell, I was more unsettled than ever.

Once there, one of the first things I did was make an appointment with my therapist, Dr La Pierre, sensing in myself a greater, more urgent need than ever for a firm, guiding hand, a kind and tender word. After all, if I'd seen Patsy, things were certainly bad enough, but if I hadn't, things were worse.

When I showed up for my appointment, I brought with me my half-dreamed, fleeting image of Patsy, bent over that cameo, as well as all my new feelings, both wanted and unwanted. I tried hard to leave these feelings at home, but they refused to stay put. Stubbornly accompanying them were all my fears, my doubts and insecurities, all in the dubious light of new and recent developments.

I carried in a great deal of baggage to Dr La Pierre that day. In fact, I thought of everything I was bringing along as a huge steamer trunk, so heavy that the customs fee on bringing it with me from Italy would leave me utterly bankrupt.

Opening its heavy lid, I took the doctor through its contents, bit by bit, not stopping, barely coming up for air. But when at last the great torrent had ceased and I was silent, when I waited for her wisdom and kindness, I found it was not forthcoming.

Instead, after I'd finished, after her cat had once again taken a running leap into my lap, landing there like a wheelbarrow loaded with terra-cotta, she sniffled a bit, shook her curly, white grandmother mop of a French head, breathed a loud sigh of apparent bewilderment, and said, 'Well, live and learn!'

And then proceeded to charge me roughly thirty dollars per word.

Part Four

Such is life.
Falling over seven times
And getting up eight.

— JAPANESE FOLK POEM

I t was just a few days later that the bell rang seventeen times in a row at 8.15 in the morning, and on the other side of the door I got the surprise of my life.

'I did it! Can you believe it? I got the fucking prize! The Nobel! I got the Nobel! Can you fucking believe it? The reporters are downstairs! They followed me!' It was Charlie, of course, panting, flushed, swaying in the doorway as if from a stiff breeze, a bottle of Dom Pérignon dangling from his shaking hand, swaying with him. It took a few moments for it all to sink in, for the enormity of what had happened to register. In the meantime, he just stood there in his raincoat, which he'd thrown over a pair of striped pajamas, looking feverish and bubbling deliriously.

'Can I please come in, for Christ's sake?' he finally asked, and dumbly, still suspended in total disbelief, I nodded yes.

'Are you sure?' I wanted to know, wondering if he was perhaps just overanxious again and had jumped the gun a little bit.

Charlie was crazily pacing, dancing around in little steps, jumping up and down, uncontainable. 'I got the call this morning, Stevie! That's what I'm telling you! They called me from Stockholm! I did it! It'll be in the papers today, and I did it! Can you believe it? I'm in the same league as O'Neill and Beckett,' he cried.

'You hate them.'

'They're *geniuses*!' He seized me by both shoulders and danced me around wildly, kissing me on both cheeks. That was just about when the men who had been painting my apartment for the last hour, Ramon and his cousin Naldo, came into the living room, which was filled with buckets, a stepladder, and big islands of furniture here and there under drop cloths. I could hear their radio blasting in the other room. The paint fumes, combined with the news Charlie had brought, were enough to make anyone swoon.

'I think if Naldo starts in the back bedroom while I'm finishing the kitchen, we can kill two stones with one bird,' Ramon told me enthusiastically.

The music was booming. Charlie was opening the champagne and the phone was ringing. It was someone from my office, looking for some scripts I'd typed, which had somehow gotten misplaced. I had a big, new-client presentation that morning and couldn't be late.

'You know, two stones with one bird,' Ramon went on, dragging deep on his cigarette, flicking the ashes on my bare wooden floor. I got off the phone and discussed his painting agenda, and then Charlie got on the phone in the kitchen. While he was talking, singing, screaming, and whispering, he poured the Dom Pérignon into some old coffee mugs he found buried away in boxes beneath the drop cloths, and called Ramon and Naldo in for some.

'I wish you'd let them work,' I told him quietly. 'They've got a major job to do here, and I've got to get to the office.'

'Do you want me to stay and watch them?' he offered.

'No, actually my mother is in town, at Leslie's, and she should be here soon.'

Well, with that, the first dark shadow moved over his face on the most spectacular day of his life. While the painters were toasting each other, Charlie pulled me over into a corner, and put my face next to his.

'You left me in Italy, Slim, but all is forgiven.'

'Charlie, I . . .'

'I know you got scared. But that's all behind us now, don't you see?'

Frankly, I didn't.

204

'We've gone and actually done this thing! We've won the Nobel, Stevie!'

'Well, you won it, I just . . .'

'What's a Bobel?' asked Ramon hazily from an opposite corner.

'A *Nobel*. It's a prize. A very important prize,' Charlie offered.

'You mean like the Olympics?' asked Ramon.

'You get any money with it?' Naldo asked.

Charlie belly-laughed loudly. Who could blame him?

'Well, just a little,' he said. 'Just about three hundred and forty thousand dollars, before taxes.'

Naldo and Ramon just looked at each other speechlessly for a moment, and then both broke out in uncontrollable laughter.

'Hey, that's some funny joke, man,' Ramon nodded.

Just then, a big pigeon flew in the living-room window, which was opened wide to allow the paint fumes to escape. As phones and now the doorbell rang, as the loud beat of salsa from the other room pounded my brain, we all chased the big lost bird around with brooms and hangers, trying to shepherd it back out the window, but it just ignored us, landing everywhere in the room but where any of us could get to it.

'Hey, talk about two stones with one bird, eh? I wish I had a stone,' grinned Naldo, a bit drunkenly.

I answered the front door and there stood my mother, drenched with rain, shaking off her umbrella.

When she stepped inside and saw Charlie, the pigeon flapping around the ceiling, and the two painters drinking champagne, I thought she'd lie down and die right then and there.

'Well, what the –'

'Mom!' Charlie embraced her. 'I won the Nobel Prize!' he beamed. 'I did it! I finally did it!'

She pulled violently back from him, she, his greatest detractor. Now she just shook her head, not believing his words about the Nobel. 'And I just won an Oscar,' she said, turning back to me.

'It's true. He won the Nobel Prize,' I said. 'They called him from Sweden this morning. Isn't it exciting?' She reached into her bag and took out a cigarette, which Ramon jumped over and lit for her.

'You shouldn't be smoking, Esta,' Charlie admonished her. 'It's really no good for you. You really should try to stop.'

She addressed me then, looking right past him.

'Kindly tell my ex-son-in-law who just won a prize which means less than nothing to me, who just left a wife with a little baby, who's wearing pajamas in my daughter's house and I'm afraid to think why, that I have *tried* to stop smoking, but I'm like a cigarette with a woman attached,' she finished, taking off her coat and going to the back of the apartment while my painters, by now as tipsy as could be, finally herded the errant bird back out into the street.

The phone rang again. It was my doctor's office calling to tell me what time I could come in to be tested for Lyme disease. I hated to cave in to what I regarded as mere Hamptons cocktail-party propaganda, but I really hadn't been feeling well, hadn't been feeling at all myself, and there was no harm in trying to find out why.

'Mom! I'm leaving. I'll call you later!' I yelled back to her.

'I'll drop you at the office, Mrs Nobel,' Charlie beamed.

'I am not Mrs anything, and you are wearing pajamas, you know,' I told him. 'I know to you and me you look like a world-class genius, but to the rest of the universe, you might look like a world-class fool.'

He danced around again wildly, hugging himself.

'I'm impervious. I won the Nobel,' he sang, just as my phone rang again. I grabbed it before anyone else could, and much to my chagrin, it was Clovis Dill, Charlie's agent.

'Who is this?' she sniffed a bit haughtily. 'Who am I speaking to, please?' she asked the air, with a chilly bit of British superiority in her voice. 'Mr Stamberg left this number on his answering machine,' she huffed and puffed, impatiently.

'It's me – Stevie – Clovis,' I told her, trying to rustle up at least a modicum of civility for this grand occasion.

'Stevie! How marvelous to get you. Isn't it just the most magnificent thing, this Nobel! I mean, I was totally overjoyed, I must tell you! Completely blown away,' she gushed. The phony obsequiousness, like thick, oily goop, oozed through the phone and practically dripped all over my floor.

'Where is that marvelous man, Charlie,' she inquired then, speaking the name as if it were worth its weight in gold, and really, if it hadn't been so to her before, wasn't it now?

'He's right here; I'll get him,' I told her, anxious to free myself from her slimy telephone tentacles.

'Oh, wait just a second, dear,' she stopped me. '*What* is this play Charlie's told me about, *Glad Tidings*? You must let me see it. He's just been raving and raving about it, more than if he'd written it himself, if you can possibly imagine it,' she confided, with a sort of girl-to-girl, Knightsbridgian snort which made the palms of both my hands begin to itch. 'The thing is,' she carried on, 'this fellow, this friend of mine out at the Mark Taper in LA, is looking for unfinished works for his summer workshop, and I thought to myself, why not little Stevie?' The air hummed with her self-satisfaction. Little Stevie? Oh, Lord.

'It's nowhere near to being finished, Clovis –'

'But that's just the point, dear. It shouldn't be. It should be unfinished. Now be a good girl and give a copy of it to Charlie before he leaves. We're celebrating tonight and he can pass it along to me. I'll read it straightaway, I promise.'

Suddenly my mind focused on what she was saying.

'Are you serious about this? Someone might want to put it on?'

'If it's even a third as good as Charlie says it is, I can practically guarantee it,' she purred into the phone.

Handing the phone over to Charlie, who had been arguing with my mother, who had been arguing with the painters, I thought to myself, well, why the hell not? The play was good all right, and why not get a little recognition? It wasn't a Nobel, but it was a damned sight better than it had been before Charlie's tinkering, even though I hated to admit it. Why not give it a shot just in case his instincts happened to be right? While Charlie babbled and gushed back at Clovis on the phone, I tore through the house, ripping open boxes, searching for my manuscript. So far, it was my only revised copy, but I was willing to entrust it to

Charlie, considering what was possibly to be gained by it. Clovis was a pretentious, self-important jerk, but she did get results. Suddenly feeling weak, I broke out in a sweat and had to steady myself and sit down for a minute on my bed. The room, the world was suddenly spinning. Was it this Nobel business? Lyme disease? The meeting I'd certainly now be late for at the office? Clovis's offer? My mother? The paint fumes? Perhaps even all of the above?

Before I knew it, I was out on the rainy street with Charlie, who clutched my play and promised to messenger me a copy of it that afternoon. A heavy phalanx of reporters and photographers tackled us before we even reached the curb. Apparently this Nobel announcement was not to be taken lightly. I stood aside watching him hold forth there on the curb in his slippers, pajamas, and raincoat like the Pope at St Peter's – triumphant, victorious, every inch a champion.

Safely ensconced in a cab after we'd both calmed down from all the excitement, I thanked him for telling Clovis about my play. 'I guess this is a pretty lucky day for both of us' is what I think I said to him.

As we pulled up to my office building and I reached for the taxi door, I let a careless thought escape from my lips, one I wasn't even sure had been tumbling around inside me until I heard my voice say it.

'You know, the craziest thing happened when I went to Florence,' I started, searching his face for a reaction but finding none.

'Is that where you ran to get away from me, you cute little thing?' His eyes flashed as he tugged a little at my hand.

'I was on the Ponte Vecchio, and I could swear I saw Patsy –'

'*My* Patsy?' he wanted to know. I had his attention now.

'*Your* Patsy, in some cameo shop.' I took a deep breath. 'Was she in Italy?'

'I have no idea,' he told me, his brow as unruffled, his face and mind as clear and guiltless as a cloudless sky.

'Was she in Florence?' I tried again, still not really knowing what to think of it all.

208

'How should I know?' he responded, not missing a beat. Then his face filled with mischief and amusement. A taxi honked at us from behind. 'Maybe it was just symmetrical, like that bag of bones from the Fireplace Inn I hallucinated in Venice. I even thought I saw him in Harry's. Can you imagine that?' he offered plainly. 'We were both very upset that weekend and our imaginations were working overtime. I'm sure I didn't really see him any more than you really saw Patsy in Florence.' He paused thoughtfully. 'Anyway, if I were you, I'd be thinking ahead now, not backward,' he instructed, just as I saw Patsy's face, all pale and watery, bobbing up and down before me like a weightless balloon, saw it take off and rise over the naked winter trees, float high up into the rainy sky and trail away.

'So how long is Esta here for?' he wanted to know then, oblivious to the honking cars behind us, and to the cab driver, who was muttering and cursing to himself in several languages.

'Just for a few days. She came up for the wedding of a friend's daughter on the weekend, then she goes back,' I told him anxiously, reaching again for the taxi door.

'Maybe I can take you both out, to celebrate my big news. Your big news,' he grinned enchantingly. 'I'll take you to the theater or something. She always loved the theater,' he rambled.

'Charlie, you may have won over the Swedes, but my mother is another story. I have to go now,' I told him, pushing past him finally.

'We'll see,' he dared, his green eyes and voice teasing me.

'I really am very proud of you. I couldn't be any prouder,' I had to tell him then, and really, I meant it. To be any prouder, in fact, I'd have to be him.

'I'll drop off the copy of your play later on,' he told me, before brushing my mouth with his lips and opening the door to finally let me out. To my utter surprise, I kissed him back then, an urgent, frantic little kiss that startled us both, and then his cab sped away, disappearing around a corner.

The rest of that day passed as if in some turbulent, ever-changing, kaleidoscopic dream. Sitting in my meeting, I was perfectly useless. In fact, I could've been a Nobel Prize winner myself, in astral projection, so far away did I travel, first to Los Angeles, where I took a deep, extended bow at the Mark Taper Forum after the opening-night performance of my play. After that, I kept picturing the green of Charlie's eyes, and the dry, feverish feel of his lips, and then in my fantasies, it was on to Sweden, where I sat back in my seat at the Nobel ceremony in the great Concert Hall. I fidgeted around in my chair, smoothed the silk of some steamy, red, classy designer creation with a gloved hand as the King of Sweden somberly presented Charlie with his medal, his diploma, and his money. This of course, was before we all repaired to the awesomely elegant banquet in the City Hall, for perhaps some marinated salmon, for elk steaks with rowanberry jam.

All the papers and the news reports that day were full of Charlie, and I couldn't even begin to count the calls I got, from friends, from relatives, even from a tiny radio station in Carbondale, Illinois, where they thought I was apparently the most current Mrs Stamberg. All of New York and beyond was brimming with pride and glory at the reality of this award, which was to be bestowed upon one of its own.

I had gotten home that evening feeling even weaker and fainter than that morning when I'd left. I thought of the blood test for Lyme disease I'd taken at lunchtime, then shrugged it off. I hadn't, after all, gone prancing naked or even shoeless through any deer paths. No. Lyme was just too predictable. It wouldn't dare come looking for me, would it?

No way, I thought to myself, ripping into the huge envelope waiting for me, sent over by Charlie, with a copy inside of my play, and a note saying he'd delivered it personally that day to Clovis, and to keep my fingers crossed. Also enclosed were matinee tickets for the following day, presumably for my mother and me, to see *Phantom of the Opera*. Good gracious, but the boy was working hard.

When Leslie phoned a bit later to tell me that she and our

mother were going to a movie, inviting me along, I reluctantly agreed, still not feeling much better, but I'd seen very little of my mother since she'd been in town, and my guilt, as usual, got the better of me. As it turned out, my mother didn't really want to go either, but off we went, to some mindless, chattering fluff that was to last about an hour and a half. Once in our seats, we asked a man next to my mother to move over one so that the three of us could sit together, but he wasn't budging. My mother pushed at him, poked and jabbed, raising her voice and calling him rude and ignorant, but it did no good. He was dead.

After the theater was cleared out, we decided to forgo any form of cinematic entertainment, feeling it was certainly ill-fated, and trooped off instead to dinner. We decided to introduce my mother to the subtle joys of Japanese food, but when it was brought to her, after she'd made her selection from a menu she claimed was as big as the Torah, she only curled her lip, wrinkled her nose, flatly refused to eat, and told the waiter, whose name was printed on a badge on his lapel, that trying to read the letters of his name was like 'reading an eye chart'. In the end, Leslie and I quickly finished our meals, and Leslie shuttled her back home for a tuna-fish sandwich, a thawed piece of frozen noodle pudding, and an evening of writing postcards to all the ladies in her building, no doubt painting an infinitely rosier picture of her stay than was, shall we say, accurate.

Now all of this did nothing, of course, to help me get her to the Majestic Theater the next day for a two o'clock curtain. To say she was reluctant would be like saying that the Collier brothers were reluctant to throw out magazines. Still, with her booted little heels digging in deep, scraping the pavement, fighting me every inch of the way rather than accept anything from her former son-in-law, I managed to get her to her seat roughly eight minutes before the heavy red curtain inched upward and the show began. However, eight minutes was just long enough for five little white papers, each with a black 'Phantom' mask in its center, to float out of her *Playbill* and land at her feet. 'At this performance, the role of the Phantom usually played by Timothy Nolan will be played by Jeff Keller,' the first one read.

'At this performance, the role of Christine Daae usually played by Patti Cohenour will be played by Dale Kristien,' read the second, and so on.

As the houselights dimmed and the conductor took up his baton, my mother leaned into my face and whispered, with more than a trace of misdirected harshness, 'At this performance, the role of your mother will be played by someone extremely disappointed.' She then maintained that theme throughout the performance; during intermission, the only comment she could make was about the chandelier, the famous chandelier, the cynosure of the enterprise, certainly. From there, she'd gone on about how Charlie still had the chandelier that had belonged to her mother so many years ago, as well as scores of other objects he had made off with after our marriage, items that had all belonged to her and to members of her family.

But the drama of the day did not end, alas, with the final curtain inside the Majestic, because right there at the curb as we stepped outside was a limo as long as *War and Peace*, and inside it was old Charlie, intent on spiriting us away to his studio in Brooklyn Heights, where he was currently living and where he'd decided to cook us dinner.

'Where's my chandelier?' my mother barked at him, as a trio of photographers surrounded us, closing in like Indians around a wagon train.

'Your *what?*' Charlie yelled back, astonished, beckoning us inside. But she wouldn't budge, at least not until he answered her about the chandelier.

'It's at my closed-up apartment,' he shouted. 'On Fifth Avenue.'

'Yeah, but it shouldn't be, Mr Hotsy-Totsy World Prize-Winner,' she called to him, loudly enough for each reporter who'd just arrived to jot down every word precisely.

Charlie laughed then, laughed louder than the Phantom himself had laughed before he'd dropped that great chandelier.

'You can have it! You can have the goddamned chandelier, Esta. Just get into the car, for Christ's sake,' he begged her, his eyes flashing wildly, the photographers feverishly clicking away.

Well, in the end we got into his car and let his driver hurry us over the Brooklyn Bridge, all the way to the townhouse Charlie had kept on Henry Street for his office and studio, but which now served as his home.

For the sight of Charlie cooking dinner for anyone, I'd gladly have limped over that bridge myself, with both feet bound in nail-spiked ropes, with my tongue dragging along the roadway. A genius in the kitchen he had never been. Tonight, however, he was promising us veal piccata and chocolate cake.

'Who's your caterer?' I asked him, cagily.

'You're looking at him,' he beamed, quite thrilled with himself all around.

'How did you find time for all this, in between your interviews and everything?'

'*And* writing my Nobel lecture, don't forget,' he cut in, just as we bounce, bounce, bounced over the bridge. 'I made the time, Stevie. I wanted to do it,' he smiled charmingly.

'And my silverware, the fancy stuff, I want it back,' my mother went on, more to herself, still enumerating the items he had made off with after our marriage.

'It's all in the apartment on Fifth Avenue, Esta,' he repeated for her patiently. 'Look, whatever you find at the studio that's yours, you'll take back with you. The rest we'll talk about some other time.'

'When you win another Nobel Prize?' she sniffed, still not trusting him as far as he could throw a limousine.

'Now, isn't this fun?' he asked her, still not giving up, as he shepherded her out of the limo and into his studio.

'I'd give up if I were you,' I whispered to him.

'About as much fun as gout. Or a chandelier falling on my head,' she yawned.

He settled us in his spacious living room, handed us each a glass of wine, and went into the kitchen to see about dinner.

'The stove is the thing with the knobs. The sink's the little bathtub with spigots!' I couldn't resist calling to him, to which I was not favored with a reply.

While my mother went snooping in search of stolen contra-band, I got up and poked around a bit in the living room, which was littered with telegrams, airmail letters, and newspapers, all announcing his award. Lying on a table strewn with magazines was that day's edition of a local newspaper, one long on gossip and innuendo and short on anything else. As I riffled through it innocently, my eyes suddenly seized upon a picture of Charlie, now humming in his kitchen to the Miles Davis tape he'd put on, celebrating his Nobel at a party at Le Cirque the previous night.

I was just about to yell out to him again when, out of the corner of one eye, I thought I spotted, in the center of the photograph, half turning and leaning away from Charlie, the tiniest smudge of a face, no bigger than the nail of my pinkie, all grainy and dotted with black-and-white specks, the crass, grinning face of Dolores, but I really couldn't be sure.

When Charlie brought out a platter of pâté and crudités, as well as a bottle of wine for us, I showed him the paper, ever so casually.

'Nice party, eh?'

'Well, yeah,' he laughed, a bit self-consciously. 'You know me. Make a fuss over me, put me in a grand setting, and it'll thrill me every time.' He shrugged his shoulders. 'It takes so little to make some people happy.'

'Is that Dolores?' I asked him then, pointing to the little grainy smudge.

He blinked a few times and his face went blank. 'Dolores, who?' he asked naïvely, making his way back to the kitchen, and that seemed to be the end of that. Again, the specter of Patsy's face bobbed up and down before me and then receded, the light in the Florentine cameo shop dimming to blackness.

When my mother reappeared, it was with a triumphant smile pasted across her face, as she stockpiled her loot in the front hallway: pictures in frames, a marble cherub brought to her from the Carrara quarry, an old camera, a rusty flute in a battered case from God knows when.

'All right,' she said to me, absolutely seriously. 'We can go now. What did he do with my coat?'

When we finally got her seated at the table, she seemed at last to relax her seething contempt for our host, somewhere between the salad and the veal piccata, with its gluey noodles and a sauce as thick as a pair of woolen socks. I looked at our chef in the candlelight and for a while I was perilously close to becoming lost in him again, poised on a precipice. It felt just like the old days, even as he and my mother kept up their now semi-good-natured ribbing. When I finally recovered my voice and found the words, over coffee and a fairly decent rendition of chocolate cake, I asked him about my play, about giving it to Clovis, and about how much time he thought it'd take her to get around to reading it.

'Oh, come on now, don't be pushy. She just got it, for God's sake, Stevie,' he admonished me. 'She has a few other things going on just now, don't forget,' he grinned. 'She'll get to it, don't worry.'

Well, it was right about then, just as my mother was asking him what sort of alimony he planned to settle on Patsy and his little son, that a great wave of fatigue and weakness overtook me, just as it had that morning, which now seemed like a few tired centuries ago. All of a sudden my muscles were aching, and I realized that my left arm felt terribly sore. Something was not right. I couldn't move my fingers. I explained to my worried host, as he packed us and my mother's recovered treasures into the four-block limo for the trip back to the city. As he leaned into my window, he whispered to me, 'Don't worry about Clovis, she'll read it. She'll love it.'

'Oh, I know. It's okay, really,' I started to lie, but then abandoned the pretense. 'It's just that –' I started, but then faltered, barely knowing what I'd been about to say. It was strange all right, very strange.

'It's just like old times, eh, Stevie?' he asked, but we sped away before I could answer, relieving me of the task of knowing just what that answer might've been, leaving him to his dirty pots and pans, his woolly-socked veal sauce, and his Miles Davis.

We dropped my mother off at my sister's where, with the help of two extremely beleaguered doormen, her evening's haul was transported upstairs. Overpowered by weariness and in a sweat,

215

I went home and fell asleep in my bed with the lights and all my clothes on.

Seconds before shutting my eyes, I thought of a snippet of conversation I'd just had with my mother in the car, and had some trouble shutting it back out of my brain.

'So, who's he running around with these days?' she'd inquired, almost spitting out the question, the minute the limo had left the curb.

'I haven't the faintest idea.'

To this she laughed. 'Well, you don't think he's actually alone, do you? A man like that, he'd never make it through one night by himself. And now with this Nobel' – she accented the word with a flamboyant hostility – 'the sea of floozies must swallow him up in the morning before he can even reach the street.'

'Why do you even think about these things?' I moaned to her. But, more important, why didn't *I* seem to?

'I just wonder what must be going on in your little brain, that's all. What you must be thinking of to be starting up with him again.'

'I'm not "starting up,"' I insisted, beginning to know better, even within the carefully deluded confines of my 'little brain.'

'Time and time again you insist upon giving these people, these men, human characteristics . . .' She shook her head. 'You just don't look out for yourself,' she went on. 'It's a good thing you have me.' With that she had reached into her purse for a small, crumpled piece of paper, which she shoved into my hand.

'What is this, now?'

'It's the number on the bottom of his answering machine, the number he uses to call in for his messages. It could be useful to you,' she bragged, clearly proud of her fast-footed espionage work.

'I really don't want this,' I told her, thinking for a second of just opening my car window and dropping it into the East River.

'All right, don't use it. Just keep it for yourself. Put it away someplace so you'll know you've got it if you ever need it. You might thank me someday.'

'I don't approve of methods like that,' I sniffed. But I put the rumpled little page into a coat pocket, after reading the number, 56, which now seemed to hold such mystery.

When I walked into the apartment soon after, I took the scrap of paper from my coat and jammed it into a crowded night-table drawer, hoping I'd never feel I had to use it but bowing once again to my mother's irrefutable craftiness. After all, Charlie was playing Mr Solitaire with remarkable humanity. I would never forget the sight of this man bending over to load a dishwasher. Given the fact that it had taken all of eight years for me to teach him to bring his dinner plate into the kitchen, this remarkable sight touched and affected me.

This was not to be my only shock over the next few weeks; in fact, it was just the first of several, starting with the news that I had tested positive for Lyme disease. It was the very last thing I'd expected. Now this meant, of course, that I had to beg for more time off from work, and I would have to submit to a regimen of antibiotics that seemed more appropriate to a herd of African bulls.

On my second day at home in bed under the influence of this pharmaceutical onslaught, I lay in a languid, forgetful haze. The fingers of my left hand were by now so sore and stiff they were like the tines of a fork. I opened the Sunday *Times* to the wedding announcements and was startled (so startled that I nearly bounced right out of bed) to find the smiling, starved, and mentally ill face of Calvin Persky and his bride of one day, grinning up at me. Married? Was he kidding? Had he become intoxicated with the female bartender at Harry's? Was Lyme an illness fraught with hallucinations as well as the several thousand other complaints I'd developed? Could it be possible? Again and again I turned back to the page with his lopsided smile and to the large face beside his, the woman who was now his wife, a slightly cross-eyed woman with a pair of the largest, flattest ears I had ever seen. Mrs Dumbo.

The accompanying paragraph explained that she was some sort of society dame from a long line of society dames, who spent her time raising money for charities and doing social work in some limited but respectable capacity. Social work? Charities? She'd better get ready for the biggest project in social work she'd ever dreamed of. Now here was a medical pioneer worthy of Dr Salk, I thought bitterly, still astounded at this quirky turn of events.

Phoning Dr La Pierre from my sickbed the next day to relay this bit of news to her, I couldn't wait to hear what she'd say. Would she admit that she'd been wrong about him, that he had, ultimately, been capable of making a commitment after all? She listened carefully, patiently, at the other end, and then said, 'Well, I'm not impressed. All that glitters is not gold,' and I hung up disgusted, unfulfilled.

At the same time, as my illness progressed ('It will get worse before it gets better,' my Lyme doctor had warned, and he certainly knew his stuff), I became increasingly bored, exhausted, and frustrated. The days all ran together and were the same. Mara came over often, as did a few other friends, to feed me, to talk me out of myself, to help me into and out of the shower, but all of the effort of receiving them only helped to deplete me. Once in a while, I tried to get dressed and occasionally even made it outside, for a labored stroll around the block, but it always took its toll, setting me back a few days.

The one bright spot was Charlie, who I must say behaved quite lovingly, stopping by at least once a day, cooking, shopping, renting and showing me movies, mostly the old, classic comedies, and reading aloud to me from books, magazines, and newspapers, usually about himself, but he was entertaining nevertheless. He was also getting ready to begin putting together his lecture, the one he'd make to the Nobel Academy in three weeks when he left for Stockholm.

I think it was quite early on during this time that Charlie came to me and asked me to help him write his Nobel speech. Actually, 'asked' sounds passive, far too casual for what he really did, which was suck me into a perfectly foolproof maelstrom; flatter me, cajole and beg me, seduce and tug me in with intensely frantic pleadings. I mean, good Lord, being asked to collaborate on this speech, wasn't that practically like winning the Nobel, Jr? The mere thought of all this, especially when approached from the depths of my Lyme haze, made me smug and dizzy, whipped me into a lather of self-importance and self-satisfaction, with all its flattering implications. Would I help Charlie? How could I not? Would Gunga Din say no to the British Army? After all the help he'd given me with my play, how could I decently refuse him?

I couldn't, and from that moment on, we began to work together, slavishly trying to write the speech that would absolutely knock every last intellectual 'herring lapper' and 'ice monkey' right on his ear. Since I was still feeling pretty poorly, I didn't think I was contributing all that much, but whatever I came up with was greeted with unmistakable respect, enthusiasm, and good cheer by Charlie (who sat at my desk, usually with a pair of chopsticks and a half-eaten carton of beef with snow peas, as he fed all our ideas, and then the various versions of our speech, into my computer). No longer was I protected by the 'work at a distance' policy I'd devised for my play. This time, it was face to – in his case, beautiful, high-cheeked, jade-eyed – face.

In spite of this, I must add, the ease and pleasantness of it all came as a complete surprise to me. Little by little, it was as if the years just fell away, and all of their pain and acrimony with them.

Night after night he appeared at my door, usually showing up with dinner for us and some sort of gift or surprise for me: a book of Dorothy Parker's poetry, a lace teddy, a bar of French-milled soap. When I felt especially awful, he took care of me. There was nothing I could have asked him at that time that he would have refused me. Gradually, although still reluctantly on my part, we let the boundaries relax, and then so did we. Soon we were once again comfortable, laughing, sharing gossip and secrets, finishing each other's sentences.

One evening, I looked over at Charlie's fine shoulders, hunched over my Macintosh Plus, like bookends, and remembered back to the time so many years before when we'd first been going out together. We'd had a silly spat probably having to do

219

with that bulldog, Dolores. I remember a stubborn week-long silence on both our parts, broken suddenly on a Sunday morning (which happened to be Purim) when my doorbell rang. Opening the door, I faced Charlie, his arms overflowing with *hamantaschen*, the Sunday *Times*, and a large box of condoms. He wore a sheepish smile as he stepped neatly inside. I marveled anew at his titanic chutzpah. But this was Charlie. He offered no apologies, no explanations.

'Wear the *hamantaschen*, eat the condoms, and give me the goddamned puzzle,' I grumbled at him, as we settled back into a lazy, uncomplicated day together. Whatever trouble had separated us had somehow melted away, dispersed like common, ordinary morning fog.

I could never forget the sight of him that day, hanging in my doorway, all will and gumption, carrying his implausible bundle. And working with him on his speech, it came back to me almost nightly, his spectacular ability to fly in the face of logic, paint over a canvas and replace what had been there with what he deemed ought to be there instead. It had always worked for him somehow. And apparently, it still did. I always asked if he'd heard anything yet from Clovis about my play, but he kept telling me no and to please be patient a little while longer.

About two weeks after he first began these working visits, I started to notice a slight improvement in myself. I was a long way from being my old self, but if I craned my neck and strained my eyes, I could just see the outline of the old me at the end of a very long, dark tunnel. And since Lyme is a sentence with an indefinite stay, with no true beginning, middle, and end, you must be glad for every drop of progress, and I was.

When I told Charlie I seemed to be feeling a bit better, about a week before he took himself off to Sweden, he sounded overjoyed, and promptly announced that rain or shine, come hell or high water, come fever, aching limbs, dizziness, or memory lapse, that night he was taking me to dinner at the Rainbow Room.

At first I laughed. He couldn't be serious.

'Even if I could summon the strength for an evening like that, which I doubt I could, we'll never get in. It takes years to get a reservation,' I said, forgetting for a moment just who I was talking to.

'I have a Nobel! Are you kidding?' his voice danced. 'I'll pick you up at eight,' he said, and that's precisely what he did.

How I made it out of the house, clean, made up, and suitably dressed, I will never know, except that I owed a lot to the diligent devotion of both Mara and my sister, who chattered breathlessly while getting me ready. Talking as if they were standing over my grave, pronouncing this the evening with the most romantic potential they'd ever heard of, they pushed me, like Cinderella's sisters, like shamelessly immoral matchmakers, back into the hot clutches of my seductive ex-husband. Only my mother, who was now safely back in Florida but whom I'd phoned in a moment of sheer lunacy, remained skeptical. She was worried, terrified even, that I was falling for him all over again.

And should she have been worried? I suppose she had every reason to be, although at the time I wasn't sure. In truth, I *had* been sliding, falling backward for him again, had been ever since Fausto was lowered into the Venetian earth, but only in meager, inconsequential stages, or so I imagined. It was only that night in the colorful light of the Rainbow Room that I realized what they all added up to, and that it was one Grand Slide.

To be fair to myself though, I cannot believe that the woman, or man, has yet been born who could resist *anyone* at the Rainbow Room. Such a place was not created for the stony-hearted, the bitter, the solitary, the hopeless, or the loveless.

As we entered, we were greeted by a standing ovation. 'Bravo!' the patrons, the waiters, even the band, which had stopped playing upon our arrival, shouted to the Nobel Prize winner.

Stunned by the view, by the magnificently tiered Art Moderne ballroom, the gently spinning dance floor, which quickly refilled itself with dancers soon after Charlie's ovation, I soon lost myself

221

in the nostalgia of it all, in the music, the Gershwin, the Porter, the salsa, in the silk aubergine luxuriance of everything.

Never one to shun theatricality, Charlie had dressed for the evening in a tuxedo ('I'm rehearsing for Stockholm. How do I look?' he'd asked me in the elevator, climbing to the sixty-fifth floor), and although it was saying a lot, I could safely assert that he'd never looked better. But, of course, he already knew that, so I didn't have to.

Over a gargantuan seafood extravaganza that was our shared appetizer, as the twelve-piece band and keyboard ensemble played and its singer belted out 'Night and Day,' the restaurant owners presented us with a bottle of their finest champagne, which Charlie dove right into like a frisky seal, and which I turned down because of my Lyme disease medications. It was during this sliver of an interval that Charlie began his pitch about my accompanying him to Sweden the following week for the Nobel ceremonies.

'Oh, I couldn't possibly.' I waved him away, waved his idea away in the gentle, moody candlelight.

'Even if I wanted to –'

'You do,' he cut in, emphatically.

'Even if I felt better –'

'You do,' he insisted again and again, and, of course, he was right about both things and we both knew it.

'You are just determined to sweep me off my size seven-and-a-half feet, aren't you?' Finally I told him coyly, 'The thing I still haven't figured out is why.'

He looked at me sweetly, patiently. 'Because I love you, and because we belong together, and if you were surprised to see me cooking, wait until you see how I sweep,' he warned. 'Let's dance,' he said then, changing the subject.

I told him I didn't quite feel up to it, but he insisted on dragging me around the floor a few times, like a rag doll, not about to let the spell we were under fade for even a single second. As we settled back down with our lobster thermidor and our tournedos Rossini, Charlie was by now knee deep into the pricey champagne, holding forth nonstop. I interrupted him only once, to

222

ask again about Clovis, once more regretting that I was at the mercy of this sneering, phlegmatic woman, and once again he begged me to be patient. From there, he eagerly skipped on to the idea of my coming to Sweden with him.

I looked all around me, at the dancers, the giant crystal chandeliers, the twinkling lights outside, the waiters in their period uniforms, at the other couples nestled all around us, at the sports jackets and tuxedos, the diamonds, sequins, and cleavage, at the blue and gold baked Alaskas that suddenly seemed to be on fire everywhere. I leaned back, listening to the bewitching strains of 'Isn't It Romantic,' closed my eyes, and had to admit that yes, it was romantic, more than just romantic, so much so that it should almost have been declared illegal. No one should have the Rainbow Room working for him, it tilted the odds so unfairly. I had a feeling that that night I would say yes to anything Charlie might ask, and just hoped he wouldn't ask for much. As it was, he just rambled on about his speech.

'I was thinking of quoting Lundkvist,' Charlie babbled, as the waiter refilled his coffee cup with a slight bow.

'Who?' I asked him, in a trance, unable to wrench my eyes away from the moving dance floor, where a couple had broken into a skillful, overemotional tango.

'Lundkvist, you know, Artur Lundkvist, the Swedish poet. Right at the end of the speech. The Academy would love that, I bet,' he bubbled, suddenly breaking out into an ostentatious display of Swedish. 'Yes, I believe I will quote from *Sjalvporträtt av en drömmare med öppna ögen.*'

Still, I couldn't take my eyes off that tangoing pair, gripping each other with a fervor that nearly made me giggle out loud, it looked so ridiculous.

'Don't you want to know what it means?' asked Charlie, clearly disappointed, breaking into a cheerless translation before I could even respond. 'Self-portrait of a dreamer with open eyes,' he explained triumphantly, clenching my hand tightly, the hand that still ached from Lyme. 'You must come to Sweden with me, Stevo. It's your speech, too, now. I just won't have it any other way.' I wrestled my hand back from him and told him I'd think

223

about it. 'We have let so much time slip by us when we should've been together . . .' he trailed off.

'Aah yes, maybe . . .'

'"Aah yes, maybe"? Is that what you said?' he asked excitedly. 'My dear, are you quoting Sartre to me?' he asked conspiratorially, with some pride. 'This *is* a night to remember.' His eyes flashed as he doubled over with laughter.

'I don't know what you mean.'

'Not much you don't. "Yes," she says with assurance. "It was in Aix, in that square, I don't remember the name anymore. We were in the courtyard of a café, in the sun, under orange parasols. You don't remember; we drank lemonade and I found a dead fly in the powdered sugar." And then she says back to him only "Ah yes, maybe . . ."'

'Do you still see Dolores?' I blurted out so unexpectedly that I was actually unprepared for it myself.

Neatly skirting the issue, his eyes seizing on the décolletage of some Spanish bombshell doing the mambo right under our noses, in a red dress with a neckline so low she'd left it in the lobby, he answered only, 'Well, no, of course not, why would I?'

He saw me nod to myself, wondering whether or not I believed him, wondering what had possessed me to even ask, and it was the first time in months I witnessed the shadow of true annoyance skate over his excellent face.

'You know, Stevie, you still see me as this ridiculous ladies' man,' he began, his eyes still glued to Miss Uruguay. 'Aren't I a little too old for that, to be making such a fool of myself?'

'Since when is any man too old to make a fool of himself?' I barked back, hearing my mother tugging on my vocal cords.

He laughed a hollow laugh and cast about in his champagne-soaked brain for examples, for evidence, for a path of reasoning that might get him away from this topic of conversation, which was, evidently, such a nuisance to him.

'You know,' he started (he always started with 'You know' when he was in a tight spot and stalling for time), 'you talk to me sometimes as if I were Marcello Mastroianni, Rudolph

Valentino . . . or even Fausto. It's just absurd. I'm not some slick, Italian lover boy. The Autostrada is not my playpen. I don't ride the young girls around in my Porsches on the road, streaked with sun or slicked with rain, at impossible speeds, with one hand down a girl's blouse and the other flicking the ashes from my cigar out the window with short, stubby, thieves' fingers,' he went on, wildly. 'I can just picture the kind of guy you're picturing, Stevie, and he's certainly not me.'

'I'm sorry,' I offered lamely. 'I just wanted to know −'

'You just wanted to know. Don't you want to know even more that I love you? Haven't I shown you that, proved that to you at least? What more can I do?' he asked miserably. 'I need you in Sweden with me. Say you'll do it. Say you'll come.'

'I . . . might come,' I offered.

His face brightened considerably, and all talk of Valentinos on rainy roads with stubby fingers was left behind us.

'Just think of it. It's what we always talked about, Stevie. We always planned it together. Over and over. The Nobel ceremony. And the Grand Hotel, and the Operakallaren,' he pushed. 'You would never have turned that down before.'

I wasn't sure I could now. As he settled the bill, I searched the dance floor once again for those tangoing fools, but they had disappeared, like Dolores just now and Patsy on the Ponte Vecchio; they had faded and joined the gallery of sights to be recalled like slides in my memory, culled from fact and fantasy, but I couldn't know from which.

That was about when Charlie took an envelope out of his pocket and pushed it toward me. 'It's a ticket for next Wednesday night, kiddo. SAS flight number nine-o-four to Stockholm. It leaves Kennedy at seven-thirty. There's also a gift certificate for three thousand dollars in there from Bergdorf's. Buy yourself some gorgeous little thing to thaw out those chilly Swedes at the ceremony.'

Well, I don't know what happened next, but all of a sudden I was crying, not sobbing or anything, just quietly leaking in, I suppose, an elegant way, appropriate to the Rainbow Room, and I was kissing Charlie, my arms around his neck, telling him yes,

225

I'd come to Sweden, and that he was a good, good man after all. The very best.

When he kissed me in the elevator as we left, I felt the evening, the gravity of my decision, and the force of my antibiotics swim over me completely.

'You know what we should do now?' Charlie asked me out in the street, as the cold night air slapped me in the face and helped to revive me. 'We should go and spend the night at some overpriced hotel,' he said mischievously. 'And then in the morning, we can have penny chocolates for breakfast on a park bench, and oranges, and stale rolls,' he finished, reminding me of the first time we'd gone to Paris together. 'I love you so much,' he'd whispered to my hair, clasping me around my waist and pulling me close.

'Haven't you spent enough money tonight? Now you want a fancy hotel?' I laughed.

'I just bought a space shuttle, and now you're asking if I have enough money to put the flag on top?' he wanted to know, clearly thrilled at his cleverness, as well as the outcome of the evening which was not yet over.

In the end, we did not go to a hotel. Since we could not agree on one and since I'd idiotically left my medicines at home and because he had an early morning meeting with some fellow from a German television company, we instead wound up spending the night, or what little was left of it, at my apartment. Tripping over furniture that still hadn't been put back in place after the painters, we drifted through the rooms as if in a dream, with Charlie remembering his life there in that apartment with glasses so rose-colored they bordered on scarlet.

If I anticipated a night of pleasurable, memorable lovemaking, which I suppose I did, I was sadly disappointed.

'This absolutely never happens to me,' Charlie muttered unhappily, over and over again, after he'd tried and tried but was repeatedly impotent.

'I can't even remember the last time,' he said, angry at himself, at the world, at me, causing me to wonder briefly when the last time was that he had tried, silently calculating the number of

226

months since Patsy's disgraced exodus back to Manhattan, Kansas. 'It must be the champagne because it certainly isn't me,' he told the ceiling impatiently. That was when I took him in my arms, but he wriggled out of them and soon took himself into the bathroom and sat down at the edge of my big claw-footed tub, the same tub I'd cried my eyes out into the night of our divorce. While I listened to him throwing up the sensationally high-priced dinner we'd just consumed, I relinquished all thoughts of our past passions and lovemaking and lulled myself to sleep instead with thoughts of Sweden, of an overly luxurious room at the Grand Hotel, with a splendid view of the waterfront and the Royal Palace, and of Clovis, that whining, sniveling sycophant, loving my play and having to admit it to me.

Over coffee and burned English muffins served to me in bed the next morning, I once again asked Charlie when I might expect to hear from Clovis. 'I'm just worried about being away when she calls,' I told him nervously, in between sips of bitter dark coffee that tasted as burned as the rusty bottom of a watering can. 'I can't wait to talk to her and hear what she thinks.'

Well, that's when he turned on me and started carrying on about how impatient I was, how my behavior was childish and how spoiled I was, raising his voice and shaking his head vigorously, with utter exasperation, saying anything but God, I'm embarrassed about flying at half mast last night, old girl, which I knew was exactly what he was thinking. After a while he finally began to simmer down and I asked him, stubbornly I guess, just why it was so wrong to be impatient, why it was wrong to want so badly to see my play produced. Wasn't that fervor, that determination exactly what had gotten him where he was?

'That's different,' he mumbled, looking away.

'How?'

He shrugged his shoulders. 'You have a good job, which you do very well.'

'But I hate it, you know that. I want to write plays.'

'Well, maybe you want it too much,' he insisted.

'There's no such thing.'

227

He closed his eyes and wearily rubbed them. 'I'd just rather you wouldn't count on this so much. I don't want you to be disappointed if things don't work out. You're too wrapped up in it.'

Which only fueled my fire. 'Well, you bet I am. I worked very hard on it and I want something good to happen.'

'I want you wrapped up in something else, though,' he sulked.

I raised an eyebrow. I knew his words even before he spoke them. 'I want you wrapped up in me.'

The next thing I remember is him going into the shower, before going home to change clothes for his German interview. Taking my breakfast back to the kitchen, on the floor I noticed a folded piece of paper, a ripped-out page from a paperback book, which must have fallen out of his pocket. I picked it up and smoothed it out. It was from a book I remembered him telling me Patsy was forever quoting to him last summer. *Men Who Can't Love*, page 199, Chapter Seven, 'Understanding the Commitmentphobic Relationship. What a smart woman can do.' Underlined in cornea-scratching yellow was the first paragraph, which read:

> *Now you know why some men can't love. So what can you do about it – or is there anything you can do? Yes, there is something you can do, and that's what this book is all about. Granted, some men are so commitmentphobic that their girl friends could move across the Atlantic, and they would still feel trapped. Most of these men will never be able to love, and the smartest, most self-protective thing a woman can do is identify the problem and get out – before he does.*

I heard the shower stop running then, and folded the page back up and stuffed it into his tuxedo pocket, but not before I read in total disbelief 'Missing you, Puppy. See you soon. Patsy' scrawled in the corner. The page, of course, was not dated and could've been sent to him ages ago, but why was he carrying it around, then? There was just no way to know.

When he emerged from the shower it was immediately clear

that he had changed cassettes, and was off and running on another topic entirely. Having neatly steered me once again from the apparently incendiary subject of Ms Dill, he was back to his Nobel lecture again. Pulling on his socks, he lambasted poor Eugene O'Neill, who at the time of his Nobel was too ill to travel to Sweden for his award, and whose speech, which was read for him in Stockholm, was, as Charlie put it, 'disgustingly humble. All that self-righteous crap, paying homage to Strindberg and Nietzsche – I mean, give me a break, eh?' he rambled on and on, without even a hint of humility himself. Some 'puppy,' I thought then. At that moment, he seemed more like a rabid mongrel.

'Take care of yourself. I want you well for Sweden' was what he said to me, I think, before he left, turning up his smile to its highest voltage, flashing those white teeth and the green hypnotic glare of those spellbinding eyes. 'Too much champagne or something last night, eh?' he muttered casually, but before I could even think of answering him, he was in the elevator, and on his way home.

That day I polled the troops, who were unanimously ecstatic about my impending trip to Sweden, with the notable exception of the doctor who was treating me for Lyme – who advised me against traveling so soon. But I knew before I called him that any physician who hadn't graduated from Bozo University would tell me that, and I also knew that I had no intention of listening to him. From there, my fingers, still happy, dancing across the numbers, made the inevitable mistake of calling my mother in Florida, who asked me right away if I'd used the number she'd gotten hold of to retrieve Charlie's messages. After hearing that I hadn't, she took a deep breath and cautioned me to remember what Dolores had said to me about Charlie so many years ago, namely, that 'a leopard doesn't change its stripes'. Hanging up with my mother, I decided to take the precipitous plunge and call Clovis, but as I expected, Lumsden Worlock, her efficient secretary, male, supercilious, and terribly British, wouldn't put me through, and I ended up leaving a message. In fact, I ended up leaving several messages with him over the next week, but none of these was returned.

On the day we were to leave for Stockholm, Wednesday, I awoke and found a terrific snowstorm brewing outside; fine if you're in the mood for dogsledding in Canada, but nasty if you've got a lot to get done after a week of deeply committed procrastination in New York City. I knew the streets would be strangled. Traffic would not move. There would be one taxi out, and the driver would have just arrived that morning from Kiev, with a chip on his shoulder the size of Bear Mountain. And if that wasn't bad enough, my friend Mr Lyme was in very obvious attendance, tackling me before I could even get out of bed.

The phone rang at around seven-fifteen that morning and it was Charlie, as breathless and manic as I had ever heard him, and I had heard him plenty.

'Next stop, Arlanda Airport, puppy,' he giggled.

'Puppy?' I fumed, feeling suddenly like this was musical chairs and I might not have a place to sit.

'Sorry, it's just habit,' he placated me, sheepishly. 'Kennedy Airport, six o'clock,' he whispered. 'And don't forget, the chauffeur will be over at four-thirty to pick you up. Don't forget the speech. Don't be late! I love you!' he nearly screamed, hanging up. It was then that I sleepily remembered back to our plan, which had Charlie going to the airport earlier in order to take care of all the press that would be there.

Somehow, over the next few hours, with all the strength of a broken-backed ant, I dragged myself out of the house and to the hairdresser for a cut, and also a manicure. In the middle of having my hair blown out in the style I'd specifically asked my stylist to avoid, deep in the throes of giddy, pretravel jitters and a feverish antibiotic haze, I felt that my fingers were on fire, and I ran to the pay phone to once again try Clovis, just once more before I flew off. But again she did not take my call.

Running about two hours late on a schedule that had been haphazard to begin with, I next pushed through the wind and the elements, the snow and the slush, to the peaceful, dry, pretentious, always pretentious, confines of Bergdorf Goodman, where I was to pick up the dress I'd purchased and had altered.

There was always something about Bergdorf's and me. Indeed, we had such a love/hate thing for each other that I could have dragged the entire store with me to a marriage counselor. Was it only me who felt that the salespeople always treated you as if your nose was running and your underwear dirty? Was it only me who thought these same people must all have enormous trust funds, mansions, estates, children in only the poshest, most expensive prep schools? Whatever, I always felt that as soon as I walked in I had to make excuses for myself, and never as much as on the day I blew in with a broken umbrella and my brand-new, two-hundred-dollar haircut plastered across my red, wet face. 'I am leaving for the Nobels tonight!' I wanted to screech at them all, as they turned their noses up and looked through me like glass. 'I am meeting the King of Sweden and you're not!' I wanted to yell at them, shattering their Aryan composure, but decided against it. I had a dress to pick up. A plane to catch.

I rode the narrow escalator up to the fourth floor, to the hushed, mocha womb – the gown department – and asked one of the saleswomen to please get it for me. 'I'm in something of a hurry,' I explained. 'I have to catch a plane.' Oh, sure you do, toots, I could see her thinking to herself, and I'm Maury Povich, a second before she decided to take as long as she possibly could to get it. While I waited for her, I thought I heard a familiar voice, two of them in fact, buried behind one of the dress racks, two English voices, spraying at each other like castrated monkeys.

'But it's not *me*,' the woman protested, again and again.

'Oh, but it is. You're wrong, you're so wrong,' the younger voice, the man's, chattered back.

'It makes me look like a waitress, for God's sake.'

'Oh, Clovis, just because it's black and white doesn't mean a waitress would wear it,' he told her, exasperated, saying the word 'waitress' as if it were 'cockroach' or 'child molester'.

I poked around the corner just in time for both of them to look up and see me. Clovis's face lit up with the plastic flash of happy surprise and civility, just like a cheap camera. As I approached her, I searched for even a shadow of guilt at not returning my calls, but there was none.

'Tell me, Stevie, what do you think of this dress for Sweden?

231

I've just decided this morning to go and I'm in a terrible rush.'

'Are you leaving tonight?' I asked, dreading her reply.

'Oh, no, no need to rush there for all those dreary speeches. I just want the main event on Saturday. That's more than enough for me. So tell me,' she asked again, holding the pricey black and white silk number up against herself. 'It's nearly two thousand dollars. But is it me?' she begged, as her young assistant fumed at this intrusion. 'Schoolmarmish cunt,' I could swear he hissed at her under his breath.

For once in my life I agreed with her. If there was an annual reunion of Schrafft's waitresses, this would definitely be *de rigueur*.

'Grab it, Clovis,' I told her. 'It's perfect, and it's definitely you.'

'See, what did I tell you?' her companion muttered miserably into his coat collar.

'This is Stevie Stamberg, Charlie's ex-wife, who's going to Stockholm tonight with him, Lumsden. Look sharp now,' she teased. 'He's my assistant, Stevie,' she explained, just as the saleswoman returned and Clovis told her she'd take the dress. As we were just about ready to say good-bye, as my dress, a tiny, electric-blue, crinkled killer of a Vicky Tiel for around three thousand dollars was brought out to me, I plucked up my courage and tapped Clovis on the shoulder as she was paying for her gown.

'You know, I've been calling you,' I said tentatively, hoping she might help me out a little, throw me a rope before the waves got too high.

'Yes, I know, darling,' she purred sweetly, patronizingly, 'but I couldn't imagine why. I mean, if you changed your mind about the play, that was your business, but you really can't keep changing your mind, you know,' she chided me.

My throat was suddenly very dry and I couldn't locate my voice. I stood there, staring at her, nearly numb. 'Charlie . . . never gave you my play?' I asked, terrified of her answer.

'Well, of course not. What do you think I've been telling you?

232

You know, you really must figure out what you want, Stevie. You can't be a playwright if you won't let anyone read your work.'

'He told you I'd changed my mind about sending you my play?' I asked, practically shivering at the thought.

'Well, you know he did. And now it's too late to change your mind back. The Mark Taper's all booked for the season. See you in Stockholm, dear.'

She left me there, frozen as a tombstone, as Lumsden, looking at his watch, pulled her away. And there I stood, flabbergasted, running a full two hours late, my Vicky Tiel slung over my arm and my mind in one hell of a tizzy.

Outside it was still snowing heavily. I tried to get a cab, but an empty taxi was nowhere to be seen. The snow and the wind were so fierce, I thought they might blow me all the way to Sweden. In true desperation, I waited as a bus pulled up, got on it, and then felt it begin to creep along like a snail on Thorazine. At this rate, Charlie would reach Stockholm before I even got to Central Park West.

I sat down across from a trio of diminutive, elegant, white-haired ladies, all bundled up under plastic rain hats, each clutching a copy of *Playbill*, chatting and laughing together. It took a while for my head to stop spinning, for my heart to stop pounding, so furious was I at Charlie for his insidious deception. I held my little, blue, silken, crinkle-puff close to me as the anger bubbled up in me again and again, each time with renewed venom and vigor.

After a while, as we inched along, getting practically nowhere, I turned to the girl seated next to me humming to herself, a disturbed-looking teenager in a plum-colored coat and black open hightops with no socks. She was carrying a plastic container with a cluster of holes poked into the top. Occasionally, she'd hold it up, tap it, and coo to it in an excited, whispery tone. Looking at it, the matinee trio and I could see that something was alive and moving inside the container. A gerbil, perhaps? Possibly a pet turtle? one of the tiny, sugar-haired ladies discreetly inquired. 'It's a rat I found in the street,' the girl answered

233

brightly, never taking her gluey eyes from her bounty, clearly transfixed. 'It's sick and I'm taking it to the vet,' she told us then. Peering closer, we watched the creature whirling about in its little plastic cage. 'I'm bringing it to the Animal Medical Center,' the girl announced with obvious pride, like the mother of a small child in a beauty pageant.

As I stared at the plastic tub I was thinking sadly, angrily, about rats, human rats. Six feet two ones, with wide-set green eyes, brilliant minds, and a way with the ladies. As I felt the walls of that miserable bus crowding in on me, I thought suddenly of a cartoon about rats (or maybe it was mice?) that I'd seen some years back in *The New Yorker*. In it, a rodent, reentering its dark rodent hole, where another rodent is waiting, says, 'I'm back. The Brie's not ripe.' I had never forgotten it.

I'm not at all sure when, or on what avenue, I decided to tear off that bus and run the rest of the way home, but suddenly I got up, rang the bell, and knew I had to get off or my lungs would burst. I kept thinking of Clovis's disapproving face and of Charlie's exasperation at my impatience about my play, and I felt like ten thousand pots boiling over. I tried to yank the back doors open but they were stuck and my dress kept getting caught as I struggled and pushed. 'Hurry up, I don't got all day,' the driver yelled back at me. Neither did I, but that didn't seem to matter very much anymore. I thought that in all probability, nothing in the world would ever make sense to me again. (Rats were okay on a bus; a three-thousand-dollar silk dress bound for the Nobel ceremony stuck in a door was not.)

I ran all the way home, getting splashed by cars at the curbs, getting shoved by angry walkers, carrying on my back a god-damned dress that suddenly felt as heavy as a corpse.

When I finally reached the apartment, the phone was ringing, but I didn't answer it. Instead, I called SAS to see if their planes would be flying in such atrocious weather, and was told they would be, along with a wealth of other details I didn't ask for, like the movie we'd be watching, and the meal we'd be eating.

'Captain Carlsson will be your pilot this evening,' the mild-mannered voice informed me, with just a touch of British reserve.

I ran a bath and sank down into that tub, so weary and frazzled with rage at Charlie that I wondered if I'd ever get out of it again. Or ever want to.

I thought back to the summer, when he had first reappeared, jogging up the road as I inspected the damage in my garden, the defenseless petunias the rabbits had feasted on, the crocus bulbs gorged on by the chipmunks, the roses punctured with the greedy appetite of Japanese beetles. I thought back to how and why I had ever begun to trust him again, to the many ways he'd cleverly, irresistibly insinuated himself back into my life, to his coldly systematic plan. From the beginning, from his heart-wrenching Bastille Day speech atop Spike Church's dishwasher, to his stunning *pièce de résistance*: getting me to work with him on his Nobel speech. Flattering me, drawing me back into the intimate confines of his wicked labyrinth, only to suffocate me once I was safely inside.

God, he was good. But not quite good enough. I thought back to the time when he was so driven by his nocturnal quest for fruit, when my key didn't work at his studio, when the perfume had sprayed my eyes and suddenly I could see. Maybe my eyes needed to be branded again so I would know and feel, indelibly this time, that the Brie wasn't ripe. That a leopard never changed its stripes.

If I called Charlie's answering machine and punched in his retrieving code, who knew what I might hear? Who knew? I knew, which is precisely why I didn't have to.

Almost certainly, there would be Patsy, there would be Dolores, maybe even the high-pitched, patronizing voice of Clovis, complaining about me. No doubt, there would be other messages that would also turn my stomach; maybe a Ginger from Bayonne – 'You left your tie here the other night' – or a reporter perhaps, from *Time* or *Newsweek*, a Janice, a Susan, or maybe someone with a foreign name like Daniella, Natalija, or Gabrielle. 'I just wanted to clarify a few points from our interview the other day,' she'd begin tentatively, nervously adding, 'By the way, you're a really great kisser,' trying too hard to make it sound like an afterthought.

I knew that right about now, Charlie would be leaving for the airport, dressed in some drop-dead suit, maybe carrying along a volume of obscure Slavic or Scandinavian poetry for the flight (with a box of double-strength Mylanta II tablets tucked safely away in a suit pocket), ready for his near-royal reception at Arlanda Airport the next morning, and it just made me seethe.

As for myself, I just lay there in the tub, furious, sinking in deeper and deeper, hearing my house phone buzzing to let me know that Charlie's chauffeur was downstairs ready to retrieve me and Charlie's speech.

At this point, my doorbell began ringing, and I knew I had to get it or he'd never go away. I threw on some clothes, and as I did, I thought of the occasion I'd be missing in Sweden, the splendid pomp and circumstance, the warm handshakes I wouldn't be receiving from King Carl XVI Gustaf and his striking Brazilian-German-born wife, Silvia, the dancing and the dinners, the elk steaks and rowanberry jam, the reporters, the Operakallaren and the grandest of all hotels, the Grand Hotel, with its spine-tingling views; I thought of my wasted, tiny, bottle-blue silk extravaganza, thought how little it meant to me now to prance about in it on foreign soil. I thought of Flora Mastroianni and of Santa and truly it all just made me want to go and smash plates or step on baby chickens. See, Charlie was no Marcello, no Valentino, no Fausto, speeding along the slippery Autostrada, hormones dancing inside him like popping corn. (No Jack Kennedy?) He was just a miserable fake, a pale imitation, a fraud. Those men were open, transparent, unfolded, and revealed. They did not pretend to be what they were not, didn't invent or deceive. He, on the other hand, had gone and won a Nobel for reinventing himself, and had lassoed me along for the ride. Bravo, they would all say in Sweden, goodwill ambassadors from all over the world giving him a feverish, white-gloved ovation. Thank God, I would not be among them.

The doorbell rang some more, and I ran over to my desk. Into a large manila envelope I stuffed a copy of our divorce decree, along with the first and last pages of my play. I handed it to Charlie's driver and, when he'd left, confused that I hadn't come too, I stepped over to my computer. With a few deft twists of the wrist, I erased all of Charlie's speech, until it was just a blank screen and a bad memory. If everything were only that easy.

Right about now, I figured Captain Carlsson and his flight engineer would be taking a stroll outside the plane, inspecting the wings, the tail, the wheels. Back in the cockpit, he would exercise the yoke, making sure there was no drag on the controls, jerking it right, left, forward, and back.

I thought of Charlie, waiting for me in the VIP lounge at Kennedy, checking his watch, fidgeting. I took my phone off the hook just at the second I imagined him rushing over to a pay phone to inquire after me.

I thought then of all I should have done and said to him when there was still time, but then I caught myself. When you live your life in *esprit d'escalier*, you are liable to trip and break your neck sliding down the banister. And if I felt tremendous sadness then for what might have been, for what had never been, it was bathed in the red-hot glow of anger; it was nothing but the pain an amputee feels for a phantom limb. The Brie was not ripe.

I had read somewhere awhile back that a strange glow had been found emanating from the floor of the Pacific ocean. 'Inferences drawn by a sharp-eyed biology student from her study of a particular eyeless shrimp have led to the discovery of a mysterious glow emitted by a scalding jet of water more than one mile beneath the surface of the Pacific Ocean.' And so I thought to myself, how terrific. Eyeless shrimp can see the light at the ocean's floor and damnit, so can I.

I left Charlie waiting at the airport for me on the eve of the most memorable event of his life. I left him there to ache perhaps just a bit for his own phantom limb. I imagined him, surrounded by reporters and photographers, boarding his plane with a smile of false composure, hiding his confusion and hurt at my failure to

237

appear, imagining that I'd been kidnapped, killed. Poor baby, I had never felt stronger.

As the meals and luggage were loaded onto his flight, as the fuel was pumped in and Captain Carlsson checked his horizontal stabilizers and flipped his wing flaps up and down, I turned on the evening news and saw the scene awaiting Charlie, all the hullaba-loo in snowy Stockholm. And then I switched it off again. What the hell. Elk steaks were probably loaded with cholesterol any-way.

In my naïve ignorance, in my stubborn refusal to recognize that knowledge is useless when we bury it in wishes, I pictured Charlie on that plane, clutching the envelope with its surprise contents, pining for me, planning even then how to win me back, perhaps even toasting himself, and it made me want to laugh. To shriek with laughter. I pictured him next to my empty seat, prematurely delighting in his own spectacular ingenuity.

What I couldn't possibly know yet was that even before Captain Carlsson had reached his cruising altitude, a saucy, hot-tempered Japanese number seated across the aisle from Charlie would decide she'd already reached hers.

I imagined him that night mired in sadness, loneliness; a repentant wretch; a shattered shell of a man, his heart splintered in a thousand fragments.

This did not turn out to be the case.

Some things never change, nor do some people, and this predictability of the universe can prove maddening or cause elation, depending on one's situation. In my own, it was thank-fully the latter, when I later learned that, gesturing at my empty seat, leaning over Charlie in a cloud of perfume, with a cagey plan for his next decade or so, the Japanese vixen had asked him, coyly, 'Excuse me, is this seat taken?'

And with that, Captain Carlsson had eased back in his seat, flicked a wrist at the controls, climbed into the clouds, and flown them on to Sweden.